PRAISE FOR *The Heart You Carry Home*

"Passionate, atmospheric, *The Heart You Carry Home* is the work of a young writer full of energy and promise."

—Jennifer Egan, author of *A Visit from the Goon Squad*

"Speaking as the daughter, as well as the wife, of a veteran, I can say this book packs an honest punch. *The Heart You Carry Home* gives voice to generations of soldiers and their families seeking understanding and forgiveness. A testimony to love's ultimate ability to heal even our most hidden wounds."

—Sarah McCoy, *New York Times* best-selling author of *The Mapmaker's Children* and *The Baker's Daughter*

"Here is a tale of family, community, love, and madness, as a woman who is both the daughter of a Vietnam veteran and wife of an Iraq veteran journeys to heal the heart-wounds of war. *The Heart You Carry Home* combines great storytelling with social questions that are both as current and as old as war. I read it in one sitting."

—Karl Marlantes, author of *Matterhorn*

"In Becca Keller, Miller has crafted a fierce heroine whom you'll eagerly follow across the country, into the depths of a madman's sanctum, and back into the light—stronger but forever changed. *The Heart You Carry Home* is a story about fathers and daughters, and how the legacy of war not only breaks families apart, but can pull them back together."

—Joanna Smith Rakoff, author of *My Salinger Year*

"A powerhouse of a novel. Miller captures the emotional minefield of veterans returning home from the battlefields of Iraq and Afghanistan with vivid, engaging detail. This novel cuts right to the heart."

—David Abrams, author of *Fobbit*, a 2012 *New York Times* Notable Book

"An engrossing tale layered in mystery, told with compassion and — at the perfect moments — wit. Miller gives us a truthful look at the fallout from war, both today's wars and the conflict in Vietnam. A damn fine read."

— Artis Henderson, author of *Unremarried Widow*

"With *The Heart You Carry Home*, Miller has crafted a thrilling, surprising, and mercilessly readable novel about the far-reaching effects of trauma, our crippling capacity for guilt, and the long road to forgiveness. Ultimately, though, it's a novel about healing."

—Jonathan Evison, author of *The Revised Fundamentals of Caregiving*

PRAISE FOR *The Year of the Gadfly*

A *Self* Best Book of 2012
A *Kirkus Reviews* Best Fiction of 2012 Selection
Daily Beast Must-Read Fiction

"Part *Dead Poets Society*, part *Heathers*. Entirely addictive."

— *Glamour*

"A darkly comic romp." — *Washington Post*

"*Prep* with attitude." — *Vogue* (Australia)

"A smoldering mystery . . . [that] recalls Donna Tartt's *The Secret History* . . . A gripping thrill ride that's also a thoughtful coming-of-age story."

— *Kirkus Reviews*

"There is a relentless authenticity in her prose . . . Miller cleverly teases the reader with sly literary allusions and cultural ephemera . . . It is the ideal crossover work." — *Atlantic*

"Harrowing, enchanting, and utterly original."

— Amber Dermont, *Daily Beast*

THE HEART YOU CARRY HOME

BOOKS BY JENNIFER MILLER

Inheriting the Holy Land

The Year of the Gadfly

The Heart You Carry Home

The Heart You Carry Home

Jennifer Miller

A Mariner Original
MARINER BOOKS
Houghton Mifflin Harcourt
Boston • New York
2015

www.hmhco.com

Library of Congress Cataloging-in-Publication Data
Miller, Jennifer, date.
The heart you carry home / Jennifer Miller.
pages cm
ISBN 978-0-544-30055-2 (paperback) — ISBN 978-0-544-29015-0 (ebook)
1. Veterans — Fiction. 2. Fathers and daughters — Fiction. I. Title.
PS3613.I5378H43 2015
813'.6—dc23
2015007140

Book design by Chrissy Kurpeski
Typeset in Mercury

Printed in the United States of America
DOC 10 9 8 7 6 5 4 3 2 1

Original translation of lines from Homer's *The Iliad* by Marian W. Makins. Used by permission.

PART I

Dwell Time

December 13, 1969

Dear Willy,

It's the middle of the night and I can't sleep. King and Reno are passed out cold, but I keep thinking about Patroclus. I wish you'd never told me about him, Willy. I wish you hadn't ruined our friendship with all that. But you did, so here I am.

I couldn't sleep the night before the mission either. I lay awake imagining myself as a Greek soldier camped outside the walls of Troy. All those men waiting for sunrise, praying that Achilles would return to battle. The fates of so many resting on the decision of one. I'm no Achilles. But I also carry men's lives in my hands: King's and Reno's.

The only part of you I carry now is Durga's heart. I feel it beating. I must be crazy. Or maybe I'm sane as a man can be. I know only that I will carry the heart for you, Willy. I promise. For Patroclus, Achilles would have done no less.

Currahee!

CO Proudfoot

1

THERE WERE FEW streetlights in town, and the army duffle, crammed with Becca's clothes, kept sliding from the handlebars of her bicycle. Still, she knew these roads well enough to take them blind. Here were the doublewides, flimsy as Monopoly pieces; the gardens dotted with plaster birdbaths; and the harried-looking lawns scattered with dirt bikes and abandoned Barbies. This was her beloved, unbeautiful Dry Hills, Tennessee.

She pushed past the town limits and pedaled on. Damn Ben for taking her old Cadillac. Only a month after their wedding and he had turned into someone else, like any other man around here—gotten drunk, disappeared, forced her to flee into the night. The foggy August air grew thick with droplets of moisture large enough to catch on the tongue. Becca stopped and looked around. Where was she? Out in the alfalfa fields, a glittering barn wavered like a mirage. And there was Ben, a distant apparition, playing the fiddle tune he'd written for her. "It's a loooove song," he'd crooned the night before his deployment. "I'm going to play it at the wedding and embarrass the hell out of you." It was one of the few promises he'd kept, and Becca's cheeks flushed again at the memory. Since then, there had been no love songs. Nothing except fighting and silence.

After another fifteen minutes of hard pedaling, she came to a crossroads. Her father's house was to the left. Right and straight meant farmland for miles. Becca had never dropped in on King uninvited, and it was after midnight. But what choice did she have? Her mother was holed up in a Colorado commune, and the girls she knew in town were asleep next to their husbands and newborns. With a queasy feeling, she looked around, as though a third road might suddenly appear. *Get on with it!* she ordered herself and pushed on.

Twenty minutes later, King's house appeared behind a bulwark of trees. The large picture window in front was dark, indifferent, like a person looking the other way. As Becca climbed off the bike, a ring of pain ignited around her waist, belly to back. She checked under her shirt. The bruises were dark, multicolored splotches, and she registered them with detachment; they matched a painting she'd made in last semester's art class. She dropped her shirt, hoisted Ben's duffle onto her shoulder, and climbed her father's steps. Then she sucked in a breath, and knocked.

From inside came a cough, followed by heavy steps, clomping *fee-fi-fo-fum*. A voice growled, "Who's there?" Becca stated her name and heard the metallic chinks of many locks sliding open. King lived beside a cow pasture, but he'd fortified the house as though awaiting a full-on assault, perhaps from a rogue government force or maybe just the government. She'd never figured out who his enemies were.

The door swung back to reveal his hulking figure. Despite the hour, he was fully dressed: black jeans and a Sturgis Rally T-shirt, steel-wool hair pulled into a ponytail. His jowls sagged with a mastiff's despondent frown. Becca's father was sixty years old, but he looked closer to seventy. When he noticed the army duffle, his thick lips sank.

"Can I come in?" She considered throwing a *Dad* onto the end of this sentence, but the word wouldn't come, not even as guilt ammunition. She waited, trying to breathe steady. He was going to send her away. But he held the door open and stepped aside.

Becca followed him into the kitchen and sat down at the table. This room usually indicated King's physical and mental state. Many times she'd arrive and immediately take up arms against the roaches, mildewed towels, and weeks of frying-pan grease. The fridge was generally a bright electric wasteland. It was a wonder her father survived out here on his own. At present, however, the room was spotless. King made coffee and, smiling, put two mugs on the table. The coffee tasted like dirt, but Becca would have accepted a mug of lighter fluid from her father had he offered it with a smile.

"What's going on?" King asked, sitting heavily across from her.

"We had a fight." Becca pressed her molars together, determined to keep renegade tears at bay. She needed to convince King that things were bad enough for her to be here but not so bad that he'd grow agitated, take action.

"What kind of fight?"

Becca met her father's eyes, then looked away.

"Becca, what kind of fight?" he repeated.

"I biked all the way out here."

King drew in a quick breath and patted her hand. It had taken many months for him to show even this much affection. He gave her a paper towel from the roll she'd bought at Costco the last time she'd gone shopping for his necessities; King did not like crowded public places.

Becca blew her nose, a brash, earsplitting honk. According to her mother, this was the single trait that father and daughter shared: a propensity to sneeze and blow like storm systems.

"Usually you'd be welcome here," King said, "but the thing is . . ."

Becca swallowed. Of course their détente of the past few months couldn't last. He was going to send her away. Her mind spun into the uncertain future. Where to go?

"Thing is," he continued, "I'm leaving on a trip tomorrow. But—" His gray eyes brightened. "I'm stopping at Kath's on the way."

Aunt Kathy. Her house, teetering on the peak of a mountain overlooking the Buffalo River Valley, had been Becca's childhood refuge when the home front turned nasty. When she was old enough to think about it, Becca couldn't believe her mother had put a six-year-old on a bus alone, but the frequent trips had taught her self-reliance. Now, secreting herself away with Kath seemed like the perfect solution. She'd be an Ozark girl for the rest of the summer. And after she'd erased the past few years from her memory, she'd continue west. Like a pioneer on the Oregon Trail, she would make her own manifest destiny. She'd take hold of her new opportunity. One that nobody—not even Ben—knew about.

"If it's not too much trouble, Dad," Becca said, finally looking King in the eye, "I'd love to come with you."

"Just to Kath's," King said.

"Of course." Becca nodded.

Despite its being the middle of the night, King retreated to his work shed. Becca was exhausted, but she was also sticky with dried sweat and, beneath that, a grimy heartsickness that she hoped a blast of hot water might dissolve. She tiptoed into the monk's cell that was King's bedroom, searching for a towel. Her father's dresser displayed the barest signs of life: a tattered spy novel, a pack of American Spirits, and a couple of photos in drugstore frames. But there, unexpectedly, was her high-school graduation portrait: her hair long and blond, like some hippie girl's. Becca had chopped it off just hours after receiving her diploma. She'd been drunk, reveling in her newfound freedom, flinging fistfuls of hair out her bedroom window. In the backyard, her fellow graduates had shouted, "Rebecca, Rebecca, let down your hair!"

King hadn't been at her graduation and she hadn't expected him. He'd been MIA for many years by that point. So where had this picture come from? Certainly not from her mother, who never missed a chance to remind Becca how much she hated her ex-husband. Another puzzle, but not one that Becca had an ounce of energy to solve.

In the bathroom, she stripped off her clothes and ducked behind the shower curtain, avoiding the mirror. Letting the tears, salt, and snot flow into the drain, she washed herself gingerly where the skin around her midsection was tender. Then she turned off the water and stood naked and dripping in the tub. The heartsick feeling had hardened inside of her, like a shell.

Back in the kitchen, a towel around her, Becca discovered a small, wiry man rooting around in the fridge. Reno, a friend of her father but a man she despised.

"Your old man doesn't have anything decent to drink," he said, not bothering to look up.

"You know King doesn't keep booze here."

Reno stood upright and flashed his metallic smile. He had three gold caps, two on his top incisors and one on the bottom left canine. "I meant all this diet crap. I don't drink around your daddy." He nodded at the soda in his fist. "Jesus, girl."

Becca rolled her eyes. Reno was a fixture. Just two years her father's junior, he'd been in King's unit in Vietnam, and her father had called him a crazy son of a bitch who'd run into live fire like he was the fucking god of war incarnate. It was one of the few pieces of information King had volunteered about the war. *He's a good doobie,* King had added. *Heart of gold.*

Reno eyed her critically. "Are you okay?"

Becca scowled and pulled the towel higher around her chest. Her clothes were in the duffle bag beside the table. "What are you doing here, Reno?"

"Is that any way to welcome a weary traveler? I've been riding half the night and my ass is screamin'." Reno snapped open the soda. "We got a trip coming up. King didn't tell you?"

Becca deflated. Even two days in Reno's company was too much. "My dad's in his shed," she said. "Go bother him, okay?" Without waiting for a response, she grabbed the duffle and turned on her heel. When she heard the back door slam, she dressed and lay down on the lumpy couch. The pillows reeked of cigarette smoke, so she stuffed Ben's duffle under her head. The fabric was rough and had its own peculiar mustiness. When she closed her eyes, she saw a thousand duffles crammed into army trucks rumbling through faraway deserts. She saw Ben trudging among blown-out buildings. So many nights she'd made mental lists of the places he'd been, the names of the people in his unit, the objects that made up his sixty-plus pounds of body armor. She'd hoped these thoughts would bring him close to her — a kind of intraplanetary mind meld. No such luck.

Finally alone and still, Becca clenched her teeth until her face turned red, and hot tears burned in her eyes. She was a twenty-one-year-old woman throwing a tantrum, however silent. But who gave a damn? As a child, she'd lashed out over every affront. *Kick as hard as you like, but you can't crack the earth,* her mother would say after she'd been called to pick up Becca early from school.

Nothing had changed. Then, as now, her rage felt like all she had.

Becca forced herself to breathe slowly in and out like her

first running coach had taught her. She thought about her well-tested strategy for winning long-distance races. First, gain momentum from a fierce burst of energy. Next, fall into a steady rhythm. And finally, when you felt confident in your movement and your breath, hit your stride. *Momentum, rhythm, stride.* Becca repeated the mantra in her mind. *Momentum* [breath], *rhythm* [breath], *stride* [breath]. She felt her body calm and her heavy eyes close. *You have options,* she reminded herself. *You're free now. Hit your stride and you can outrun anything.*

2

BENJAMIN THOMPSON SURVEYED the litter of glass at his feet. He'd poured at least four beers down his throat in twenty minutes flat. Then, belly bloated, he'd thrown the remaining bottles against the side of Becca's car. Even now he could feel the swing and release, followed by the glorious *smash!* It had been downright cathartic, breaking things, alone in a field, nobody to judge him. Now he was calm — at least calm enough to go home. To be in bed with his wife, where a newlywed was meant to be.

If only an awful headache weren't gathering behind his eyes. He rooted in the car for another beer. Finding none, he decided to make a quick pit stop. He needed to be as clearheaded as possible when he walked in the door. He had taken Becca's car and he felt bad about it, but with his own in the shop, how else was he going to leave? And he'd had to leave. Otherwise, he might have done something horrible. Just a month before, he'd stood before all of their family and friends and pledged to protect her. *I do solemnly swear that I will support and defend Rebecca Keller against all enemies, foreign and domestic. So help me God.* He'd taken the car as a protective measure. She would understand.

Crunching on glass, Ben walked to the driver's side and slid into the Cadillac. Becca had dubbed it the Death Star — the vehicle was so hulking, so full of menace. But to Ben, the car felt more like a hearse. Which made him the corpse. Except the dead were not supposed to feel pain, and tension pulsated in the middle of his forehead like a third eye. He put the key in the ignition and realized that he'd been thinking about the wrong pledge. *Support and defend* the Constitution; *love* his wife. But it was all the same. Loving, honoring, supporting, defending: each word was a stand-in for commitment. And Ben did not renege on his commitments.

He drove home on high alert, casting his eyes back and forth like searchlights. The lush alfalfa fields—welcome assurance that he was no longer in Iraq—did nothing to allay his fears. He needed that beer. Home for eight weeks, and little but the taste of hops could force the dark shadows—tree branches and crows' wings—back into their proper shapes, prevent them from morphing into snipers and camouflaged IEDs. Ben kept telling himself that he knew better. He knew the difference between imaginary and real, between Iraq and Tennessee. But then he'd get behind the wheel, helpless against the urge to scan, to tap his foot, to speed.

He stopped at the first bar he came across. The sight was a relief, like home base in a game of tag. Just one beer and then back to the house to be the kind and loving husband he'd vowed to be.

It was late Sunday night—or was it early Monday morning? Either way, look at these drunks and insomniacs. How pitiful! He ordered a beer and slid into a booth. Just one more, he promised himself when he realized the first was gone, and he ordered another. But next, a whiskey appeared. Time began to unspool, and soon, Ben was lost. He hadn't moved, but in his mind, he'd flown over the ocean, across the continents, and landed heavily on the potholed surface of Ali's Alley. The sun was very hot, and the air smelled of burned metal. There was music, but instead of the Arabic scale, it was a fiddle tune called "Sally in the Garden," his father's favorite. And Ben was walking to the command outpost—the COP—to meet Corporal Eric Coleman for a game of pickup soccer. After a while, Ben realized that he was having trouble walking, because he was dragging something attached to a rope tied around his waist.

And then, out of nowhere, Ben's father appeared in the middle of the street. His cheeks were gaunt, his body withered, his lips cracked with sores.

"What are you doing here, Dad?" The fiddle music was so loud now that Ben was forced to shout.

Ben's father raised his arm and pointed at whatever Ben was dragging.

"What's wrong?" Ben called, louder this time. "What's behind me?"

George Thompson just stared, horrified. Ben turned to see for himself—

"—I said, you've been sitting here awhile. Do you want another?" There was a hand on his arm, but only for a moment, because his arm reacted, snapping from the table like a live wire. He barely registered the arm as his own, but it must have been, because the waitress was stumbling backward. She collided with a table, her tray toppling. "What's wrong with you?" She rubbed her back where it had struck the table edge. "You're fucking insane."

One of the insomniacs rushed over to help the waitress up.

"*You* touched *me*," Ben spat.

"You oughta leave," said the man.

The guy wasn't so big and he had a belly. Ben could take him. But he wasn't looking for a fight. "I'm just sitting here having a drink!" he protested. "And then she comes over and puts her hands on me. I didn't do anything."

"Out," the insomniac said, thrusting his thumb toward the door like he was a goddamned umpire. Now two additional bodies appeared, their faces bug-eyed, like cartoons.

"I've been serving for you all for fifteen fucking months! And you're kicking me out because I don't want some dumb bitch touching me?"

Fifteen months forced a brief pause in the bar and the man who'd originally helped the waitress took a step back. "Come on," he said gently. "Let's go, son."

Ben stood, knocking over his empty bottles. "I'm not your fucking son and I don't want your pity. Do I *look* like an invalid?" He stomped out of the bar and, after a couple of jabs at the keyhole, managed to unlock the Cadillac.

Back home, he ran into the house calling Becca's name. He paused at the open door of her childhood bedroom, saw his father's fiddle lying in splinters on the floor. What happened here? In a moment, he remembered and shut the door. Frantic, he called for her again.

In the silence that followed, Ben knew she might be gone — as in *left him* gone — and the house spun madly around him. Without her, there was nothing. He rushed into the master bedroom and saw her phone on the nightstand. If she had left for good, she would have taken it. He called some of her friends; they hadn't heard from her. Finally, he called King. "King can't talk now," said a grubby voice on the other end.

"What about Becca?" Ben demanded. "Is she there?"

There was a brief pause and then the dial tone buzzed in his ear. Ben grabbed the keys and took off toward the town limits.

Ben had been to King's only once before, on a sunny afternoon before the wedding. Then, the house had looked peaceful, almost quaint. Now, well past midnight, as he pulled up the dirt drive, he saw the place as a booby-trapped cabin out of some horror movie. He thought about the homes he'd staked out on nighttime missions, the sand-colored world seen through his night-vision goggles, cast in a sickly green light. He wished he had his NVGs now. He wished for the protection of his body armor and his weapon.

He charged up King's front steps and banged on the door. A thin rectangle of light glowed behind the picture window. And then King appeared, his belly pressed to the screen-door mesh.

"Ben," said the old man gruffly. "It's late."

"Where's Becca?" Ben was breathing heavily, as though winded from a long run.

"I know you two had a fight," King said. "But it appears you haven't calmed down yet."

"I'm calm," Ben said. "But I need to talk to her."

"You're drunk."

"I'm fine," Ben said. He grabbed the handle of the screen door and pulled it back. It was far lighter than he expected, and the door banged violently against the side of the house.

"What's that fucking racket?" said another voice. That grubby voice from the telephone. A short, sinewy man with thinning hair appeared beside King. This must be Reno, Ben thought; he'd heard plenty about the guy from Becca. "Aw, fuck," Reno said, as though Ben's presence on the doorstep were a personal affront. "You're the sergeant King's been blabbering about all night."

"I want to talk to my wife," Ben said.

"He's drunk," King said to Reno.

"You think?" Reno said.

They were talking about him like he was an animal under observation and the two of them were goddamn zoologists.

King looked suspiciously at Reno. "You been drinking too?"

"Just your sissy diet soda." Reno smiled, flashing metal.

"What is this bullshit?" Ben said. Who were these men, the

fucking odd couple? "Becca!" he called. "Becca, we need to talk!"

And then she materialized from the gloom, hair mussed and eyes squinting with sleep. She wore sweatpants and a worn-thin army T-shirt that revealed the shape of her small breasts. He felt a deep flush of desire for her, then tenderness.

"Becca, how'd you get all the way out here? I'm so sorry about the car."

She didn't respond. She just stared.

"I think you'd best leave," Reno said. "And leave the car. It's not yours to take, and you're in no condition to drive it."

"Becca!" Ben kept trying to see her behind the men, craning his neck until he was sure it would snap. She looked sad. Was she crying? He needed to get closer. "Becca," he pleaded. But she seemed to float away from him, to fade into the darkened living room. "Why did you come out here?" he asked, but King and Reno were like a wall that his words couldn't breach. Why wouldn't they let him in? Just to talk. That's all he wanted. "I came back!" he cried. "I came back for you and you were gone!"

Was he wearing his body armor? He felt so heavy. Heavy enough to knock through the men in his way. He lunged.

In the next instant, pain exploded in his face. It was less of a feeling than a sound: a bubble of white noise, like a broken television set. Then Ben was weightless. He reached his arms out as though to grab Becca's T-shirt. But there was nothing to hold on to as he flailed and fell. His body hit the ground, his head knocking hard against the earth. Then he didn't see or hear anything.

3

RENO HAD REACHED the Smokies and still no sign of life from Ben. He peered at the inkblot bruise between the kid's eye and upper cheek; he hadn't intended to knock him out cold, but the sergeant had come at him like a bulldozer. At first, Reno worried King would be furious. But King said only "Better you than his own father-in-law" before lifting Ben baby-like into his thick arms, buckling him into the Cadillac, and telling Reno to drive him home.

Reno hoped Ben didn't have a concussion, hoped that the punch combined with the booze had just temporarily carted the sergeant off to la-la land. And he was grateful for some quiet time to think. All night, right up until Ben showed up, King had been talking his ear off about the wedding. Reno couldn't quite get his head around the thing. Not the wedding itself—he supposed kids did much dumber things than get married just weeks after coming home from war. But the way King had been all mushy about the event—now, that was odd. He'd insisted on describing Becca's dress, waving his meaty hands in the air in a futile attempt to convey a sense of its shape, beaming at how she'd sewn it herself.

"Was it silk?" Reno had asked, trying to be helpful. "Satin maybe? How about chiffon?"

King shook his head, helpless. "How do you know what chiffon looks like?" he demanded. But he'd pressed on. He said that his heart nearly stopped beating when Becca appeared at the top of the aisle. And not just because of how stunning—how glorious—she looked, but because of the expression on her face. She'd looked at Ben like she couldn't believe her luck. "Like she'd won the Powerball jackpot!" King exclaimed. And when the music started—Becca's cue to walk—she didn't move. She just stood there, her eyes locked on Ben, the two of them laughing hysterically. It was awkward, King said. People grew restless. But he understood that his daughter and her intended had been transported to some other, secluded place. Their bodies were only decoys, keeping the secret of their private communion.

Still, King worried. Ben was twenty-five. Becca was barely drinking age and had another two years of college ahead of her. Maybe that was normal here. Even late, compared to many of the guests, who weren't in college and never would be. But King knew that as soon as Becca started down the aisle, time would begin moving again. Her joy, frozen and pure, would begin to thaw.

Hearing this, Reno, who'd been King's own best man many years before, said, "You sure you're still talking about them?"

"That was a different time," King said. "Different circumstances."

Different time, same circumstances, Reno had thought. But he'd kept his mouth shut.

"Becca doesn't deserve a life alone," King had said.

"She's not alone anymore," Reno told his friend. "You're back, which I gotta say was a shocker."

But King didn't meet Reno's eyes. They both knew this business of being back wasn't going to last. They knew King's days of living in Dry Hills were numbered.

• • •

Ben stirred in the passenger seat and made a familiar, unwelcome sound. Reno pulled over and unsnapped the kid's seat belt. No sooner had he yanked the sergeant's shoulders out of the automobile than Ben vomited onto the grass. "You better not have spilled any of that on my shoes," he warned. In response, Ben heaved again. "Jesus, boy, what in God's name have you been drinking? I've never seen anything that color."

Ben coughed, spat a couple of times. "I'm not a boy." He panted. "I'm—"

He puked again. Reno stood back, chuckling. "Yeah, fine, *Sergeant*. How about *busted drunk*. That title suit you better?"

Ben hung his head between his knees. His skull felt stuffed with cotton. "Where are we? Where's Becca?" He looked around with alarm.

"She's still at King's. Since she wasn't so successful in getting away from you, I decided to get you away from her." Reno walked back around to the driver's side of the car and climbed in.

"But you took her car," Ben complained, pulling himself inside the cavernous vehicle. "Does she know that?"

"No. But she didn't exactly put up a fight when I punched you in the face. I think she won't mind." In fact, after Reno knocked Ben out, she'd said nothing, just disappeared inside the house.

"You wait until she finds out," Ben said. "You'll have another think coming."

"You're criticizing me?" Reno shook his head and pulled onto the road.

"Where the hell are we going?"

Reno recoiled from Ben's stinking breath. He rolled down the window and told Ben to do the same. Ben's hands were shaking and he had some trouble gripping the handle. Reno watched, frowning. He was not, as King had suggested, driving the sergeant home. "You're in bad shape," he said. "I'm going to help you."

"Like fuck you will." Ben closed his eyes and pressed his head against the seat. If only he could fall into oblivion. Part of him wouldn't mind if Reno decided to punch him out again.

"I've been worse than you," Reno said as they sped down the road. "I know you don't believe it. But trust me on this. King yabber-jabbered about your wedding, and the way he explains it, you aren't a lost cause. You showed up that night—now, stay with me, 'cause I'm talking metaphorically. You, Sergeant, were present." Reno shoved his index finger at his own temple. "Up here," he said. "And in here." He beat his palm twice against his chest. "That ain't nothing."

Ben knew that if he nodded, he'd vomit again. He felt waves of nausea rolling over and over him, in huge swells.

"And frankly," Reno kept on, "to be in your general condition and *still* to have shown up means—and I have a particular intuition about these things—that you can unfuck yourself."

"Jesus Christ." Ben moaned. Reno had suddenly veered off the road and onto grass. They bounced along on the spongy surface before stopping short. Ben threw open the door and retched.

"We're here!" Reno announced.

Ben heard crickets. His vision was fuzzy, but it looked as though Reno had driven them into a field. "Where are we?"

"Get out and you'll see," Reno said brightly. He unbuckled his seat belt. Slowly, Ben followed. They were in a meadow surrounded by slopes of trees.

"There's nothing here."

"Exactly. See, on the way out here, I came up with something. It's called the Reno Caruso Veteran-Unfucking Program."

"What are you talking about?" Ben sagged, nearly fell to his knees.

"Here's what I'm thinking, Ben. You went off and got yourself fucked up. You didn't plan for it. It's not your fault. But you're home now and you're newly married, and it just so happens—and I wouldn't underestimate the importance of this fact—that you love the person you're married to. So now the question is, what part of you is going to win out? The part that's loving or the part that's fucked?"

"Please," Ben groaned. "Crawl back into whatever hole you came from. Becca's told me all about you."

"Becca knows me *so* well." Reno chuckled. "What'd she say? Cavorting, drinking, fucking? Truth is, Ben, I grew out of all that a long time ago. I've got a business. And I've got to look out for your father-in-law."

"*You're* looking out for *King*?"

Reno nodded solemnly. "He and I were in-country together. You know what that means."

Ben nodded and the world tumbled over itself. He rested his head against the car and let his body go limp.

"I help him, even when he's not interested."

"What's that got to do with me?" Ben could barely manage a whisper.

"King believes in you, Ben. He believes in the *two* of you."

"So do I."

Reno laughed and shook his head. "I'm going to pretend that we're on the same page about all of this."

Ben slid his face down to the window. The glass was soothing and cool. He'd be all right if Reno would just shut up.

"Sergeant, we want to give the loving part of you a head start over the fucked part. Welcome to the Great Smokies, Tennessee side. Specifically, to a section of country I like to call the Dry Isle."

Ben realized how far east they'd traveled, how far he was from Becca, and his heart sank.

"True to its name, the Dry Isle is a thirty-square-mile region where you will not find a single ounce of purchasable alcohol. Trust me on this. No liquor stores, no bars. If you wandered around long enough, you might trip over somebody's still, but I'm guessing you'd get eaten by a bear before that happened, or get shot for trespassing."

A throbbing sensation suddenly announced itself on the side of Ben's face. He touched the skin and winced. "Yeah, that's gonna be nasty by the morning," Reno said. "Sorry."

Ben finally gave in to the pain and dizziness. He dropped to his knees and shut his eyes. He looked like a man awaiting execution. Reno pulled a pen from his pocket and took the cap off with his teeth. Then he grabbed Ben's arm.

"Get off me!" Ben opened his eyes and leaned away, but Reno held tight.

"If I don't write down the instructions, you'll forget." He yanked Ben's arm straight. "You're gonna head due southeast," he said and scribbled. "Your destination is a town called Sparta." Reno wrote this too. "Get yourself to the auto garage. You can't miss it. Introduce yourself to Miles." Reno wrote *Miles* on Ben's arm. Then he stuck his face right in front of Ben's, so close that Ben could see the stubble points on the older man's cheeks. "Miles'll tell you what's next. Do you follow?"

"No," Ben moaned. But then, looking into Reno's uncompromising eyes, he realized one thing very clearly. Panic set in. He leaped to his feet, then stumbled from dizziness. "You can't just leave me here."

Reno felt a tug of pity, but he let it go. Until a couple of months ago, Ben had been on active duty in the U.S. Army. He had two sturdy legs and there was surely GPS on his phone. *No such thing as GPS during* my *service,* Reno thought, taking a moment to muse over what navigational gizmos and gadgets the military must be giving soldiers these days. Not that any of it mattered.

War was confusing as fuck. *Different time,* he thought, *same situation.*

"Once you get to Sparta, you'll get your wheels back. Then, if you straighten yourself out, you can come get Becca. Sound like a deal?"

"No."

"Good." Reno got back in the car.

Ben stumbled toward the passenger-side door but tripped and fell. "Asshole!" he shouted as he heard the car's locks engage. He watched Reno turn onto the road and speed away. "Fuck!" he shouted at the car. "Fuck!"

To say that Reno was unmoved by the image of Ben screaming furiously at him as he drove off would not be accurate. Twenty miles later, he could still hear the boy shouting and see his wide, furious eyes. Reno did not like to hear men scream. He did not like to see men's eyes popping from their sockets. But this action was necessary. Reno wasn't doing this for Ben, really, or even for Becca. He was doing it for King. And there was a chance — the smallest, slimmest chance — that if the kids got their shit together, they could protect King from the madness ahead.

December 13, 1972

Dear Willy,

Durga has been talking to me. Ever since I got back Stateside, she's been whispering directions. She let me know that keeping the heart in my hometown was pointless, that my home wasn't my home any longer, and that my parents were relations only in name. Durga showed me that I'd been reborn. I had new organs — a new heart. So I bought a motorcycle (Durga wasn't vehicle-specific; she simply said, *Get going, Proudfoot!*), and I set out. My mother stood at the end of our block crying as I drove away. I felt bad about that, but what could I do? I haven't been back since.

I bummed around in the upper Midwest, college towns, pretending to be a student. You once told me that the ancient Greeks knew everything there was to know about war. So I went to lectures on Homer and Hellenic warrior culture. I even took language courses so I could read the work in the original, though I didn't get far. In a way, I was trying to finish what you'd started — to go down the path you'd been on until the U.S. government diverted you, brought you to us. To me.

After a few years of this, Durga grew restless, so I trekked over to Washington State and found a job on a dairy farm. I shoveled cow shit. I can't say I liked it much, but I learned humility. I learned to care for creatures who could not care for themselves. I learned to balance the life of the mind with the life of the body. But again, Durga grew restless, so I rode my bike into Oregon. Eventually, I ended up in a hippie commune, where I'm writing you from now. They grow good herb here and this other hallucinogenic they've cultivated from a strain of some South American plant. Willy, the trip from this plant is unlike anything I've ever experienced. Inside of it, you can relive the past — people, events. It's the one place where I can talk to Durga freely and plainly. She allows me to fly, and sometimes she plunges me into the depths of the ocean, which feels like drowning. It's her way of testing me. To make sure that I can still be trusted with her heart, to protect it always. Also, the plant sells. The hippies are raking in some serious cash.

I don't care what anyone says, Willy. They aren't bad people. They know I was in the war and they don't care. I think they feel bad for me, wandering alone. The hippies are smart. They understand that family is about choice. But I wonder if true family isn't really about need. Your family isn't the people you want to be with but the people without whom you would perish. The problem is, I don't know where the members of my true family are. King, Reno, the others who came along after you. We all came back alone, and then we dispersed. Scattered by the wind.

Sometimes I think that I see you, Willy. In a bar or pumping gas. Sometimes, every face has a flash of your face. I don't like to be around strangers, because I worry I'll catch a glimpse of you. And that hurts. I don't mind being alone when I have to, though. Even when I'm alone, Durga's heart is with me.

Currahee!
CO Proudfoot

4

WHEN BECCA AWOKE on her father's couch the next morning, everything was briefly beautiful. Dust motes sparkled in the sunlight, and her pillow was dry. Lately, she'd been crying in her sleep, which she hated. Ever since she'd started running, in junior high, she'd learned to keep her emotions in check, channeling excess frustration into winning races. It was not okay that her feelings were again acting against her will.

She decided that her present sense of calm was a sign. She was right to have left home. Ben's appearance the night before had only strengthened her resolve. Through all his shouting, her heart was numb, anesthetized. If only that meant her bruises didn't hurt. She stood up, trying to reason with her nerve endings. She was sore, but she'd experienced worse pain after meets; she could handle this.

Neither her father nor Reno was around. Her car was gone, which meant one of the men must be driving Ben back to the house. They'd leave him there and bring the Cadillac back to her. Then she could go to Kath's on her own steam.

Outside, Becca squished her toes into the damp grass. The air smelled of hay and honeysuckle and if she did not breathe in too deeply, she could ignore the ache of her abdomen. She sat down in a plastic lawn chair and turned toward the pasture. She imagined her father sitting out here, night after night, his body still as a garden statue, his beard overgrown as the grass. When she was a girl, he had terrified her. Sometimes it took only a single question—*Dad, will you sign this permission slip?* Or *Dad, are you coming to my soccer game?*—to make King breathe fire. Drunk or angry or both, he'd tromp through the house, smashing and screaming. Then one day, when Becca was fourteen, her mother had kicked King out. There'd been neither warning nor fanfare. "I sent your daddy packing," Jeanine said, and that was that.

In her mother's stolidness, Becca learned a powerful lesson: their kind of women were not victims.

Only then, eight months ago, in October 2007, after six years of radio silence, King came back. Becca had started seeing him on a bimonthly basis, mostly because her aunt Kath had asked her to keep an eye on him. She didn't mind. Ben was in Iraq, and having someone to look out for—even if it just meant trips to the grocery store—was a welcome distraction. King was sober and had steady work. He'd even offered some money toward the wedding. The new King was a decent person, even a gentle one. Over the phone, Jeanine warned her daughter about getting too close. But as Becca told Ben during one of their video chats, "It's not his fault the war screwed him up. Why not show the man some kindness?"

Now, maybe for the first time, King was doing some actual fathering. Becca still kept her mother's words close—King was not a man to rely on. But that was fine. The moment he stopped offering to help, she would say thank you very much and move on.

Becca resumed her walk across the backyard. She found her father in his work shed with the air-conditioning unit rattling loud and fast, like it was about to explode. Without it, the smell of leather oil was overpowering. "Morning," Becca said.

King looked up briefly and nodded hello. He was softening a small leather bag, rubbing the oil into it in slow, deliberate circles. The motion was a meditation. Working leather, he could ignore the clutter in his brain, like his daughter's husband ranting and raving on his doorstep, and his best friend punching said husband in the face, and the presence of his daughter, who stood watching him now, clearly full of questions that he did not want to answer.

"Dad?"

At the question, King couldn't help but look up. Physically, Becca took after her mother; they were both small-boned women with big brown eyes and heart-point chins. Becca was shorter than Jeanine—no taller than five foot four, 110 pounds tops—but she had strong muscles, especially in her legs, from running. She'd always been strong. And scrappy. As a kid she was not beyond biting and clawing. With her hair cut short, she looked even feistier. But he had things reversed. It was the old, long-haired Becca who had eagerly invited trouble. He liked the photograph on his dresser because in it she looked familiar, more like the girl he knew than the strange woman she'd become. It was astonishing. Without his help or his input, she'd grown up.

"What happened last night?" she asked. "Where's Ben?"

Questions number two and three.

"And where's my car?"

Four.

Her eyes narrowed. Even though she was backlit in the doorway, King could sense the fierceness of her expression, a demand to be answered. This toughness hadn't come from him. He was, at heart, a quiet man. And it hadn't come from

Jeanine, who was, at heart, a restless woman. But his daughter had learned fortitude somehow. Still, he felt certain that some of her resolve—probably a large portion of it—was a defense mechanism. And defense mechanisms were like the shitty M16s they'd taken to the jungles, weapons that jammed up when you most needed them. Still, when the weapons worked properly, they could kill a man.

"Ben's with Reno. Black eye, but fine. Not sure where Reno took him."

Her eyes widened. "What? What do you mean?"

"Like I said."

She walked farther into the shed. Marched, really. Her body was vibrating. This wasn't good.

"I'm sure Reno will be back soon. And I'm sure he'll have your car. And then you can follow us to Kath's."

Becca nodded, but he could feel her all wound up, like those skittering toy trucks he'd played with as a child. Since returning to Dry Hills, he'd noticed that his daughter was more temperamental than she believed herself to be. She was decent at hiding her confusion and stress, but King was a barometer for anxiety. He registered, and internalized, even slight emotional disturbances. It was why he lived out here, alone. It was the reason he was going west. He was exhausted. He wanted the jitters and the nightmares and the sweats to stop. He realized that it might frustrate Becca to watch him leave again, and so soon. But his daughter was doing fine. Sure, she and Ben were in a rough patch, but that was to be expected this soon after his time in the war.

King continued rubbing oil into the caramel-colored pouch. Becca asked what he was working on, but he gave a terse answer about fixing something, and she knew better than to press him. Instead, she studied the engraved belts, knife holsters, wallets, and flasks. The leather surfaces were tough but their undersides were soft as chick down. *Chicken,* she thought and then banished Ben's pet name from her head. She poked through shoeboxes of King's knives, needles, and awls. It was strange to think of her father as a craftsman, though perhaps this was another thing they shared. At school, she was majoring in graphic design and had a knack for layouts and fonts. She understood what it meant to be absorbed in a single project for hours on end without even bothering to use the bathroom, let alone eat. Her father, working in his shed, was the same way.

King had introduced Becca to his trade eight months ago by way of a key chain. On one of her first visits to his house, he'd taken her out back and showed her a menacing Cadillac parked on the grass. King explained that his friend Rusty had passed away and left him the car. "He wanted her to be useful. I thought she could be useful to you."

Without thinking, Becca had jumped on her father, squeezing her arms around his belly. It was a mistake. King stiffened, became a block of stone. "Don't!" he growled, and Becca stumbled backward.

"I was just excited," she'd apologized. "I forgot you don't like — I'm sorry."

"Don't," he spat and lumbered away, shaking his head. Becca looked down to find the key on a key chain in the grass. Her initials were stamped in the impossibly smooth leather, and she read those letters for the lesson they were: however much her father had changed, he wasn't better. Deep inside, he hurt and could hurt others as much as he ever had.

"Can I call Reno and find out what's going on?" she asked now.

King nodded to the phone on the table. His contact list was short, though she was surprised to see her mother's name. As far as Becca knew, her parents had not seen each other — had not spoken — in years. Jeanine had not even come to the wedding, in part (Becca assumed) because King was going to be there. But then she remembered the graduation photo in King's bedroom.

Before Becca could think on it further, Reno came roaring up the drive. He rode a sports bike, the kind that a certain brand of Southern asshole gunned, lethal, down the highway. Reno's model was shiny and black with acid-green embellishments. Seen from head on, the front fairing resembled the face of a cheetah. But Becca's disapproval was immediately replaced by dread. Where was her car? She rushed to the driveway and stood stiffly by as Reno parked. "What the hell?" she demanded the moment he pulled off his helmet.

"What—you don't like her? This here's a 2007 Kawasaki Ninja 2X-6R with a four-stroke, liquid-cooled, DOHC, four valve, inline four-cylinder engine. Just look at these fairing flares. They're like Wolverine's blades! Makes the thing look fast even when it's dead still."

"You know I'm not talking about the bike."

Reno swung his leg over the racer and dismounted. "Man, I've been yelled at a lot in the last twelve hours. Did you and Sergeant Thompson shout your wedding vows at each other?"

"Fuck you, Reno."

"Whoa, girl. Profanity is uncalled for. Especially since I've been up all night long helping out *your* husband." Reno slipped the helmet under his arm and walked past Becca toward the house.

"Hold on," she said, following. "You can't just disappear with my car."

"Funny how you seem so much more concerned about the car than the man."

So much for her early-morning calm. A fireball of exasperation burst in her stomach and sent shards of panic ricocheting through her body. Any second, she'd start shooting metal from her fingertips. She rushed up and grabbed at Reno's shoulder, but the leather jacket kept her nails from digging in. Reno froze, and, for a moment, Becca feared he'd go ballistic, like King. She braced herself for a verbal slap or worse. But Reno gently lifted her hand from his shoulder and placed it by her side.

"Your car is at my shop in the Smokies. It needed to be fixed up, which I am going to do for you, free of charge. Your husband, if you still care, is sobering up. Until he's in a better state of mind, he won't be back to bother you."

"I don't want him back."

"If you say so."

"Don't patronize me, Reno. You have no idea." She'd calmed a little, but her panic began to hum anew. She saw the electricity snapping across black space, collecting into a new ball of fire.

"Not only *do* I know, but I'm the only one looking out for you."

The idea of Reno as her guardian was too absurd. "My dad is looking out for me," she said.

Reno shook his head. "King can barely look out for himself."

"I'd say King's doing pretty good," she retorted. She knew she was walking on dangerous ground. Still, the idea of Reno being right about *anything* killed her.

"I don't want to argue with you. Can we please call a truce?" he asked.

"So what now?" she said.

"We'll take you to Kath's. Ben'll bring the car to you." And then he mumbled a word under his breath; it sounded like *hopefully.*

"I don't want him coming after me." She swallowed hard as she spoke these words. Reno did not know the situation—

why she had run. The fireball was pulsating. At any moment, it would explode and tears of fire would spray from her eyes.

Reno turned and fixed his eyes on her. They were hazel, flecked with yellow and brown, set deep into his skin. Skin that had seen too much sun and resembled the untreated leather in King's shed. He looked tired. "It'll be okay," he said, his voice quiet.

But he couldn't know that. She turned and began walking away. She felt him watching, but she willed herself not to turn around. And before Reno could hear the sob escape her throat, she took flight. She wasn't wearing shoes, so she hopped the neighbor's fence and sprinted across the cow pasture. For most of her life, she'd chosen not to rely on others. But then two years ago, Ben had arrived, not only promising his help but insisting on giving it. Another person could make things easier, he'd argued. It was vital to have a load-bearing beam. And so, tentatively, she began to share with him: her long-held frustrations and disappointments; her triumphs and regrets; her awful memories and ambitious plans. She allowed herself to need him. And then that load-bearing beam had started to crack.

As King and Reno packed up their motorcycles in the driveway, King gushed over his new bike. A Honda Gold Wing, it was a touring vehicle made for long rides with passengers. It was also bright purple.

"Did a woman with tsunami bangs pick that out?" Becca joked and then wondered why this prompted King and Reno to exchange strange glances.

"What do you really think?" King asked. It was difficult to tell which was brighter, his enormous smile or the bike's gleaming exterior. He pointed out the five-disc CD changer and GPS screen.

"Does it shave you and give you pedicures?" Reno asked. "One of them metrosexual bikes?"

King ignored him. "Feel this," he said to Becca. He put a meaty hand down on the seat. "You can bet my ass won't hurt anymore."

Becca brushed her palm across the plush velour. "Are those armrests?" She pointed to the passenger seat.

"They rotate!" King said happily. "You can relax, snug as a baby in a cradle."

"Yeah." Reno snickered. "And after you've been rocked asleep, you can fall off."

King's smile faded. Why, thought Becca, couldn't Reno just let her father enjoy this moment?

But King nodded. "He's got a point. Becca, you've got to stay vigilant. But you'll also wear this." He handed his daughter a black helmet the size of a large bowling ball. It wobbled around her ears. "Sorry," he apologized. "It's the only other brain bucket I've got."

Becca did not like this term. She pictured her brain sloshing around in the helmet like a dumpling in soup. Her nerves were igniting like pistons. She'd never been on a motorcycle before. Many years ago, King had been in a horrible accident and had lain mummified in bandages and casts for weeks. Becca's class had just learned how caterpillars turned into butterflies, and she'd hoped her father would emerge kinder and quieter from his plaster cocoon. But trapped inside this artificial skin, the anger had only become more concentrated. Once home, he unleashed a fury that shook the glasses on the shelves. Jeanine ended up sending Becca to Kath's for a full ten days, despite school being in session. A very good reason not to like motorcycles.

Now she hoisted herself onto the passenger seat and sank

into the backrest. The bruises made real comfort impossible. But her father was right; the seat was nice. She glanced at Reno, who'd traded the flashy Kawasaki for his all-purpose Harley. The motorcycle was the bare-bones variety. With its valves and spokes and tubes, it looked turned inside out, less like a motorcycle than an x-ray of one.

"Buck up, girl. That's no bike you're on." Reno smirked. "That's a parade float."

Becca located the foot pegs, terrified that her father would take off before she was ready. King turned the ignition, and the bike expelled a deep-bellied grumble and began to vibrate. Without thinking, Becca grabbed her dad around the gut. For a second, she was sure he'd have an attack. Instead, he patiently instructed her to hold the armrests and sit up straight. "You won't fall," he said.

Reno shouted something at her above the engines. It sounded like *neophyte*.

King put up his hand, signaling that he was ready. He clicked the gear lever into first with his left foot and then, twisting the throttle toward him, started slipping the clutch. Reno, meanwhile, made a big show of revving his Harley. The bike barked, Doberman growls devouring them all in a mouth of sound. The ground beneath Becca bucked, and suddenly, she was racing, the wind punching at her face. Her heart flew up into her throat and she gripped the armrests. "Holy shit!" she whispered, but the wind ripped the words from her mouth. She looked down —a big mistake. There was the road, rushing mere inches from her sneakers. It seemed soft instead of hard, like the bike was afloat on an asphalt sea. How would the road keep them buoyed? What if they capsized? What if her father spooked at her closeness and crashed them both?

King tapped Becca's leg and she flinched. But then she saw that he'd raised his hand and was giving her a thumbs-up.

Slowly, she raised her hand to return the gesture. The wind battered her arm like a twig, as if it would shake the very skin from her bones, blow her fingernails out of their nail beds. She gripped the armrests again and focused on her breathing. And, just then, King slowed. The shift was small, but Becca's relief was indescribable. It was like King had sensed her terror. *Thank you, Dad,* she thought. *Thank you for keeping me alive.*

King had found his stride. If she didn't resist the wind and the speed, if she let herself become part of the bike, she could skim the road's surface and, like a sailboat, glide. For the first time, Becca held up her head and looked around. She took in the smooth green quilt of pasture and the fields of alfalfa, the cows freckled across the hills. She felt something well inside of her and realized it was joy. It was, it seemed, a perfect day to ride.

Around five that evening, the trio rode into Memphis and crossed the Mississippi River. Reno sped by, his legs stretched out straight like a little kid racing downhill on a bicycle, daring gravity. Becca pushed up the face guard on her helmet and gulped down mouthfuls of wind, each draft filling her with lightness. They weren't quite halfway across the river when she looked down the bridge and imagined she saw Ben standing at the far end, grinning. She'd been here before — the familiarity was powerful — though she couldn't think when or how. And it didn't matter anyway, because soon the motorcycle had gobbled up the last few feet of bridge and hit land. They'd reached Arkansas, and there was nothing but road ahead.

PART II

AWOL

December 13, 1975

Dear Willy,

I have come to believe that certain anniversaries—holy days, if you will—deserve a formal commemoration. Sad as it may be, your story will never appear in the history books. It will never be cataloged by scholars, or published in journals, or immortalized by poets. This is wrong, Willy. It's unjust. It's enough to make a man grow angry . . . But that is not Durga's way. So instead, I have decided to mark this holy day by writing your story. Which is my own story. Which is, above all, the story that Durga herself put in motion.

I will begin with December of 1969, that irreversible slash in time after which neither I nor the war I'd been fighting was ever the same. Before you, of course, everything was awful. I was on my second tour. This time around, I'd spent months sloshing through the Mekong Delta swamps, up to my knees in stinking water, shooting blind through the mosquito haze. Though our squad lost three in the swamps, we somehow managed to distinguish ourselves. The leadership said we'd displayed uncommon heroism and bravery, and as a reward, they were promoting us—me, Reno, and King

— and tapping us for something special. The next thing we knew, we'd been transferred to a Civilian Irregular Defense Group camp — a CIDG — near the Cambodian border. Then for months, we saw no action at all, just built barracks and surveillance posts. In the neighboring Montagnard village, we put up a school and taught the tribesmen to shoot. We handed out C rations to local kids in exchange for back rubs. It didn't matter that no amount of beer could wash the fetid taste of swamp water from my mouth. I'd developed my routine: drink too much, sit up on patrol, try not to think.

And then one morning, you arrived. You sat in the major's office, this skinny kid with an acne-blasted face and lashes so dark and thick, you looked like you had on makeup. You were eighteen, nineteen tops. I remember thinking: *No way this kid's ever been laid.*

The major introduced you as "Private Wilfred Owen McKenzie, anthropologist." He said we were pulling a mission the next week and that you were coming with. "Willy Owen," you said and stuck out your hand to shake mine. Your fingers were pale and your skin seemed translucent. I noticed your hands were trembling.

Reno's mouth was wide open and King had this slack-jawed look, like you might be a mirage. I thought: *No way in hell am I going to let some Fucking New Guy get my men killed.* Of course, the major knew exactly what was on my mind and tried to set me straight. He said you'd been through basic, reported you were a decent shot. Normally, I trusted the major. He was experienced, a picture of confidence, straight as a pencil, his head squared off like a worn-down eraser. But right then, I was feeling a whole lot of panic.

The major waved his hand over a map on his desk, loosely identifying a village called Li Sing. "Some minority related to the Cham lives there," he said. "You know the Cham?"

Of course we didn't know the motherfucking Cham.

"They're Hindus or Muslims or some kind of mix," the major said. And then he looked at you for confirmation.

"Yes, sir," you said, your voice shaking as bad as your fingers. You swallowed so hard, your Adam's apple practically shot up into your chin.

"Headquarters suspects the people of Li Sing have important intel. Private McKenzie'll explain. This map came with him, direct from HQ."

That night in the mess, you told us that you spoke seven languages, had gone to college at sixteen, and had read Homer in the original. (I was impressed, Willy. I'd always considered myself something of a scholar. Growing up, I had a shelfful of books they don't even think about giving you in high school. But advertising your brains out here, to these men? That was a big mistake.) In any case, you told us that three months before, an army colonel had arrived at the university where you were studying the anthropological and linguistic origins of indigenous Cambodian tribes. Apparently, you were the only American the army could find whose linguistic skills might let him communicate with the people of Li Sing. The colonel gave you a patriotic spiel, but you were already in; you'd do anything to see Li Sing with your own eyes.

But here's what you didn't tell us, Willy. Only forty-eight hours after you landed in-country, snipers attacked your convoy. They killed the private sitting next to you, the bullets blowing blood and shreds of skin onto your face. You sat like that, beside a dead man, for the thirty minutes it took to reach a medical facility. You were the Fucking New Guy and you'd been fucked over real good. That's why your fingers were shaking. When the major told me this, I thought: *Well, maybe he was a good shot in basic, but not anymore.*

Currahee!
CO Proudfoot

5

BEN WALKED IN the dark. He'd wasted no time after Reno abandoned him, just headed down the road according to the directions on his arm. He was too exhausted to hate, too tired to think. Periodically, he felt a tug at his waist, like he was pulling something along the road. But whenever he turned, he saw nothing. When he touched his bruised eye, a swampy, queasy feeling overtook him. But he couldn't leave it be. He'd never been sucker-punched before. *Congratulations, Benjamin,* he thought. *At last, you're a man.*

Ben walked down the center of the road, wary of the shadowy woodland around him. The Smokies were cooler than Dry Hills and he wondered how far into the mountains Reno had taken him. He needed a couple of beers to dull his throbbing face, settle his stomach, and clear the fog from his head. He doubted the county was actually dry, but it didn't matter. He was alone. Nobody for miles.

As dawn broke, the wall of shadow dissolved. Red and silver maples appeared, clustered among hornbeam and yellow birch. The thickness and freshness of it all, the mesmerizing color—Ben had forgotten such lushness existed. He left the road and tromped toward the forest, not minding the dampness of the long grass that seeped into his shoes. At the base of a maple he stopped and placed his hand against the sap-stained bark. There, on his finger, a gold band. It seemed impossible that he'd spent all those months in Iraq without it. Ben pressed his palm harder against the mottled trunk, as though to intentionally drive splinters into his skin. How had he ended up out here, so far from her?

He made himself walk back to the road. He was nervous, wanted to crawl on his belly to avoid bullets that at any moment could come whizzing from the trees. *You're not crazy,* he told himself. *So you won't act crazy.* He felt better once he reached the pavement.

By ten a.m., Ben moved in a full-blown haze of dehydration and nausea. Pinkish-red light poured from a gash in the sky, and sometimes, when he looked at the road, he saw the sticky black floor of Corporal Coleman's Humvee. Shortly after noon, he passed a sign that read *Sparta, Population 3,046.*

A few hundred feet on, Ben came to a gas station with an attached convenience store. Beside it sat an auto shop and, beyond that, two Airstreams. Shiny and silver, they seemed to hover like blimps. About twenty yards back was an impressive junkyard of old automobile parts, lawn mowers, television sets, dishwashers, scrap metal, tires, and wood stacked under blue tarps. It was the most orderly junkyard Ben had ever seen, the items arranged in rows according to color and size. A sign on the chainlink fence read *Last Chance Garage and Junkyard. Reno Caruso, Proprietor.* Below this in letters that were comically small: *Miles Swanson, Apprentice.* Ben entered the convenience store and headed straight for the refrigerators. Not a beer in sight.

He grabbed a bottle of water and drank greedily. Then he opened a bag of chips. When nobody came to take his money, he headed out in search of Miles. Classical music floated from the garage. Ben walked in and let out a relieved sigh. At last, the Death Star.

"You're Ben?" said a soft voice. "I'm Miles."

The man who appeared quite suddenly resembled a desiccated cornstalk. He wore khaki coveralls, and his sloping forehead was topped with a dandelion puff of brown hair. "Reno do that to your face?" Miles asked and barked a loud, awkward laugh. His gaze was fixed midway between Ben's bruised eye and his earlobe. His left hand trembled against his leg. *Something off about this one,* thought Ben.

"Reno said to get you some food. Come on." Miles led Ben into one of the Airstreams. It was a tidy little compartment. Ben noted a cluster of yellow wildflowers in a vase, checkered curtains, and a photograph of a pretty young woman.

"Nice place," Ben said.

"Thanks. I'm happy enough with it." Miles opened cupboards and gathered glasses and plates. His hand continued to shake. He glanced over his shoulder and motioned for Ben to sit down. "This place used to be a real pigsty. But I realized that I was letting the sick tell me what to do instead of the other way around." Miles pulled a bowl of chicken salad from the fridge. He put a few slices of white bread on the plates, poured iced tea into Ben's glass. He did all of this with his right hand. "I thought you'd rather eat something fresh. You know, instead of that crap we sell at the gas station."

Ben pulled out his wallet and offered to pay for the water and chips, but Miles shook his head. He nodded at the lunch items. Ben made himself a sandwich, but the mayonnaise turned his stomach. "I really should get going—" he began, but Miles interrupted him.

"So what's your story, Ben?" he asked, and then, without giving Ben a chance to answer, he launched into his own personal history. "Before I came here, I was on the street in Chattanooga. And before the street, I was in a shelter. And before the shelter, I was in a house in Chattanooga and working at Hardee's. Prior to that I was at Fort Benning. And before that I was in Fallujah and Nasiriyah. And then," Miles said, scratching his balding crown, "let's see, before that, I guess I was just a regular kid living outside Macon, Georgia, and going to high school. My wife and I were both JROTC. We were high-school sweethearts. More iced tea?"

Ben held out his glass. "So your wife is in the service?" he asked, thinking too late of the Airstream's narrow bed and lack of feminine objects.

Miles nodded, then shook his head. "I was pretty shook up after she died," he said. "You know, because I'd been stationed in the same place only a few months before. It was like she was walking in my footsteps. Only I walked out and she didn't."

Ben had imagined what it would be like to have Becca in Iraq with him. He'd sometimes envisioned himself standing outside the COP and her suddenly jumping from a Humvee shouting, "Gotcha!" But these daydreams quickly turned dark. As he thought of burying his face in her hair and breathing her in, he'd start to panic. He'd picture bullets flying into her small body, flinging her to the ground. He'd picture her eyes dead and open to the sky.

"I've got steady work now," Miles continued. "I was lucky to meet Reno. He helped me get my disability. And there are nice people in Sparta. Even with the Vietnam and Korean guys fighting over me. The VFW and American Legion are across the street from each other, and I'm stuck in this tug o' war between them."

"What do you mean?" Ben shifted uncomfortably. Now that he'd learned about Miles's wife, he felt stuck, obliged to listen.

"Vietnam guys refuse to set foot in the VFW ever since one of the Korean vets told Reno that he wasn't welcome there."

"Did Reno get in a fight?"

"No, sir. See, the VFW is for veterans of foreign *wars,* and this one guy from Korea told Reno that his war didn't count."

"Why not?"

"Because Congress never made it official."

"That's ridiculous."

"Everybody wants his truth to matter, I guess."

"You'd think these guys could find some common ground," Ben said.

"You mean like you and me feel common ground with marines?"

Miles had a point. And yet. If you'd been fired at, you'd been fired at. Who cared if the conflict in which said firing occurred had been authorized by Congress?

"So what's your story?" Miles asked.

"Well, I served in—"

"No." Miles shook his head. "I mean what happened that our friend Reno sent you out here? You'd think since he's so much shorter . . . but his fist is like a rock."

Ben wondered how many people Reno had punched in recent months. "I was trying to talk to my wife. I guess he didn't want me doing that."

Miles nodded. "You were angry? And drunk?"

"Yes." Ben looked directly at Miles, tried to make the guy hold his gaze. "But I would never hurt her." He didn't know why he felt compelled to explain himself to a man who was as busted as the junk he lived next door to. Looking at Miles, Ben realized that he, Sergeant Benjamin Thompson, was doing pretty well for himself. "So can I have my keys?" he asked.

Miles shook his head. "Reno gave me instructions. Not till you're okay to drive. When was the last time you slept?"

Ben couldn't remember.

“You can rest here, no problem,” Miles said. “I even made up the bed for you.”

Ben did not like this option, but what could he do? “Just a catnap.” He picked up his plate to rinse it and realized that he’d finished the sandwich. When had that happened?

“I’ll just be in the shop,” Miles said and left the Airstream. Ben lay down on the bed and set his watch alarm for one hour. Miles wasn’t so bad, he decided. He was only following orders.

6

KATH KELLER STOOD on her front porch waiting for the wind to carry the sound of growling engines to her ears. She looked calm, as always, her plump body draped in a simple tunic, her face serene as a mountaintop monk's. But inside, Kath was full of trouble. It wasn't just that she'd spent the morning wearing an executioner's mask and wielding a fiery torch. (Kath made sculptures from gun shells and kitchen appliances and told gullible tourists—usually Northerners—that the pieces were statements about the military-industrial complex.) Today, the trouble was about her niece. Only a month married, Becca was already running from her husband, on her way here.

"Well, isn't this a sight!" Kath said when the bikes finally crested the hill and parked in front of her cabin. She enveloped her niece in an embrace that smelled of cake flour and solder. "Rebecca Keller—er, is it Thompson now?—whatever caused you to join ranks with these barbarians?" She nodded at King and Reno.

"A lovers' tiff," Reno said.

Kath studied her niece. She saw how hard Becca was struggling to keep her expression even, saw the panic twitching like muscle spasms under the girl's skin. Whatever was going on, King had not one clue about how to fix it, so he'd simply chosen to deposit the problem with her. *Not so fast, big brother,* she thought and smoothed Becca's short hair. "Men are swine, honey," she said aloud. "Young men . . ." She paused and cocked her head toward Reno and King. "And old men."

"So nice to see you too, Kath," Reno said.

"No love for me?" King butted in.

"How *is* your heart, King? You still taking your explosives?" Among King's many medications were angina pills, hard nitroglycerin tablets he sucked on like candy. "And that belly!" Kath exclaimed. "King, honey, you know your heart and your stomach are connected, right? Reno, are you endorsing this mad-ass trip?"

"No, ma'am."

"What's mad-ass?" Becca asked.

It was like the wind had died. Nobody spoke. Nobody looked at her.

"Reno was the one who insisted we stop at McDonald's," King said quickly. "And for the record, I had a salad."

"Kath, you know your brother does what he wants."

Now the wind picked up again and shifted toward Reno. Kath and King stared at him, the former with overt suspicion and the latter with self-satisfaction. Becca realized that an entire conversation was being had behind her back and yet right in front of her face. But before she could ask questions, Kath said, "Well, never mind. Thank you for bringing my beautiful niece to me. Come on, honey."

She led Becca into the house. Reno and King followed like sulking dogs.

That night, the men dug into Kath's homecoming spread. "Your father has this theory that a body on the road needs to refuel often, just like a bike needs gas," she said after they'd filled their plates.

"But why?" Becca protested. "All you do is sit." She hadn't been on a proper run in three days and she could already feel her muscles starting to atrophy.

"It's because you're part of the bike's nervous system, isn't that right, big brother? Veins fusing with the wires, blood turning to oil?"

"Kind of like in *The Matrix*," Reno said, shoveling a fork loaded with multiple foodstuffs into his mouth.

It seemed an obvious contradiction for Kath to be so concerned about King's heart and yet feed him a lard-soaked meal of grandiose proportions. But Becca knew well enough that this was just the usual hospitality—both the concern and the contradiction.

"A man's heart beats with the great machine, King?" Kath continued.

"Not according to Proudfoot," Reno said and shook his head. "Who needs a bike when you've got a—"

"Enough." King glared at his sister and best friend and then resumed eating.

The second time in just a few hours that things had gone weird with those three. But maybe Becca was merely imagining it because she was on edge. Because she'd just run away from her husband. And her marriage. Oh, and her long-dreamed-about future. Maybe *that* was the weird thing.

"Now, this is the life," Reno said, leaning back in his chair after brother and sister had disappeared into the kitchen to wash up. Becca stood.

"Hey, wait a second, girl. Tell me how you're holding up."

She threw him an impatient look. "I'd be better if I knew when my car was getting here. And Ben too."

"All in good time."

"Then why bother to ask how I am?"

"If you want to know about Ben," Reno said, "why not call

him?" He held out his cell phone. She looked from his outstretched arm to his face. There was something approximating concern in his eyes, and yet he'd called her bluff. He put his phone away. "Suit yourself," he said.

Outside, moths and mosquitoes vied for a chance to self-immolate in the porch light. Kath's dog Shep lay in the dirt, breathing heavily, and Becca sat in a deck chair with closed eyes. She was *here,* physically and metaphysically. Nothing to be done about it. Betrayed as she might feel, she blamed herself more than Ben. A more vigilant person would have avoided this outcome, but she had let her guard down. She stamped her foot against the wooden porch boards. How had she let this happen? She should have been prepared! She had spent years training herself in readiness. When she ran a race, she always scoped out the course beforehand. She'd walk it or, at the very least, study it on a map. And yet where her own life was concerned, she'd failed to do the most basic work of planning for possible contingencies.

Becca stood and walked to the railing. She leaned forward, and her stomach lurched. Beneath her stretched a deep basin of trees, what the tourist guidebooks called the Arkansas Grand Canyon. The precipice was only a few yards away. Still, in the dark, it was easy to imagine this abyss as a solid blacktop, across which she could run.

In the distance came a rumble, and Shep released a whine of distress. Becca edged away from the railing and returned to the safety of her chair. "What kind of guard dog are you?" she complained as the rumble grew closer, its aggressive growl resonating in her bones. Soon enough, an orb hit her like a spotlight. She shielded her eyes until the white circle shut off. Clad in leather from head to toe, the rider seemed to ooze out of the darkness, like he was surfacing from an oil slick. The front door banged and King and Reno clambered down the steps.

"Bull, this is my daughter, Becca," King said, and he swept his arm out stiffly, like a novice game-show model. He was showing her off, proud of her. Bull removed his helmet and flashed a slick, white-toothed smile. He was the tallest of the three men, though less meaty than King, with razor-sharp cheekbones. He looked less bull than lynx.

"Becca's about to start her junior year of college," King said and Becca again noted the pride in his voice. "She's a track star." This was the first time her father had introduced her to someone. This was only the second friend of her father's that Becca had ever met.

"It's nice to meet you, Rebecca." Bull's voice was rich and deep, and the way he used her full name stirred something in the pit of her stomach. Maybe butterflies. Maybe bile. She was grateful when the men went into the house.

7

BEN STOOD OUTSIDE the COP, watching a pickup soccer game between his soldiers and some of the local kids. As usual, his platoon corporal, Eric Coleman, had kicked off the game. Coleman was gawky and tall, but his toothy grin and oversize ears were like kid-nip to the haji children; they flocked to him. He had such an easy way with the local population that Ben always brought Coleman along when they needed to interview people.

Ben, however, never felt comfortable around the Iraqi kids. The young boys were especially friendly, but slippery too, like their innocence was a ruse. You wanted to love those children but you couldn't trust them. And then you felt like a jerk for not trusting them, because weren't they only kids and wasn't their country going to shit? Ben suspected that if he looked less soldierly — less muscular and serious, with eyes that did not frown — then he'd feel less self-conscious. Becca had assured him that his smile more than compensated for his eyes. But how often did you smile when you were interrogating a family about the militants next door?

On this particular afternoon, Coleman was being schooled in fake-outs by a twelve-year-old boy named Majid. The kid called Coleman Soldier Eric, and the two of them appeared to have bonded over Corn Pops, which the corporal smuggled out of the mess. Coleman talked about Majid a lot, actually, how the kid could be a soccer star one day if his godforsaken country ever got its act together. Now, watching Majid dribble and fake, Ben understood Coleman's interest. But Ben worried. Soldiers should not be so attached—or involved. You had to put people in boxes in your head. You had to be able to tape those boxes up and stow them away. If you couldn't do that, you might very well lose your mind. Ben had seen it happen more than once.

He'd spoken to Coleman about this, but though a sergeant outranked a corporal, Coleman wasn't green; he'd done a previous tour in Afghanistan. And he and Ben were friends. Ben wondered if attachment was more his own problem than Coleman's.

"Aren't we supposed to be winning hearts and minds?" Coleman had rebutted when Ben asked about Majid. The comment was likely meant as sarcasm, but who knew? If he let Coleman cultivate Majid, then down the line the kid might provide some useful intelligence.

But now, in the middle of the soccer drill, Majid skidded to a stop. A man stood across the street, shouting. He had a black mustache and was dressed like any number of local shop owners.

"What's the matter?" Coleman shouted in Arabic.

The man ignored him. "Majid!" he called angrily.

Majid's eyes widened as though he'd been caught stealing. Suddenly, Ben understood that Majid was not allowed to play soccer with the soldiers.

"It's just a game," Coleman said in English. "It's harmless. Look, your son, Majid, he's really good." Coleman pointed fervently at the boy. "Really good," he said in slow, exaggerated English. *"Mumtaz."*

Ben did not like where this was going. "Let's go in, Corporal," he said.

"It's only soccer," Coleman protested. "Look." He turned back to Majid's father, who was becoming increasingly irate. "Don't be angry with him. You really don't understand how talented he is." Majid's father crossed the street and grabbed his son's arm. "Now, that's uncalled for," Coleman said.

"I understand you," said Majid's father in heavily accented English. "And I do not care. I do not want my son around you." He practically spat on Coleman. As his father pulled him away, Majid looked back over his shoulder with sad, frightened eyes.

Coleman stood there, shaking his head. Ben walked over. "What were you thinking?" he demanded. "That could have escalated. We talked about this."

Coleman looked pained.

"Hey, man," Ben said, finding it impossible to pull rank. "It's okay. Majid'll play soccer with his friends."

Coleman looked at Ben like Ben just didn't get it. "He's going to learn to hate us," he said, and he glanced back at the COP. It had been a school once, then an insurgents' arsenal, and now it was a makeshift base, fortified with blast walls and barbed wire. He watched a Humvee head out to patrol the trash-strewn streets. "The father — he's the reason that Humvee might not come back. Because his son will grow up to fucking hate us."

For a moment, Ben didn't comment. He considered this a simplistic view of the situation. But what if it really was that simple? Coleman's oversize shoulders sagged, and Ben felt compelled to make the guy feel better. Somehow.

"Maybe you're right," he said at last. "But by the time Majid grows up, it'll be our unlucky successors who get the brunt of his hate. You'll be playing soccer with your own kids. You won't even remember Majid's name."

"Yeah," said Coleman. "Sure."

Ben shot upright. "Majid!" he exclaimed. But the only person there was Miles, sitting in a chair beside the bed.

"Who's Majid?" Miles asked Ben's ear.

"How long have you been sitting there?" Ben demanded. He felt thoroughly creeped out.

"You were gone, man. I finished two cars while you were out."

Ben rubbed his eyes. "What time is it?"

"Almost one thirty. It's a good thing I didn't let you get in the car yesterday. You needed those z's."

"Yesterday? Oh, Jesus." Ben scrambled out of bed. "Why didn't you wake me?"

"You needed the sleep, man."

"Get me my keys, Miles!"

Miles nodded with a wormy smile. He led Ben back to the garage and handed him the leather key chain stamped with Becca's initials. Ben unlocked the car and climbed in. He stuck the key in the ignition, but the engine wouldn't start. He tried again, with no luck. Ben leaned his head out. "What's wrong with it?"

Miles crouched down beside the open passenger door. "Nothing. But you have to blow into this if you want the car to go." He reached across Ben's lap and pulled a small device, roughly the size of a primitive car phone, off a patch of Velcro on the dash. The object was black with a panel of buttons, a narrow screen, and a tube sticking out from the top like a short, squat antenna. A spiraled cord connected this object to a box installed beneath the steering wheel. "Ignition-interlock Breathalyzer," Miles said, not waiting for Ben to ask.

"You're not serious."

"Reno's instructions." Miles shrugged. "I'm only the apprentice."

"So if Reno says jump . . ." Ben scowled, inspecting the installation. It looked easy enough to dismantle.

"Reno doesn't *make* me do anything. You're in no shape to be on the road without some kind of check. You think I'm so pathetic?" Miles shook his head. He looked angry. "I feel sorry for *you,* man. I mean, fuck. I lost my wife over there. But I'm pulling myself together."

"I never said you were pathetic." Ben did not like to be blamed for things he had not done. Miles was just like those asshole men in the bar—and the waitress. Why was everyone ganging up on him?

Miles snorted. He was no longer looking at Ben's ear; he'd managed to fuse his eyes onto Ben's face. The guy's expression was ugly and as twisted as a mechanic's rag. "Anyway," Miles said, composing himself, "if you turn that thing on and blow, the car'll start. But don't try to take it apart. I've fixed it so that if you do, the car won't go at all. That was my idea, by the way. Not Reno's."

Ben gaped. He would not—could not—bend over and blow into the tube. But what choice did he have? He needed to get back on the road, get back to Becca. Also, if the opportunity presented itself, he needed to plant his fist in Reno's face.

In one swift motion, Ben picked up the Breathalyzer, switched it on, and stuck the plastic nub between his lips. He could feel Miles's eyes on his neck, but forget pride. He was doing the necessary thing. If Becca were here, she'd say the same. *Do what you need to do.*

He blew and the system beeped approvingly. Ben turned the key and the car started.

Miles leaned through the window. "Do you want to know where Becca is?"

Ben was bursting with impatience. "Of course. Why wouldn't I?"

Miles shrugged and his eyes drifted to the ground, like the pupils were too heavy to stay level. "I mean, this could be your getaway vehicle. You could start over. If it's too hard to go back. I don't know. Maybe that's the best thing for you and your wife."

"You don't know my situation."

Miles smiled as if he did, in fact, know Ben's situation.

"You think because we fought in the same war, you know me?" Ben said. "You don't know shit about me."

"Once you know where she is, you won't be able to walk away," Miles said, seemingly unruffled. "You'll go back, and this whole mess will probably just repeat itself. But if you leave now, you'll free her from all that. After all, if you're not with her, you can't hurt her."

Ben knew this. It was the reason he'd taken Becca's car and left in the first place. But he hadn't considered it in a big-picture kind of way. At least, he hadn't admitted the option to himself. It could be that Miles understood the situation precisely. Or that Miles was spouting more of Reno's manipulative bullshit. "Where is she, Miles?"

Miles nodded, but whether the nod was one of approval, acquiescence, or disappointment, Ben couldn't tell. "She's at her aunt Kath's. In Arkansas."

Without so much as a goodbye, Ben reversed out of the garage, swung the car around, and accelerated, heading back the way he'd come.

December 13, 1976

Dear Willy,

A week after your arrival, we set out into the wilderness. Of course, all of fucking Vietnam felt like wilderness to me, but Cambodia even more so. Because we were searching for a place that possibly didn't exist.

A Huey dropped us off in the dark, fifteen klicks into the jungle. We headed due west, using your map. I walked point, followed by King with the radio, then you, then Reno. I was worried Reno would end up shooting you out of sheer frustration, but I needed somebody competent watching the rear.

It didn't take long before I was ready to drop your skinny ass faster than a grenade with the pin pulled out. You were so skittish—starting every time a twig snapped—and you kept pulling at the collar of your uniform like it was trying to strangle you. You had no business being in the jungle with us.

Meanwhile, when you weren't letting every goddamn thing scare the bejesus out of you, you were giving us a lecture on the Cham of Li Sing: How they came from some ancient culture of Hindu origin that dated back to the seventh century. How they worshipped Durga, the ten-armed warrior goddess. You said the ten arms of Durga represented ten alliances—ten indigenous minorities throughout Cambodia and Vietnam. Apparently, we—meaning the United States Army—didn't know exactly where these tribes lived. We knew only that Li Sing was the center point of all ten groups, their heart.

You told us a saying among the Cham: "The body follows the heart." In other words, if the people of Li Sing agreed to fight Charlie, then the other tribes would follow them.

I wanted to know how you were so sure the people of Li Sing wanted to follow us. And you said maybe they didn't.

But you were so excited to actually meet them, you didn't care.

By midmorning on our first day in Cambodia, on our journey to find the Cham people of Li Sing, the sun had burned away the fog, and the jungle was as stagnant as the inside of a mouth. When we stopped for water, I noticed Reno cursing and scratching at his arm. "Something bit me earlier," he complained and rolled up his sleeve to reveal a nickel-size circle on his forearm. It was perfectly round and inflamed, but we paid it no mind. Reno said he was fine and we had endless miles of brush to hack through.

By the late afternoon, it felt like we'd been humping for days. So it was something of a relief when we stepped into an open sweep of low grass and put our machetes away. The clearing was a strange place, admittedly. In direct sunlight, it should have been much hotter, but it was cool, like a cold spot in the middle of a lake. I shivered as wind rustled bushes around the perimeter. I held up my compass, but the needle was frozen stiff. I borrowed Reno's compass and discovered his had the same problem. Meanwhile, you sat on your helmet, staring into the jungle. Reno stripped to his undershirt and inspected his arm. The skin was flushed between his hand and shoulder, and the circle had turned black. He pulled out his cigarettes, but his fingers were shaking so much, he could barely get one lit. Sweat glistened on his face and neck.

King walked over. "You feel that breeze?" I nodded. "We're too exposed out here." He held out his canteen to Reno, but Reno choked on the water and spat it out. "Tastes awful." King drank and said the water was fine.

"This place is like some kind of Cambodian Bermuda Triangle," I said and told King to dial camp. He did, but all he got was static. He adjusted the controls. More static. You,

Willy, just sat there through all of this, resting your head in your hands. I wondered briefly what you were thinking and whether you were replaying the ambush in your head — the private's face splattered all over your freshly pressed uniform. I thought that some people just have bad luck. Shit had happened to all of us, but not on our first day.

I'd just given orders to move back under cover when something crackled. We snapped to attention — except for you, still fumbling to get your helmet on — and flexed our weapons.

Then a figure stepped into the light: a woman. She wasn't more than five feet tall, and her clothes hung from her little body like rags on a line. Her eyes were glazed over with the look of a mortally wounded soldier, a man who doesn't know he's dying.

"What's she doing out here?" Reno demanded, moving forward.

"Search her," I ordered and I nodded at King to follow him.

"On your knees!" Reno said.

The woman didn't move. She didn't even look afraid.

"Get down on your knees," said Reno, "or I'll put a bullet through your flat-ass chest."

I moved closer behind Reno and saw that the rash had crawled up the back of his neck and into his scalp.

"Get the fuck down!" Reno brandished his gun.

The woman opened her mouth and uttered something unintelligible.

"Now!" Reno screamed, and I could have sworn he was going to shoot her, except suddenly you bounded forward and thrust yourself between him and the woman.

"Move out of my way, kid," Reno said.

"Take it easy!" King yelled and glanced back at me, panicked.

"She can help you," you said, looking the woman dead in the eyes. "She says Reno's sick. He's in trouble."

"Like fuck I'm—"

"She knows what bit you, Reno."

The woman babbled quickly, the words pouring from her mouth as though from a faucet.

"Does the water taste bad?" you asked, and the urgency in your voice sent a pulse of fear through me. Then Reno's legs buckled. King rushed forward to catch him.

"She has medicine," you said—nearly cried—to me.

"I don't trust her, Willy," I said.

You shook your head madly. "Proudfoot, listen to me. This woman's from Li Sing."

Currahee!

CO Proudfoot

8

THE MORNING AFTER her first night at Kath's, Becca woke up with her stomach clenched tight. One more day before her dad left—put the pedal to the metal, burned rubber. Why did she feel so nervous? She peeked out the window to find the porch looking like the aftermath of a college party: crumpled beer cans and cigarette butts everywhere.

Downstairs, she made coffee, grabbed a biscuit, and went outside. The air was wet, and a thick fog hung over the valley. As a kid, Becca had desperately wanted to move out here and live with Kath, but her aunt had never invited her. Later, in high school, she'd asked why Kath and her late husband had never had kids. "A lot of people have kids because they think they have to," her aunt said, "but that only leads to trouble for everybody. I'm not the parenting kind."

"Just like King," Becca offered.

"Maybe," her aunt answered. "Maybe not."

King was no parent, Becca had thought back then. But in the past few days, she'd begun to reconsider that assumption. If only he'd hang around a bit longer now, realize that his only daughter was in need of some TLC. But this was a dangerous road to walk. She should not expect more from her father.

"Well, if it isn't the lovely Rebecca." Bull materialized at the cabin door holding a can of Bud Light.

"It's Becca," she said.

Bull took a sip of his beer and pulled up a chair. For a moment, they sat in silence enjoying the view. The valley was beautiful, the Arkansas Grand Canyon an enormous basin of green tufts. *Like heads of broccoli,* Kath used to say. *And the sun shining down over the top — that's the melted butter.*

"We keep you up last night?" Bull asked.

"Yes." She wanted to piss him off so that he'd leave. But he only smiled. Some of her frustration dissolved. "You weren't in the army with my dad, were you?"

"Do I look that old?" Bull shook his head. "First Gulf War."

It wasn't like King to befriend younger vets. "Where'd you meet?" she asked.

"At the Rolling Thunder Rally in DC, about five years ago now. I was having a real hard time." Bull kicked his legs up on the porch railing, settled back into reverie. "I figured if a guardian angel didn't swoop down soon and save my ass, it was goodbye, Bull. But then your dad and the CO appeared. Now, I'm not a superstitious man, but what are the chances? Three hundred thousand people at that rally and they find me — a guy who so badly needed to be found? They took me out to Utah, got me straightened out."

Utah. Was that where King had been all this time?

Bull drummed his fingers on the top of his beer can. "Guys have a lot of opinions about the CO. Reno thinks his whole salvation thing is a load of crap. But I can't help it. I'm a believer. Hey, look there." Bull pointed at a hawk winging across the sky.

Becca had not heard her father mention a commanding officer. "A believer in what?"

"That there's a way out. That us vets can be free. It's a shame, though, you know? No matter how enlightened you are, the Agent O gets you in the end."

So a friend of theirs was sick. That's where they were going, and why.

Bull sat up straight, suddenly and inexplicably enraged. "Those motherfuckers in Washington. Just shrugging their shoulders like, *What did I do?* Like even though we bathed in that toxic shit, they're not responsible. Like they don't *owe* us." Bull glared at Becca as though she, specifically, owed him. Becca wanted to point out that Bull had never served in Vietnam and therefore had not been exposed to Agent Orange. But that was a technicality, at least to Bull. Also, as a child, Becca had watched her father fly from kind to cruel faster than a sports car going from zero to sixty. She'd never grown used to this behavior, and when she saw it happening with Ben — lethargy running to rage and back again, not to mention the drinking — she didn't want to believe it. Ben had promised her — sworn to her — that he would never, ever turn into King.

"What if I don't know you when you come back?" she'd asked on the morning of his deployment. But Ben reminded her that this was his second tour. "I've done this once already. And I came back fine," he said, pulling her close. "Fine enough for you to fall in love with me."

But he'd been wrong. After the second tour, he wasn't fine. The wedding had been the eye of an emotional storm. The days on either end of the event were beautiful and brilliant. But afterward, especially, things turned bad. Ben had gotten drunk and crashed his truck; he'd destroyed his father's fiddle. He'd broken everything.

"Everybody judges us," Bull said, dragging Becca away from her own misfortune and into the glare of his own. "And the kids your age are the worst. Everybody's entitled. Nobody appreciates what they're given."

"Not me."

Bull chuckled. "Right. You're different."

"I am, actually," she said. "Nobody else in my family went to college. I worked hard for that. I know nothing'll be handed to me on a platter."

"Last night, King said you'd gotten into one of those fancy schools up north – they gave you some money to boot. But you didn't go."

She wasn't sure why she'd confessed this to King; it had kind of just spilled out one day. He'd seemed a little disappointed in her decision, though she couldn't imagine why.

"What's that got to do with entitlement?"

"Not that part, Rebecca. The appreciating-opportunities part."

"It made more sense to stay close to home," she said.

"You want to appreciate the freedom I fought for? The freedom your daddy fought for? Then don't be afraid to confront your fears. The CO taught me that. Too bad you can't meet him. You could learn a lot."

"You don't know me, Bull, so I'd appreciate you not judging my decisions."

"College girl thinks she knows so much." And then, as though the whole conversation had never happened: "It's grub time." Bull downed the rest of his Bud Light and licked his lips.

9

LATER THAT DAY, while the men were in town, Becca used the cabin's landline to call her boss and ask for time off, pleading a family emergency. If she was going to stay at the cabin for a while, she'd have to find an Internet-connected computer in town, and no way the local library was going to have the necessary design programs. Now she sat in the kitchen and explained the situation to her aunt, but Kath abruptly veered off topic. "Why'd you really come here, honey?" she asked, pointing her mixing spoon at her niece.

"Just postwedding stress," Becca said, avoiding her aunt's eyes.

"What's that phrase your mother uses? 'Too blessed to be stressed.'"

Becca thought about her mother at the Hands of God Church out in Colorado. There, a group of Christian faithful tended an organic garden and knit socks for orphans. And prayed, obviously. Jeanine probably had to feed her smoking habit on the sly, sneaking cigarettes behind the quinoa patch.

Kath continued. "The stress is supposed to come before the wedding, honey, not after."

"Ben's been touchy since he came back. King says he just needs some time." Becca knew full well that if she was leaving

Ben for good—divorce leaving—then eventually she'd have to fess up about it. But she felt like somebody had poured cement into her mouth. Kath said nothing more. With one hand, she cracked eggs into a bowl and tossed the shells into the garbage. She added oil and sugar. She did not use measuring tools. Her silence was heavy and dense as a ball of dough.

"So they're going to Utah to visit an old commanding officer," Becca said, unable to tolerate her aunt's stoniness. "They're talking about this trip like it's a big deal."

"Your father can't help you if he doesn't know what the real problem is," Kath said.

"I don't know what you mean."

Kath stopped what she was doing and turned to her niece. "Earlier today. You went for a run down the mountain? Trip Meester was out on his porch."

The run had been painful; with each footfall and each breath, sharp flashes had shot out from the ring of bruises. It was nearly too much to bear—nearly. But Becca decided to bear it. The pain was a necessary reminder of her weakness and stupidity; she would not go back to Ben and she would never, ever, let anything like this happen again.

"You were in your sports bra, honey. Trip knew the men were here. Seeing you—" Kath nodded at Becca's torso. "Well, he was worried. So he called me."

The backs of Becca's eyeballs stung, but she gritted her teeth until she was certain that not a single tear would fall. "Momentum, rhythm, stride," she whispered to herself. Let the electricity burn itself out. Let the despair ease up. Let go of every hope you had for your life and be free. You're running. You're already gone.

Becca felt Kath's warm body beside her, hovering close. "It's not what you think," Becca said, though her voice sounded very small.

"How is it not what I think?" Kath's face was pitying. "Either he put his hands on you or he didn't."

"I'm not one of those women — the 'he didn't mean it, it was just this one time' women. But we were asleep and then . . . I don't actually know if . . ." Becca felt ill-equipped to explain. The events of that night lay broken in her memory, scattered like the shards of the fiddle Ben had smashed. What frightened her most of all was that Ben apparently didn't know what he'd done. Didn't realize that he was incapable of controlling himself. "I'm not naive!" she burst out. "I didn't think that he'd come back and everything would be fine. I tried to get ahead of all of this."

"Honey, you're not making sense."

"In the beginning he told me stories. On the phone, video chat, e-mail. He made me feel like I was with him. There was an Iraqi soccer-star kid who ate Corn Pops, and a platoon corporal with weird superstitions, and kitty litter to cover the latrine stink, and every other thing you could ever want to know. And then one day, out of the blue, he just stopped talking." Becca knew she was rambling incoherently, but she didn't much care.

"Who knows what might have happened," Kath said. But Becca, who'd started pacing around the kitchen, wasn't listening. She felt like an attorney arguing to a jury of one: herself.

"It was like somebody flipped a switch! He shut down and I didn't know what to do. I asked him questions, but he wouldn't answer. And I couldn't stand it — the not knowing. So I tried to fill in the gaps. I read all this stuff — books and articles. You would have laughed at me."

Even in her keyed-up, frantic state, Becca was too self-conscious to confess aloud all that she'd done. It had involved rereading all the books from a war-lit class she'd taken her freshman year, renting every war movie at the video store, and obsessively consuming soldier blogs. Anything for a glimpse into his world—and his head. She'd tried to bone up on information so she'd know what questions to ask him. But during their conversations, he was either too tired to talk, or they'd had a bad patrol (whatever *bad* meant, he never explained), or he was too stressed due to new orders from HQ. Nothing Ben told her was consistent. It was like running a race where the ground continually shifted beneath your feet.

Becca often felt lonelier after talking to him, but she refused to believe that all was lost. There were moments when he still laughed. When he shared some funny detail or anecdote. And he always signed off by saying, "I love you, Chicken." Other women were *baby* or *sweetheart* or *hon*. But it was there, in the silly nickname Ben had given her, that Becca felt him close, as he had been before. So she continued to hope. And she continued to read and study and prepare. Just in case.

Kath asked no more questions. She walked to Becca, who had drifted to the far side of the kitchen, and reached for her, but Becca did not want comfort and pulled away.

"I've been thinking, honey," Kath said. "If you want to go with your dad to Utah—"

Becca looked up with surprise.

"Well, why did you run to him if not for advice? For some insider knowledge? So he happens to be taking a trip. Even better. Perfect for bonding."

Becca stared at her aunt with genuine confusion. She'd run to King because she could think of no place else to go. To speak of bonding was absurd. Traveling with her father, she'd be nothing more than extra weight on the bitch pad. Once she explained all of this, Kath's face grew stern.

"Sit down, child," she said and Becca obeyed. "I'm not saying you did wrong trying to get inside Ben's head but there's only one way to really know a person, and that's to be with them."

"I know that now."

Kath sighed. "I don't think you're being honest about why you went to King. You could have called me. But you called him. And if he hasn't given you what you came for, then just letting him go on his merry way would be a real waste." Kath's stare was more powerful than truth serum.

"He can't advise me unless he opens up, and we both know he won't. It's not like I can guilt him into sharing."

"Not guilt him, honey, communicate with him. Your father's not so great at that, but I don't think you're giving him enough credit. You can't expect him to do a thing for you, though, if he doesn't realize he *has* to. And besides, you're not staying here cooped up with me. I'm an old misanthrope. You're young and adventurous. At least I thought you were."

Becca remembered what Bull had said about confronting her fears. And her aunt was right; this cabin was the physical edge of what she knew — like one of those invisible fences that keep dogs from running into the street. Her father's motorcycle would be more than sufficient to bust through. "Maybe I'll talk to him tonight," she said, searching Kath's face for encouragement.

"Come on." Kath breathed, exasperated. "You need to confront him soon and be forthright. Say you want to go with him. You're a runner, Becca. It's not in your blood to stand still."

Just then, the growl of motorcycles blasted the windows.

"This is a horrible idea," Becca said, but she marched outside anyway. Partly, she was allowing herself to be baited; she was not a person who stood still. But mostly, she wanted to show her aunt that King had zero interest in helping her.

"Rides like butter," King was saying to the others. "I mean, it cruises like a yacht." Reno and Bull saw Becca first and they must have noticed something in her face or her walk, because they hopped off their bikes and shuffled out of the way. Becca stopped her march and watched King dismount, trying to get a sense of this person—this father—who had produced her. Yes, he'd returned after a long absence, but Kath had made it clear that he was only halfway back—no closer than shouting distance.

The sun was setting into the valley, and the light glowed halo-like around her father's head. He looked truly king-like and prophetic. Then he coughed, and the spell was broken.

"Dad, listen," Becca said, closing the final feet between them. "I know it's out of the blue. But Kath thought—well, not just Kath but me too—that I might be able to stay with you a little longer. The road's good therapy, right?" These were King's words. He'd said them to her many times.

"Oh." King glanced around for backup and realized his friends had retreated to the porch. "It would be nice to take you out at some point . . ." His throat released a grating sound. "But this isn't the right time."

Becca hoped Kath was watching. She'd taken the plunge and the outcome was exactly as she'd predicted: her father was letting her sink. But then, King turned away and started toward the steps. He was literally turning his back on her.

"When?" Urgency welled inside of her, a feeling that bordered on panic.

King halted, looked back. "I know you and Ben had a fight, but if you two really love each other then I'm sure—"

But King stopped talking midsentence because Becca had pulled up her T-shirt. She did not glance down. She was already familiar with the sight: it looked as though Ben had tried to wring her out like a rag.

The trio on the porch—Kath had joined Reno and Bull—cast their eyes away. King looked stunned, his mouth slack. Quietly he said, "I'm so sorry, Becca. I don't know what to say."

"Say you want to kill him!" Becca screamed. "Say you can't believe my *husband* did this to me. Say you want to take me as far away from him as you possibly can!"

But why would he take up her crusade? They were barely more than strangers to each other—which was precisely why she'd vowed to expect nothing from him. And yet she could not take her own advice. Her brain and her gut were working at cross-purposes, slowing her down. *Momentum, Becca,* she thought. *Momentum.* She turned from her father and took off down the mountain at a sprint.

Dinner that night was tense. Bull hid behind a phalanx of beer cans. Reno leaned back in his chair like an apathetic teenager, and King affected a forced normalcy, as though nothing much had happened. Eventually Kath stomped down to her metal shop. Becca took this as her cue to stomp upstairs to her bedroom.

Many hours later, insistent voices roused her from sleep.

"Everything will not be fine, and you know it." Her aunt's voice was uncharacteristically bitter. "If you insist on going through with this nonsense, then you've got to at least let her in. Leave her with something she can keep. That girl's on the verge of losing everything. And if you think her mother's going to step in once you depart, then you're a fool."

Becca didn't know what nonsense her father was involved in or what her mother had to do with anything, but it hurt to hear her life discussed like this. She was just starting to sneak out of the room when King's words froze her still.

"Jeanine came to the wedding," her father said.

Aunt Kath gasped. "What?"

"Too much pride, that woman. She said she didn't approve of the marriage—of Becca yoking herself to the military and all that—but in the end, she couldn't stay away."

"She came because she knew *you'd* be there, more like."

"She knows there's no chance of us —"

"You just go around breaking everyone's heart, big brother. Your wife's, your daughter's. It's a wonder that Elaine —"

"Enough!" King growled. "We're done talking." He stomped down the stairs.

Becca shrank away from the door and into the dark of her room. Had her mother really been at the wedding, hiding in the shadows? It was confusing and sad and Becca just didn't want to think about it. But she also didn't want to think about this other thing that her aunt seemed to be suggesting — that her mother was somehow hung up on her father. It couldn't be true. Jeanine had kicked King out. She *hated* him. It made no sense.

Becca crawled back into bed. Stumbling into her family's past was not part of her escape plan. She needed to keep moving forward. Running, after all, was what she did best. And running was a solitary activity.

10

BEN DROVE WEST from Sparta at ninety miles an hour. He could not retreat, not from his wife and not from the war. The former was beautiful and the latter was hideous. Logically, they should repel each other, like two positive charges. But they lived together inside of him, fused like Siamese twins.

An hour outside Dry Hills, Ben came to the exit for Pretoria, Becca's college town, and, as though some external force were guiding him, he followed the signs to campus. He parked and, still being led along by powers unseen, entered the cloistered college green. He told himself that he was traversing the campus only to get lunch, but he soon found himself drifting off course, moving toward Frederickson Hall, where he and Becca had first met.

Ben had come to campus in the fall of 2006, a few months after his first tour had ended, as part of an army recruiting team. Generally, such positions went to career soldiers in their early thirties, but Ben was distinguished. He'd made sergeant at an almost unprecedented speed, and his commander at Fort Campbell prided himself on creative thinking. Which in this case meant sending a soldier who was not much older than college students to help recruit college students. Ben wasn't thrilled about the position. Anyone with the motivation and smarts for college would obviously prefer to lug around sixty pounds of textbooks than the equivalent weight in body armor. Ben decided that since he was being forced to play car salesman, he'd insist on a decent commission. Having never attended college himself, he requested permission to audit a class.

The commander acquiesced on the condition that Ben choose a subject related to his recruiting effort. And that's how Ben ended up in Literature and Film of War, a seminar the commander thought would attract army-friendly students. Ben knew this assumption was way off base, but he couldn't argue. Sure enough, the students arrived on the first day sporting Free Palestine patches and buttons that read *Bush, the Fascist Gun in the West*. The syllabus, meanwhile, displayed its own bias, filled as it was with Graves, Remarque, Kubrick, and Coppola. Still, Ben settled in. He'd asked for this.

On the last day of registration, a new girl arrived. Ben liked the way her jeans molded to her muscular quadriceps. He liked her large, challenging eyes and delicate chin. As she sized up the other students, he saw the fierceness in her face dim to circumspection before blazing forth with double brightness. Ben realized that he'd witnessed a moment of vulnerability, and that it was rare for her. He was smitten.

The girl's name was Becca and she kept to herself. The others were vocal; highly critical of war, eager to "support the troops" (whatever that meant), and indignant about the recruiters on campus. One of them, a girl named Leah, was even trying to get the recruiters kicked out. Ben found his classmates' ignorance and smugness infuriating. They'd all walked within inches of the recruitment table and never even looked at him. To them, he was almost invisible, nothing more than a uniform, a symbol.

A few weeks in, Leah volunteered to read aloud from a story she'd written. The piece featured a Vietnam vet who refused to acknowledge that the war had ruined his life. It was only after befriending a young antiwar protester that he faced facts. "If only I'd run when I had the chance," said the vet in the story. "Now I know I fought for nothing, killed for nothing."

Ben listened, and he boiled. Who was this girl to claim that she knew why anyone had fought or what someone had gained or lost in the process? As he tried to gauge the others' reactions, he noticed Becca's mouth tightening. Then, to his astonishment, he watched her hand go up.

"Do you know any Vietnam vets?" she asked before the professor had a chance to call on her. It was the first time Ben had heard her speak. Her voice was deeper than he'd expected based on her size.

"I've been to plenty of rallies," Leah said.

"But you don't actually know anyone? Personally, I mean." Becca was perfectly calm. There was nothing overtly aggressive in her voice. And yet.

"Does it matter?" Leah shrugged.

"Well, I don't think it's right for you to act as if you know what other people are thinking."

"And you're an expert?" Leah said.

"My father was in Vietnam. So, yeah, I guess I know something about it."

Hearing this, Ben felt his annoyance toward Leah vanish. Let her float inside her self-righteous little bubble. She would not be a party to his future. But Becca, he now knew, would. Ben's own father had served two tours in Southeast Asia between 1969 and 1971. *Thank you, Dad,* Ben thought as his heart swelled. *Thank you for this gift.*

Class ended and Becca booked out of the room. By the time Ben caught up with her, she was on the front steps of Frederickson Hall engaged in a heated argument with Leah, who had half a dozen people, mostly her compatriots from class, standing behind her in a blockade. They seemed to be one body: a giant Goliath staring down the diminutive David.

"I'm terribly sorry that your family was screwed over by the war," Leah said. "But anyone with half a conscience would have gone to Canada."

"You'd do that?" Becca smirked. "If it were you? You'd give up your home and your rich parents who buy you whatever your ungrateful heart desires and go live in *Canada?*"

Even from where he stood, Ben could feel the air around the group change, and he started down the steps, pulled forward by a feeling honed by months of training and patrolling.

"I'd leave in a heartbeat. It's been forty years and we're *still* at war," Leah retorted. "Jesus, I feel sorry for you." And then, under her breath: "Brainwashed hick."

Becca's shoulder muscles tensed and she shifted her weight in a way that told Ben exactly what was coming. The silent, beautiful, indignant Becca was about to punch Leah in the face.

"Hey!" he said jovially, jogging over. "What's going on?" The girls fell silent and looked at him, annoyed.

"What do you want?" Leah snapped. She seemed eager to get back to her tirade, oblivious to the fact that Ben had just saved her from a bloody nose.

Ben glanced at Becca, who observed him coolly. *She knows why I came over,* he thought. *And she is not happy about it*. Becca turned back to Leah. "You think because your father got a deferment, that makes you better than me?"

"I think you're an ignorant bitch."

Ben cursed himself. His intervention had accomplished nothing. "I love my freedom," he said. "How about you guys?"

Becca and Leah, momentarily united in their confusion, just gaped.

"You love life, liberty, and the pursuit of happiness?" Ben

continued. "The right to get an education? To go to college? To meet people who don't think the way you do and be incredibly rude to them? I mean, it's not everywhere in the world that people can trash-talk each other so openly. It's actually kind of beautiful. I mean, you *could* go to Canada," Ben said to Leah. "But you probably wouldn't find anybody there who'd want to fight with you."

That was it. He'd killed the argument. Leah gave him a look of perplexed disgust and left with her friends. Becca started off in the opposite direction. She walked incredibly fast; he was impressed.

"You were going to punch that girl," he said. "You were going to throw away your scholarship on her! I'm happy you didn't. Even though she deserved it."

Becca stopped and looked at him. "You're not a student," she said. "What are you doing here?"

Ben was equally impressed by the fact that she made no attempt to deny her intentions – or, for that matter, her scholarship. "Come by the student center at noon tomorrow and you'll see," he said. He walked away, ordering himself not to look back. He couldn't help it, though, and when he did, she was still standing there, watching him. Playing coy could easily have backfired, but the following day at noon, she walked through the doors. Ben stood there, dressed in his uniform, right down to the regulation cap. "Figures," she said. But she was smiling.

In the following months, Ben learned that as a child Becca had played POW in the grocery-store cart and that King was known in their town as the Landmine due to his unpredictable outbursts. He learned that kids called Becca Rabid Dog because of her constant fighting. From the outside, Ben's childhood had looked very different. He was well liked, and his father had no obvious battle scars. But Ben too was an only child who wore the uniform of confident, jocular athlete to hide a deeper loneliness. His father had demons too, quiet ones that the family did not discuss.

In Becca, Ben saw a similar—albeit stronger—version of himself. She didn't just own her isolation. She gloried in it. Ben's favorite example of this was her admiration of Durga, the Hindu goddess of self-reliance and strength. For reasons unknown, King had gotten the ten-armed deity tattooed on his forearm, and on his sober nights, he regaled his daughter with stories featuring the goddess and her tiger bound for battle. Becca admitted that it was often Durga she channeled at races. And Ben could tell. It was an awe-inspiring thing to see her hurtling toward him, fierce as a tiger, proud as a goddess.

Having reached Frederickson Hall, Ben decided to visit their old classroom. He felt almost giddy—the first wave of positive emotion he'd experienced in a while. He walked quickly down the long entrance hall, his shoes echoing against the floor, and stopped outside the seminar room. The knob turned easily. Except that the room Ben entered was a metal cave. And it smelled not of chalk but of charred aluminum. He knelt down and touched the floor. His palm came away sticky. He raised his hand to better examine the substance, and a terrible smell assaulted him. Ben knew what it was. Of course he knew.

Gagging, he stood and backed out of the room. He tried to run, but his body felt leaden, like something heavy was tied to his waist. He could feel the enemy approaching, but when he turned around, he saw nothing. How could he fight an invisible enemy? With considerable relief, he exited the campus and hurried into the first bar he saw. He needed to be somewhere else. Somewhere safe.

The college green was soft like a rug, and the stars floated like swimmers in the sky. Ben was blitzed. After many beers, each with a whiskey chaser, he was blitzed to the perfect point of blitzedness: not so drunk that he was going to pass out, but drunk enough that Coleman's Humvee and the load attached to his own waist had no power over him. He imagined the nightmares draining out of his ears and into the grass. He imagined that a tree would grow where his thoughts had soaked the earth. Years from now, some innocent student—a twenty-first-century red riding hoodie—would happen along the college path. She'd pluck a poisonous berry from the tree branch and pop the succulent thing into her mouth. Once the poison took hold, she'd skip over to the recruiter table and sign her name on the dotted line.

It was here on this green that Ben had first played the fiddle for Becca. His relationship with the instrument had always been complicated—just like the relationship with his dad—but when he played for her, the melodies sounded different: bright and new and layered with astonishing color, much like the lushness he'd experienced in the Smokies. Even without the instrument in his hands, the music swirled around them, a score to the life they were building.

But now, as Ben lay drunk on the college green, the fiddle lay in pieces on the floor of Becca's childhood bedroom. Except at the wedding, he had barely played since leaving for his second tour. He couldn't take the violin to Iraq, and then, when he was back home, the music hurt. The nightmare of the seminar room—that was how he felt when he held the bow now: disgusted, trapped, sick with shame.

Ben pulled himself to his knees and looked skyward. From some unexpected place inside himself, he began to pray. "Tell me what to do, Dad," he said. "Help me. Please."

He'd heard many stories of people being filled with the Holy Spirit and driven to upend their lives, like Becca's mother deciding to move to her Christian commune or a college friend who'd gotten the Call one Saturday afternoon while mowing the lawn and felt the force of God so powerfully, he later told Ben, that he'd jumped off the mower and fallen to his knees as the machine kept going and crashed into the house. But no such guidance for Ben. His father wasn't listening. His father was dead.

Ben staggered to his feet and stumbled back to the car, but the Breathalyzer beeped at him with disapproval. "Fine!" he snapped at the instrument. At a twenty-four-hour diner near campus, he ordered breakfast and a large cup of coffee. He sat there until sunup. He'd lost an entire day.

11

BECCA HOPED TO sleep through her father's departure, but the clomp of boots yanked her awake. It was just after six, and when she looked out the window, there was only blankness. The cabin was hidden in a cloud. Moments later, she heard the engines rumble, then grow faint, then disappear. Becca closed her eyes, hoping to forget that she'd ever asked her father for anything. A second later, though, Kath burst into the room. "You better get dressed," she said. "We can't waste time."

Becca clamped the pillow over her face.

"The men're stopping for breakfast in town, so that'll buy us half an hour."

"He doesn't want me going." Becca groaned, realizing what her aunt had in mind.

"He doesn't *think* he wants you. But he does." Kath wrenched the pillow away. "I'm his sister. It's my job to know what's best for him."

"Seems more like it's your job to be a big pain in his ass."

"That's a girl!" Kath smiled. "Now, clock's a-ticking."

Becca was doubtful, but she wasn't ready to quit running. And she wanted payback — wanted to show King that he had to accept her, to *deal* with her. He'd invaded her life, not the other way around. She'd been fine without him. "Give me ten minutes and we're out the door," she said.

Kath liked classic rock, so Becca sat through hours of Neil Young, CCR, and ZZ Top. All the way through the Arkansas Grand Canyon, snipping the corner of Missouri, and blazing into Kansas, her aunt belted out songs at the top of her lungs. "Looks like we beat them," she said, pulling into a Love's gas station outside of Oswego.

"Here?" The Love's was a small concrete island in the middle of endless prairie. Surveying the landscape, Becca saw nothing but grass and sky.

"Your father and his friends stop for gas every hundred and twenty miles, otherwise somebody throws a fit. Also, I know that King prefers Love's. He's partial to the heart logo."

"You've got to be kidding."

"Honey, those men're like children. They need things constantly. They're going to stop here and you're just going to have to trust me on that."

"Can't you at least wait until they get here before you go?" Two hours back, Kath had announced that once she'd dropped Becca off, she was turning right around.

"We can't give those fellas an excuse to send you home. Call me on the pay phone if you run into trouble." She planted a wet kiss on Becca's cheek, then squeezed her niece's shoulder with a grip that seemed to concentrate the strength of her entire body. "Don't look so somber, kiddo. You're on an adventure."

Reluctantly, Becca climbed out of the truck.

"Oh, wait!" Kath rolled down the window and held out a blank envelope. "Give this to Reno. Reno, and only Reno."

"If the men don't show up, I'm reading it," Becca threatened.

"They'll be here," Kath said. Then she waved and pulled onto the highway.

Large flat clouds had materialized, literally from the blue, and floated by, casting gulfs of shade and sunlight across the Love's. At least there'd been radio reception in the truck, which had made Becca feel slightly more tethered to civilization. King once told her that across large swaths of America, you couldn't get anything but static or, if you were lucky, a single station blaring Christian rock. He said he liked to hit the scan button sometimes, simply to remember his place in the world. "It's like they tell you in AA," he'd said. "Some things are beyond your control. Accepting that is a kind of freedom."

Becca wanted to ask King about those travels, but she'd learned it was best not to come too close—with either hugs or questions. Only now, Kath was instructing her to defy the warning. In the truck, her aunt had sung loudly to "Break on Through to the Other Side." A not-so-subtle message.

Becca sat down on the curb with Ben's duffle and Kath's old motorcycle helmet, which fit her much better than King's spare. After about twenty minutes, a minivan pulled into the Love's, and out of it came a father, a mother, and a spool of children. It was like one of those circus acts where more and more clowns pour from the car. There were six kids in all, a mix of boys and girls, and the mother herded them into the store. In the sudden quiet, the father looked relieved. He leaned against the van and discreetly scratched his butt.

Becca could hardly imagine growing up in such a family. The very notion of a family vacation was strange. Where were they going? she wondered. What was it like to ride in that van? She was too young to think seriously about having her own children, but she wanted them. So did Ben. They'd spent long hours discussing what theirs might be like, laying the imagined foundations of their future home.

Soon, the kids funneled out of the Love's, sucking on various candies, laughing, and complaining. Becca watched the mother shepherd them into the van and then the van pull away. That life was not to be, at least not for her and Ben.

Shortly thereafter, she spotted the bikes. All black leather and chrome, Reno's and Bull's resembled oversize beetles. Beside them, the purple Gold Wing was like a My Little Pony. Becca felt the bubble of a laugh in her throat but was too nervous to let it out.

Bull saw her first. He wasn't wearing a helmet and she didn't like the sauntering kind of look he had in his eyes as he drove slowly toward her, like he was preparing a come-on. "Well, look who showed up," he said when he'd cut the engine. "You're just like an angel, aren't you, touching down from the sky." Bull waved his gloved fingers, simulating sprinkling fairy dust. Couldn't he just let her be? But Bull was the least of her problems. She got up and walked to her father, but when King saw her, his eyes widened in an old, familiar way. A way that made her stop walking. He shook his head, slowly at first, then faster. He shook it as if he could will his daughter to disappear. Then, without warning, he kicked a large trashcan, sending it toppling onto the cement. "I said no," he growled, his belly heaving and his face turning red. "*No,* Becca."

She was at least ten feet away, but she shrank from his outrage.

"Why did you come?" Spittle flew from King's mouth. "Why didn't you tell Kath that you weren't going to be part of her crazy shit? Goddamn it!" His voice lunged at her. "I helped you the best I could. You could have shown me a little respect." He kicked the trashcan again, and it barreled into the pump. Becca felt like he'd kicked the wind out of her.

"Not much love out here at the Love's," Bull said and followed King into the convenience store.

"Your aunt really fucked up," Reno said, though he was clearly accusing her too.

It was true, she thought. King *had* helped her. She had no business demanding more. That's what her brain said. But her heart begged to differ. She deserved her father's attention! King knew what Ben had done to her. He'd seen the evidence and barely responded. It wasn't right.

"So what's Kath's brilliant plan?" Reno said. "Surely she's got one."

Becca handed him the letter, and he tore it open. She watched his eyes move back and forth over the page. "Shit," he said, crumpling the paper in his palm. "Shit."

"What?"

Reno uncrumpled the letter and read it again. "Shit." He took a couple of deep breaths, then put the letter in his pocket. He pulled a half-smoked cigar from his jacket and lit up.

"Are you gonna tell me what she said?"

"Not right now."

"Well, can you —"

"Look." He opened and closed his cracked lips around the cigar, exhaled a cloud of smoke by her ear. "This is what's gonna happen. You're coming with, for now." Reno broke into a cough, his lungs rattling like they were full of spare screws. He put his hand up to hold her off. When he'd recovered he said, "I'm responsible for you, so don't give me a hard time, please."

"I'm responsible for myself."

"Yeah, but thanks to the ever-cunning Katherine Keller, you're stranded unless somebody is kind enough to give you a ride."

"Give me your phone so I can call Kath."

"She ain't gonna tell you different."

"Give me the phone." Becca held out her hand and Reno obliged. Kath picked up right away.

"So they showed up! O ye of little faith!" her aunt declared.

Becca presented her case. For a moment, the line was silent.

When Kath finally spoke, her voice was cold as chilled milk. “It’s complicated, honey. I’ve instructed Reno to explain. But you’ve got to let him do it on his own time. And don’t worry about your father. He’ll come around.” Kath hung up.

“You’re not fucking serious!” Becca practically threw the phone back at Reno.

“I can take you to the nearest Tennessee-bound bus,” Reno offered. “I’ll remind you that you’re the one who wanted to come, or who let Kath talk you into coming, or however it happened. But if you want to stay, you can’t go making a fuss. I got enough on my mind.”

He looked so haggard, so genuinely stressed, that Becca backed down. “I just don’t understand what’s going on. My dad’s kicking trashcans, and my husband—”

Reno hung his head and nodded. “I am truly sorry. If I had known, I would have punched him harder.” Reno rubbed his eyes with his thumb and index finger. “Listen, as you may or may not already know, we’re headed to Utah to see our old commander. But the rest of it—Kleos and all that. It’s gonna take a while to explain.”

“What’s Kleos?”

“It’s where the CO lives.”

“And?”

“And we’re hitting the road in about five minutes, so if you want a drink or something, you’d better get it quick. It’s gonna be a hundred and twenty miles before we stop again.”

That afternoon the landscape flew by in alternating stretches of farmland and prairie. Sometimes there were cows, sometimes horses, sometimes just grass. Once in a while, there were windmills in the distance, massive white trees stripped of their limbs. Two rest stops and two hundred and forty miles later, Becca looked at a map and realized they’d hardly gotten anywhere. She felt like they were swimming against a current, like they were spinning their wheels. When they finally stopped at a trailer park in a nothing town called Bluff, they still had three-fourths of Kansas to cover before they would even get within shouting distance of Colorado.

Becca set up the small tent that Kath had loaned her. When she'd finished, she found Reno crouched over a camping stove making coffee in a French press. "What are you doing?" She gaped.

"What does it look like? You think I'm not *sophisticated* enough to use one of these?"

Becca's face turned red.

"You've got to be one of the singularly most judgmental people I've ever met," Reno said. "You know that? Nearly as bad as your mother."

Becca looked at her father for support, but King wouldn't meet her eye. Miserable, she made herself a peanut butter sandwich and sat down by the stove to eat. Kleos — the name felt lodged in her brain like a splinter. She tried to pry it loose, but it wouldn't budge.

After dinner, she climbed into her tent and curled up on her side, but the bruises ached. She turned over, but it made no difference. She took some ibuprofen and folded her hands in a ball against her chest. She was more than lonely; she was downright homesick, a foreigner in a strange land.

12

HELLO, BEN," SAID Kath. She opened the door but made no move to hug him. She was exhausted from the long drive out to Kansas and back. And now her blood boiled up against her tiredness; to think her lovely girl had endured pain at the hands of this man! There were many reasons to have sent Becca off with her father, among them the possibility that her presence might actually divert King from his dangerous project in Utah. But most of all, Kath had wanted to keep her niece away from Ben.

"She's not here," Kath said, inspecting the bruise on his face. She smiled to herself. Reno always pulled his weight. Still, in this moment, Ben did not look enraged or capable of violence. He looked worn out and sad.

"When will she be back?" he asked.

"She's not coming back."

"What?" He looked horrified. "Where'd she go?"

Kath just shook her head. "You think I'd tell you that? Jesus." Ben looked down at the ground. "Oh, for Christ's sake, come in." She led him into the kitchen and motioned for him to sit. "I want some answers," she said. "Then I'm going to kick you out."

Ben looked more fearful than guilty. But she launched into an interrogation.

"Were you just really drunk? Were you so enraged that you couldn't control yourself? No—" She didn't stop to let Ben answer. "I just cannot believe it."

Ben hung his head. "That fiddle was the only thing I had from my father, Kath. I didn't mean to destroy it. I swear."

"Who gives a shit about a fiddle?" Kath pounded her fist on the table. "Ben, I'm talking about what you did to your wife!"

"What?" It was the tremble in Ben's voice that made Kath halt in her fury. She sat down across from him and studied his face. Was he playing her? He seemed legitimately confused. "Ben," she said quietly. "Why did Becca run?"

He pushed his hand through his short hair and looked past her out the window. He bounced his leg rapidly. "Sleeping is tough. Staying awake is tough. Not freaking out about every little thing is tough. I busted up my car last week; she probably told you."

"Ben," Kath said. "The night she left."

Ben nodded. "We had a fight about something earlier that day. It had to do with the fiddle and why I refused to play anymore. It was dumb. But I got mad and I left. I went to a bar. She was asleep when I came back. So I went to bed too."

He stopped talking. He seemed conflicted about whether to continue. "And then?" she prodded.

"The next thing I knew, I was standing in her old bedroom. I guess I sleepwalked? But I was seeing and hearing things—don't ask me to describe them." His leg vibrated so quickly it shook the table. "The fiddle was causing it. The only way to make it all stop was to smash up the fiddle. Obviously, I wasn't thinking straight. But I did it. I broke it to bits. And then Becca came in. She was crying, Kath, screaming at me. I'd never seen her like that. And then I saw what I'd done to the fiddle, and I realized that if I stayed in that house another minute, I might hurt her too. So I bolted. Got out as fast as I could. I'd wrecked my car so I had to take hers."

For a moment, they were both silent. Kath wanted to put her hand on Ben's knee, but she didn't think touching him was a good idea.

"When I came back she was gone. I was angry. I admit it. I shouldn't have shown up at King's drunk like that. I know that now. I want to fix myself, Kath. I don't want to be like this anymore." Ben hit the table, but there was no force in his hand. It was the gesture of a man who'd given up. "Please don't keep me from her, Kath." Ben's voice broke. "Please."

"That's exactly what happened?"

He nodded.

Kath stood up. He truly seemed not to know. But how was that possible? Had he snapped? Been in some kind of fugue state? Had he done it in his sleep?

"Kath! Please. What's going on? Why are you looking at me like that?"

"She's all beat up, Benjamin. A ring of bruises around her middle, front to back."

Ben shook his head. Kath nodded. Ben shook his head more vehemently.

"Do you have nightmares, Ben?"

Ben looked at the table.

"What happens in them?"

Ben didn't answer. "I'm sorry," he said, jumping up. "I can't."

A moment later, Kath heard the screen door slam. She sat back down and pushed the hair out of her face. Was his ignorance real? Did that even matter? She was willing to take intentions into account. But what had Ben really done to avoid this situation? On the ride to Kansas, Becca explained that he had been evaluated upon his return, according to standard protocol, and was prescribed a variety of medications. But were they necessary? Were they working? Were the dosages correct? Becca didn't know. She said that after the wedding, he'd stopped taking them altogether. He'd also filled out a questionnaire about his mental state, but based on how evasive he'd been, she doubted that he'd reported honestly. "Or maybe he did," she told Kath. "And then things changed later. Or maybe he just couldn't bring himself to write down how he really felt. You know what it's like with those guys."

Kath did know. Thirty-plus years after Vietnam, the same old codes and expectations persisted. As did the excuse that civilians just didn't understand. And the possibility that the army just didn't care what happened to those boys after they came home. Growing up in Fayetteville, Arkansas, she'd been one of those civilians. Just thirteen when her twenty-two-year-old brother came back from the war. Before, he'd been her protector. Afterward, he was sullen and short. His clothes hung off him like oversize pillow cases, like hospital gowns. He couldn't hold a job. And he fought with their parents, who eventually told King to pack his bags.

At the time, Kath blamed them for giving up on him. Only after they'd died did Kath question her childhood assumptions: first, that King's coming around was inevitable, and second, that he deserved infinite leeway. Brother and sister had mended their relationship, but King was slipping again. "It doesn't matter that I'm sober," he'd told her the previous night. "Time piles up, but that just means I have farther to fall. And I always fall. It's like my dreams are full of trapdoors releasing me into the old cesspool. It's harder and harder to climb out."

"Your sobriety matters," Kath had argued, terrified that King was giving up. But King said he *did* care about staying alive, which was why he was returning to his old CO's compound in Utah. "I tried to live out here, Kath," he said. "It didn't take."

Ben eventually returned to the house and asked again for Becca's whereabouts. "Even if I did tell you where she was," Kath explained, "I don't know how to get there."

"Then why can't you give me the destination?"

"Because you're enterprising. Somehow, you'd figure it out."

Ben nodded as though he understood. As though in her position, he'd do the same thing. This broke her heart. "Follow me," she said, wanting to do *something*. In her bedroom, she handed him *The Iliad* of Homer. King had brought it from Tennessee — he carried it everywhere — and Kath had filched it before the men left. She knew this book had tremendous symbolic meaning for King, as it did for the CO and his whole Utah operation. She'd stolen it, hoping that King might come back to get it and thereby give her another chance to wear him down: Do not go to Utah! However much *The Iliad* had helped King in his darkest hours, he'd taken its help much too far. Ben, however, was not under the CO's command, neither physically nor mentally. For him, the book might be just an empathetic voice.

Ben was surprised to be holding *The Iliad* in his hands. It looked like it had been carved up into chunks and then glued back together again. It had obviously belonged to a succession of readers. The first name, written on the inside flap in faded black pen, was Wilfred Owen McKenzie. The second name was CO Proudfoot. The third name was King Francis Keller. This was followed by half a dozen other names, some of which were repeated. The last name on the list was King's again. Ben couldn't imagine Becca's father reading epic poetry.

"King and his friends seem to find something useful in

here. I thought you might like to give it a look," Kath said. Ben waited, but she did not elaborate. "You're welcome to stay here tonight," she added.

"And Becca?" Kath had done him this kindness – given him a gift. She was softening toward him, and he felt a weak ray of hope warm his neck. But Kath shook her head.

"I'm sorry," she said. "But it's best not to think of Becca right now. Get some sleep. Then go home and get yourself straightened out. Focus on that."

Later, Ben lay on the guest bed, staring at the ceiling. The sheets were rumpled and he wondered if Becca had slept there. He tried unsuccessfully to pick out her smell. Had he really done what Kath claimed? For hours after leaving Kath's kitchen, he'd walked in the woods, replaying the events in his head. He remembered – mostly in the form of a feeling – that he'd smashed the fiddle because of Coleman's Humvee and the unknown thing dragging from his waist. He'd smashed it because nothing else would stop "Sally in the Garden" from playing. It was either that or cut off his ears.

Ben propped King's *Iliad* up on his chest and opened it to the first page.

> *Rage, Goddess, sing of the murderous rage of Peleus'*
> *son Achilles,*
> *which caused the Achaeans incalculable pain,*
> *sent many brave heroes' souls down into Hades*
> *and their bodies left rotting as spoil for dogs*
> *and a feast for the birds, while Zeus' will was fulfilled.*

Over and over, Ben read these lines. "'Murderous rage,'" he said out loud, his tongue relishing the words. "'Their bodies left rotting for dogs.' Rotting for fucking dogs!" Ben's pulse picked up, each word shooting into him like an arrow. The rage was part of him. The incalculable pain: part of him. The bodies: all part of him. He closed his eyes and saw the image of that waitress. The one he'd called a dumb bitch. She'd barely rested one finger on his arm and he'd sent her flying into a table.

During a similar moment of unconsciousness or semiconsciousness, he'd done the same to Becca. According to Kath, smashing his father's fiddle had been only the aftershock.

"'Goddess, sing of the murderous rage,'" he whispered. Ben didn't know if the damage he'd done to his wife—to both of them—could be repaired. But he had to try. He closed the book and put it on the nightstand. He had no use for it. He didn't need solace, didn't care whether anybody could relate to him or his situation. His situation wasn't important anymore. He was on a mission to find her, bring her home, prove his love. Nothing else mattered.

December 13, 1977

Dear Willy,

Currahee! That's what we say in the 506th Infantry Division of the 101st Airborne. To think that you—one of the world's great linguists—had never heard a man shout *Currahee!* It's our version of the marines' *Oorah!* They say *currahee* is Cherokee for "stand alone, together."

But you couldn't do that. You put your faith in the Cham woman, despite the very real possibility that she was leading us into an ambush. And we had to follow her. Reno was burning up. He could barely walk. You went first, talking to the woman, Lai, in her scrambled tongue. King helped Reno through the thick, waxy jungle, and I kept watch in back. After half a klick, the woman led us through a net of vines and onto a plateau. In the gully below sat the remains of a village: blasted heaps of stone and wood.

"Oh my God," you said, standing over the escarpment, gaping at the destruction below. You'd been in-country such a short time, were too fresh to realize what must have happened: air force gunships swooping overhead like steel monsters, breathing fire. I hadn't known the United States was bombing Cambodia, but I wasn't surprised. Nor did the army's idiocy rattle me. It was almost funny, sending soldiers to make peace with a village it had already obliterated.

But then you saw something. At the north end of Li Sing stood the village's single intact structure: Durga. She was hewed from gray rock and stood at least thirty feet tall. Ten arms sprouted from her sides like stone branches, half of them curving upward toward her right ear, half arcing toward the ground. Durga's nostrils were flared and her eyes mischievous. Her mouth nearly smiled. She seemed half disdainful, half delighted at the rubble below.

I felt the breath sucked right out of my chest.

"Just look at her, Proudfoot. She's beautiful." You whispered to Lai, who nodded. She held up her hands as though to say *Don't shoot* and pointed to a bamboo hut at the jungle edge. I nodded and she hurried toward it. Shortly, she returned with a tower of bowls. She had us build a fire. Then she boiled a pot of water and crushed a handful of herbs. As she worked, she talked to herself like we weren't even there. Meanwhile, you stared at Durga, transfixed. When I tapped you on the shoulder, you nearly jumped out of your boots. "Looks to me like she's cooking up some voodoo." I nodded at Lai.

"Do you see how sick he is?" you snapped and pointed at Reno. He lay flat on his back on the ground. The awful rash had spread to his face and he was moaning quietly, his eyes clenched shut. You shook your head like you were disgusted with me, and for a quarter second I felt chastened. It was an unfamiliar sensation; my men never made me feel that way. You said, "A spider bit Reno. Lai says he'll become paralyzed if he's not treated."

"You think she knows what she's doing? You trust her?"

"She's the only surviving person from the village, Proudfoot." You squatted next to the woman. "She's all alone."

Was any man ever as green as you, Willy? Was it possible that a year before, I'd known nothing of this war, this land? I remembered breathing in my first lungful of the stifling Vietnamese air. It had felt like drowning.

"She claims to be the only survivor," I said and looked uneasily at the tree line.

Lai poured some of the liquid down Reno's throat. Then she scooped dirt into the remaining substance. When she'd formed a paste, she spread the thick brown stuff over his arm, shoulders, and chest. Reno's eyes fluttered, but he was barely conscious.

"Ask when he'll be better," I said.

You complied and Lai answered, smearing a second layer of paste over Reno's arm. "She says by morning."

"We'll take turns guarding her," I said, surveying the tree line again.

"She's our prisoner?" You sounded alarmed.

"We can't let her wander off and bring back her gook friends, Willy."

"She's not our enemy."

For a moment, you and I just looked at each other. You were trying to tell me something, Willy, but I refused to listen. I was too proud, too hard. I considered myself a leader, a warrior. But I was the weak one. So very weak.

"We guard her," I said and put King on first watch. "Over there." I flicked my gun at Lai. She stood, seeming to understand what you did not, and moved toward the trunk of a nearby banyan tree. Then she sat cross-legged on the ground. "You keep that gun at the ready," I told King. Clearly miserable, you sat down and pulled out *The Iliad,* which you'd cut into hundred-page chunks for easy transport and wrapped in scissored swaths of poncho to keep dry. It was almost cute, the way you'd done all that. But when you saw me smiling at you, you didn't smile back. You looked disappointed in me, your commander. It was an assault on the order of things; I was supposed to look at you like that. But why did I even care? You were a grunt, a pretty boy. I didn't expect you to make it through the week.

Currahee!

CO Proudfoot

13

"How are you enjoying your first day on the road?" Reno asked. They'd spent the morning following a long, quiet highway into Wichita and were now eating sandwiches in a park beside the Arkansas River.

"I've been on the road for five days already," Becca said, bristling. To her, it felt more like five months.

"Technically," Reno said and balled up his sandwich wrapper. "But until now, you've been familiar with some part of each day—either the bed you woke up in or the bed you went to sleep in. Today, everything's new." He snapped open a Coke and took a long sip, then added, "The road's not just a stretch of asphalt. It's a state of mind."

"How philosophical."

"Not philosophy, girl. Fact."

"I thought you all like predictability, routine," Becca said, nodding at her father. King lay a good twenty feet away, napping against a tree trunk. Still mad, he'd elected to eat his lunch alone.

"It's mostly true," said Reno. "But on the bike, it's a different story. Eighteen-wheelers, bugs in my teeth, the worst Mother Nature can throw at me—I'll take it all. As long as I can have that feeling."

"Which feeling is that?" she asked, impatiently eyeing her dad. It was not Reno she wanted to be having this conversation with.

"That everything's wide open. That I can just be. The feeling of nobody saying no. Your father, me, even Bull—we've had a lifetime of hearing no, of hearing we're not good enough."

"I've already heard this lecture from Bull," Becca said. "About how my generation is so entitled and we treat you all like crap."

Reno shook his head. "I got nothing against you or your generation," he said and seemed to really mean it. "But you know that I got spit on?"

Becca raised her eyebrows. She'd heard about this happening, but it seemed like such a cliché. "It's true," Reno said, as though he'd read her thoughts. "I got off the plane in California—I'm in my uniform, of course—and there was this boy, about your age, I think. And here I am, back in the United States for the first time in a year, and all of a sudden a big loogie lands on my leg."

"I would have gone apeshit."

"I was jet-lagged, mentally and physically exhausted. So at first, I was just confused."

Becca waited to hear more. At the very least, Reno must have cursed the kid out. Probably he'd taken a swing at him.

"I looked at him, but he couldn't bring himself to look at me. So I kept walking."

"That's it? I don't believe it."

"How do I explain this? I felt marked—and not just 'cause of the uniform. I wouldn't have been able to articulate it then, but I knew that for the rest of my life, I'd be either an object of people's hate or a source of their shame. I also realized that I wasn't going to get any kind of credit for the time I'd served, so I was going to pay myself what I was due. We fought for freedom, right? So that's what I claimed. My freedom is a piece of the road. Your daddy and I have talked about this. He'd say the same."

Listening to Reno, Becca felt ashamed. When she thought about her father, she saw a man ruled by his emotions whose fury bulldozed through any kind of self-reflection. But this wasn't true at all. Kath had called the men children, but in fact they were grown. They might not be wise. They certainly weren't respected. But they'd worked tirelessly to clear the various and formidable roadblocks in their lives. That had to count for something.

After lunch, Becca walked along the Arkansas River toward a cable-stayed bridge, where a crowd of fanny-pack-wearing tourists snapped photos of a giant steel Indian. The thirty-foot-tall statue stood atop a rock promontory and reached its arms in supplication toward the sky. A sign said it was called the Keeper of the Plains, but for Becca, it brought to mind the invincible goddess Durga. She felt an urge to raise her arms high like the statue, as though the gesture could fill her with similar implacable strength.

The Keeper of the Plains faced east. Behind it stretched the rest of Kansas. And beyond that, the west. Becca felt herself at a threshold and saw the statue as a warning: Pass at your own peril. But unlike Durga, the Keeper was hardly invincible. What remained to be protected, with the Indians' entire history pillaged? Becca hurried back, worried the men might leave without her.

Kansas, she quickly discovered, was hell. The state was flat and hot. Hot and flat. Exactly the same forward and backward. The wind filled her head with its pounding, and her body ached from hours of sitting in the same position. Not even running the dreaded hour of power—sixty minutes sprinting up and down the stairs of her college's tallest building—had left her ass so sore. "Maybe if you had an ass to speak of, it wouldn't hurt so bad," Reno joked when he saw her limping.

If only Becca could transfer her nonexistent ass to the luxurious Gold Wing, but King hadn't softened. Reno assured her that uncomfortable bikes were safer. He said the plains states worked a kind of hypnosis on bikers. The monotony might lull you to sleep or create mirages on the horizon. He claimed to know men who'd lost their minds riding after phantoms—beautiful women and wild buffalo. Clouds that resembled the gates of heaven.

Meanwhile, King's mood worsened. He raged about *The Iliad* disappearing from his saddlebag. He interrogated Reno and Bull. He'd even shouted at Becca: "What did you do with my book? Did Kath put you up to this?" Becca shook her head. She knew her father had a soft place for *The Iliad*. But to be *this* angry? She offered to call Kath and have her search the house. But he growled for her to stay out of his business. He spent the rest of the afternoon riding out ahead of the others. Whenever Reno's bike got even mildly close, King accelerated.

For the first time, she understood how Ben had felt, growing up with a father who had been there, but not really. So many nights, Ben told her, George Thompson would leave with his fiddle and not return until dawn. Even when he played in the house, he was distant; so far away, Ben said, as to be untouchable. When Becca asked why, Ben said he didn't know.

But didn't he?

When Ben was nine years old, his family had taken a trip to Colorado. Ben said he remembered camping out at a bluegrass festival. He remembered waking up in the middle of the night needing to pee and finding his mother asleep and his father missing. When he stepped outside of the tent, music wafted toward him from every direction, the sounds of fiddles and mandolins swirling in the flickering darkness. People laughed and stumbled by. Nobody seemed to notice him. As he searched for the bathroom, he saw musicians sprawled out in open-air living rooms. The whole place was a maze of colors and lights, fabulous and enchanting, and as Ben wandered, he realized he'd lost his way.

Then he heard a familiar melody. "Sally in the Garden." Ben followed the notes like a trail of bread crumbs and entered a crowded tent lit by Christmas lights and the glowing nubs of cigarettes. Sure enough, sitting on a wooden bench between two other musicians was his dad. George Thompson's eyes were closed and he played his fiddle with furious energy. Behind him, a red-bearded man accompanied on the harmonica. The man was shorter than Ben's father and burlier, and Ben watched, mesmerized, as his hands fluttered across the holes, dexterous as wings. He'd seen this man before, he realized, in his father's hardware store. Years later, after his dad died, Ben would discover photographs of this man among his father's things, pictures from their time together in Vietnam.

Ben watched the red-haired man touch his dad's shoulder. He waited for the man to take his hand away, but it stayed, cupping the checkered print of his father's shirt.

"Are you lost?" A young woman with blond hair and sleepy eyes appeared before Ben. He glanced at the woman, then back at his dad. According to kid logic, his father's presence meant that Ben was no longer lost. And yet, he'd told Becca, he knew that he must pretend not to know his dad or his dad's friend. Which made him feel even more disoriented. He asked the woman where the bathrooms were. Then he ran.

George Thompson died when Ben was sixteen. "He was sick" was all Ben told her. But it was enough. She wanted to convince him that she would never judge. That she did not think like other people, and that even their own rigid culture was starting to change. But she sensed that Ben was still resolving things for himself. That it would be better for him to confess the complete truth on his own time. What mattered was that he was trying — doing his best to reveal to her this secret part of his life.

Ben never talked about why he'd taken up the fiddle, but Becca suspected that he was attempting to access his father, which he'd never been able to do in the man's lifetime. For all of Ben's talk about familial duty and a line of soldiers that stretched back to the Civil War, she guessed that he'd enlisted in the army for the same reason. He was searching for his father, much as she was searching for hers. King Keller and George Thompson could not have been more different. But they'd passed the same legacy on to their children: too many unanswered questions and the feeling that no matter how fast you scrambled along behind them, you'd never quite catch up.

14

THE MEN IN Ben's platoon were superstitious. They kissed photographs of their wives and kids. They said a lucky number of Hail Marys before they left the command outpost. They chewed an even number of times on each side of their mouths and pissed standing on only one foot. One dumb bastard even refused to wash his socks. Ben told them that all of this was bunk. Save for knowing how to aim and not being extremely stupid, there wasn't much you could do to protect yourself.

Of course, Coleman was Ben's most vocal opponent. He advocated following what he called the movie rule: embrace the war-movie clichés and you'll avoid turning into one. "In war movies," Coleman said, "it's always the guys who swap places with their buddies and say things like 'Promise me you'll take care of Johnny if I don't come back' who bite it. If you want to avoid becoming that guy, then you've got to do the counterintuitive thing."

"Which is?"

"Do *exactly* what the unlucky movie hero does. Offer to swap places with your friend and say the dumb, clichéd thing before you head out on patrol. It's like a wink to the universe: *I know your game.*"

"The universe isn't *aware,*" Ben argued.

"It's worked for me so far," Coleman said. "I took Carlyle's slot on that mission last week and before I left, I said, 'Carlyle, if I don't make it back today, I want you to give good head to my girlfriend for the rest of her life.' And, see, I came back alive. God willing, I will go home and the head will be forever given by me."

A few days after this conversation, Ben's unit was sent out to patrol Ali's Alley. They called it Ali's Alley after an ex-girlfriend of one of the specialists; he'd come home from his first tour only to find his house cleared out, right down to the flat-screen TV. Ali (the girlfriend) had fucked that soldier over good. Which was exactly what happened when you drove patrol on Ali (the street). And still, the leadership routinely ordered patrols there. Like if the men proved their willingness to get blown up often enough, the local population would finally start to trust them.

On this particular day, Ben had woken up with a fever of 102, and the sergeant major had ordered him back to bed. He'd obeyed, half reluctant, half relieved, and was lying there aching when Coleman came in. "Fuck you for being sick, you bastard," Coleman said. "I'm taking your place." Ben groaned. His whole body felt stuck full of needles.

"Just do me a favor," Coleman added. "If anything happens to me and the kid Majid shows up again, promise me you'll keep him in Corn Pops."

"You can keep him in the fucking Corn Pops." Ben moaned. "And fuck your superstitious bullshit."

"You'll see," Coleman said and left.

Two hours later, Ben heard about the explosion. He stumbled down to vehicle sanitization to wait for the mortuary affairs people to haul the Humvee back in. There'd been four of them in the Humvee, and the report was one casualty and three injured. There was a 75 percent chance that Coleman was still alive, so Ben allowed himself, just this once, to have faith in the corporal's theory. After all, how could a guy like Coleman, with his goofy smile and cereal-smuggling operation, end up dead in some random and pointless explosion?

Ben opened his eyes in the Arkansas darkness. It was three in the morning and he was wasting precious time. He dressed hurriedly, scribbled Kath a note of thanks, and left it on top of King's *Iliad*. Then he blew on the Breathalyzer and headed down the mountain. His heart raced the way it always did when he woke up for a dead-of-night mission. He was headed for Colorado to see Becca's mother—a woman he'd never met but who, he knew, hated the very fact of his existence. Was it too much to call her his enemy? It didn't matter. Not if there was even the slimmest chance that she could help him get Becca back.

Jeanine had told Becca that she did not want her daughter to be a military mule, a person yoked to an army marriage. And because of this, she had declined to attend the wedding. But a few hours into the reception, Ben caught sight of two figures in the shadows behind the garage. At first, he didn't think much of it. But when he approached, he realized that one of the people was King and that a sound he'd initially heard as laughter was crying.

He'd gone up to his bedroom, grabbed his NVGs, then stealthily pressed himself into the shadows between the garage and a large tree. He felt a little ridiculous—doing recon at his own wedding—but he recognized Becca's mother from pictures. Why was she lurking here, crying in the arms of her ex-husband? And what if Becca found out?

Ben hurried back to the party. Becca was standing by a table of cupcakes, holding a beer, showing off the red cowboy boots she'd chosen to go with her dress. Her red dangly earrings swung with the movement of her head, tapping gently at the sides of her neck. Ben touched her upper back, and her laughter swung toward him, bright and clear, like the pluck of a mandolin. His stomach flipped over with happiness. He would never tell her about Jeanine. He would do nothing, as long as he lived, to upset her.

But now his spying had paid off, if only as confirmation that Becca's parents were in touch. It was the longest of long shots, but what if Jeanine could help him get his wife back?

Ben drove through Wichita, spent the night in a nowhere trailer park, and then sped into Colorado, barely cognizant of having left one state and entered another. Soon, however, the grassy flatness swept into hills, which mutated into low, humpy mountains. The Death Star climbed up to the plateau that was Pueblo; a nice enough town, but Ben drove on through. He was gunning for the snowy peaks. He wound along a narrow road where pines towered like massive spears, and small waterfalls ran through creases in the rockface. He kept the window down, breathing in the chill air, and eventually pulled into a scenic lookout for a piss. He hopped out of the car, jumped the guardrail, and picked his way a few meters down the embankment. Balancing on a rock, he unzipped.

"Hey! That's dangerous!"

Ben started, certain that the ground was sliding out from under him. But it was only a few clattering pebbles. He craned his neck to see a child-size spot backlit by the sun.

"You want to get me killed?" Ben snapped as he climbed back to the parking lot. The voice did indeed belong to a boy. A child of nine or ten, small and brown with eyes that were too big and hair that was too long. He wore a puffy silver parka despite it being August. He gawked at Ben's black eye like it was the most exciting thing he'd seen in days. "We sell frybread," the child said, indicating a food truck parked at the other end of the lookout. "It's good and cheap." He nodded, concluding his well-rehearsed sales pitch.

Ben's stomach rumbled, but he'd allowed himself to be derailed too many times already.

"Sorry, kid," he said. Then the child smiled, and in the boy's face, Ben saw a flash of Majid.

"Come on," the boy said and ran out ahead, his silver coat flashing in the sun.

The woman beside the food truck stared at Ben's eye with open disapproval. "Two dollars for the bread," she said, her voice deep and flat. Apparently, the boy had already negotiated the transaction. "You want a Coke? Fifty cents. You want jewelry for your wife? It's handmade." She indicated the spread in front of her and stared at Ben as though challenging him to dispute the fact.

Ben handed over some money. As they waited for the boy to get Ben's food, the woman continued to stare at him. He was starting to feel uncomfortable. "Do you live around here?" he asked, ordering himself to behave normally. The woman made a motion that was either a nod or a shake of the head. He tried again. "Do you know the Hands of God Church? It's a Christian commune in Lewell. The town's close, right?"

Before she could speak, the boy reappeared. "Frybread!" He handed Ben a paper plate. On it sat a puffy, crust-colored circle full of air bubbles. Its golden surface glistened with grease.

"Hot sauce," the woman snapped. "Honey!" The words burst forth from her lips like small explosions, and the boy ran back to the truck. "Coke!" she screamed even louder.

Ben sniffed the bread. It was fragrant and warm, and when he put it into his mouth, he felt every nerve ending on his tongue burst into life. The bread was salty and sweet and chewy and it released wave after wave of flavor. He'd barely been able to taste anything since his first tour; the doctors thought his olfactory nerves had been damaged by an explosion. Or maybe even by something as simple as a cold. They didn't know if he'd get better.

The frybread was a small victory, but it felt profound.

"So, Hands of God?" he asked again, chewing and savoring.

"I know it," the woman said. "But you can't pray there."

The little boy was now standing beside the jewelry table balancing on one leg, his toe trailing behind him in the dust. Ben felt a visceral affection for the child, a feeling he didn't like or trust. "I just need to see someone."

"The white woman."

Ben furrowed his brow.

"Who else would you be going to see?" The woman looked him up and down.

Ben thought he should feel offended but he was mostly confused.

"They've all been gone for two weeks now. To Utah. On a mission."

Mission. Sights and sounds flooded through him: heavy breathing, boots against the ground. He could almost feel his weapon in his hands.

"Healing mission," the woman was saying. The images dissolved, and her face reappeared, her brown skin and wide cheeks, material and solid. *She is real,* he thought. *Focus on what's in front of you.*

"Where in Utah? How far away are we talking?"

"Couple hundred miles. How badly do you need to find the white woman? You planning to drive there?"

"Why?" Ben asked, feeling uneasy.

"My sister—his mother," she said, nodding at the boy, "is with them, but I haven't heard from her since she left on the mission. Phone goes straight to voicemail. Doesn't answer my e-mails."

"I can tell her to call you when I get there," Ben said. "If you tell me what town it is."

"I'm trying to raise bus money," the woman continued.

"If you're worried, why not call the local police — what town did you say it was?"

The woman snorted. "My boyfriend won't let me use the Tucson powwow money. He's got it in a wallet around his waist and *under* his shirt. But I'm worried about my sister." The woman's eyes drifted over Ben's shoulder toward the Death Star, then back to Ben. She wasn't making a request so much as issuing a demand.

"Hold on," Ben said and dialed the number for Hands of God. The answering machine explained that the church was temporarily closed and that its congregation was away on "spiritual business." Ben scowled and hung up.

"So," said the woman, "are we going after them or not?"

Before Ben could answer, the woman began dumping her jewelry into a pillowcase. As she did so, she gave Ben instructions. "I'm gonna get a few things from the truck. You'd better start up the engine. I'm Lucy, by the way."

"Are we making a break for it?" He was kidding, but Lucy didn't laugh. She pulled her nephew over to the truck and disappeared inside. Ben stood by the car and considered leaving right then, but before he could move, arguing erupted. Moments later, Lucy hurried out with a backpack slung over her shoulder, pulling the child behind her. "Come on!" she shouted and ushered the boy into the back seat.

"Whore!" shouted a man — presumably the boyfriend — as he barreled down the stairs. "You good-for-nothing cunt. You ugly, worthless bitch."

"Fuck you!" Lucy yelled and slammed the passenger-side door.

Ben just stood there, stunned to be caught in the middle

of two strangers' domestic dispute. The nephew had his nose pressed to the car window, his eyes wide and worried. The boyfriend came closer. Ben braced himself. But the man stopped short. He was obviously drunk. His balance was off. "Enjoy your Navajo whore, white man," he said and spat a glistening wad of saliva onto Ben's shoe. Then he turned around and stomped back to the truck.

15

IT HAD BEEN six days since Becca fled Dry Hills and she was still searching for her stride. She practiced leaning into the speed and power of Reno's bike, closing her eyes for long stretches of road, feeling the engine rumble through her bones. She wanted to absorb the machine's power, to reach that mechanical Zen state in which she and the bike were one. But most of the time, she was bored and in pain. And still in Kansas. She perked up when a sign welcomed them to Colorado. But the landscape still looked like Kansas and smelled like Kansas and felt like Kansas, so little had changed, and Becca was convinced that she was going out of her mind.

As they headed deeper into the state, Becca realized that they were nearing her mother. Not that they were exactly close; Hands of God Church was at least a hundred miles away from the bikes' location. But Jeanine did not come home for holidays and made excuses whenever her daughter suggested a visit. Becca grimaced, thinking how happy her mother would be to discover that she'd left Ben. This outcome was more or less what the woman had predicted from the beginning. But since the men had no reason to visit Jeanine, her mother would be deprived of the pleasure of issuing a well-deserved "I told you so."

Two Easters before, Becca had gone home to tell her mother

about the proposal in person. Ben had wanted to come with her, but the situation was delicate, so she went alone. As soon as she'd walked into the house, though, she knew something was off. Her mother was no housekeeper, but the house was clean. Streaks from the vacuum cleaner ran like jet trails through the sky-blue family-room carpet. Upstairs, she found her mother packing. Trash bags full of clothes were lined up against the wall, and a suitcase sat open on the bed.

"The college girl has arrived," Jeanine said with uncharacteristic enthusiasm. She kissed Becca on the cheek, her breath thick with cigarettes. Becca asked what was going on. Jeanine sat down on the bed and folded her hands in her lap. "I can't be a good enough Christian in Dry Hills," her mother had said. "I need to take my faith to the next level."

"You're a Christian, not an aerobics instructor," Becca said.

Jeanine frowned and began explaining her newfound sense of purpose. She told Becca she'd be leaving Dry Hills for good the next day, right after church. "I need to await the Resurrection with my fellow faithful," she said, as though salvation were coming any day now. Maybe even tomorrow, and if she waited too long before driving to Hands of God, she'd miss it. "It would be ungodly for me to stay any longer."

Ungodly to spend Easter with her only child whom she had raised alone?

Not knowing what else to do, Becca went for the jugular. In one brusque sentence, she spat out the engagement, Ben's current job, the fact that he'd already served a tour in Iraq and was heading back the very next week. Oh, and they planned to get married as soon as he returned, in about fifteen months.

Her mother's eyes narrowed and her jaw tightened. "What's his name?" Jeanine said.

"Ben. Benjamin Thompson. He grew up in Kentucky. He's twenty-four."

"You foolish girl," Jeanine replied, turning away. "Go yoke your life to the army. You do that."

"The army isn't going to be the rest of our lives," Becca said.

Jeanine slammed the dresser door. "Your father didn't make a career in the army, Becca. He enlisted to avoid the draft and went for a year, and it ruined the rest of his life. It ruined ours — his and mine, yours and mine!" She stomped to the bed and shoved socks into her suitcase. "Are you stupid? No, you can't be. You're a college girl."

"Ben's unlike anyone I've ever known. He loves me. I mean, really loves me." Only after Becca spoke did she realize how this sounded. "I didn't m-mean —" she stammered, but her mother's face closed up. She turned toward a statuette of Jesus on the dresser.

"I wonder," Jeanine said, appearing to address the statue, "has my daughter taken up with this man in order to spite me? For all the love I didn't give her?"

"Mom," Becca pleaded.

Jeanine whipped back around. "Don't throw your happiness away because you think I've wronged you!"

Becca had never seen her mother so frantic or heard her voice strain a full octave above its usual husky pitch, but she was too hurt to care much about Jeanine's distress. "You don't even love me enough to stick around for Easter lunch!"

Jeanine rushed from the room, leaving Becca alone with the suitcase and trash bags. When her mother didn't come back after a few minutes, Becca crept into the hallway. To her horror, she could hear sobbing on the other side of the bathroom door.

The next morning Becca helped load the trash bags into the car. Then she watched her mother light a cigarette and pull away. When the car was gone, she looked up at the house. She'd never given the tiny structure much thought. It was just her home, nothing special. Now it was the only part of her family that she had left.

By nightfall, they reached Alamosa in south-central Colorado and headed to a bar on the outskirts of town. The men parked in a lot that was overstuffed with motorcycles. With considerable relief, Becca climbed off Reno's bike and followed the trio to a long line of bikers who were waiting to enter a tented pavilion beside the bar. A large sign read *Motorcycle Mountain Festival Fundraiser.*

"You're in for a treat," Reno said as they drifted slowly toward the entrance. "You've never been to a party like this before."

"I bet," Becca said, her teeth chattering with cold. Ever since it had gotten dark out, she'd been freezing. Now her entire body felt numb.

"Might consider getting yourself a leather jacket in there," Reno said. "You'd be warmer. And you'd be less at risk of getting skinned if anything were to happen on the road – not," he added quickly, "that I'd let anything happen."

It was true, Becca realized, that Reno was a responsible driver. Despite his penchant for unnecessary revving, he wore his helmet, even in the states that did not require it, and, unlike Bull, he avoided lane splitting. "I trust you," she said and noted Reno's surprise at the compliment.

The entire motorcycling population of southern Colorado appeared to have congregated at Motorcycle Mountain. They were like nocturnal critters who'd crawled out from their logs and up from their holes. They swarmed and buzzed, and for the first time in days, King smiled. Becca was shocked; her father hated crowds.

They moved through the tent, full of people eating and drinking, and then passed out into the night, where fields full of camping tents rolled gently into the dark. Among kiosks peddling biker paraphernalia, Becca fingered the leather vests and bras and Daisy Dukes that were hung up like the decor of an S&M dungeon. There was an entire stand of accessories to keep long hair from tangling in the wind, which, amusingly, was less of a problem for her than it was for most of the men.

Bull arrived with beers. As Becca drank, he held up a suede demi-bra dotted with rhinestones. "You should try something on," he said. "Leather could be your look. As long as they carry extra-small."

"Fuck you," Becca said.

"I'm just playing, Rebecca. Can't a college girl take a joke?"

"As long as we're talking extra-small, Bull, I think I see a child-size helmet that'll fit you like a glove."

It wasn't King who came to her defense but Reno. Only a few days ago, he'd been the one accusing her of a weak sense of humor. He was growing on her, and she didn't like it.

"Listen," he said to her now. "You're not riding safe. We need to get you fitted out." He leaned over the counter and spoke to the biker chick manning the register. She disappeared among the racks and returned with a leather jacket and a pair of gloves. "I think these'll fit," she said with a smile and passed the items to Becca.

The jacket was heavy and stiff. "I feel like I'm holding an animal carcass."

"That's because you are," said Bull.

"Go on." Reno nodded. So Becca put on the jacket and zipped it. She felt constrained, almost corseted. "I know it seems uncomfortable at first. But once you wear it in, you'll never take it off."

Becca looked at the price tag. "Two hundred dollars? Forget it."

"Your life isn't worth two hundred bucks?" Reno asked. "And

at the very least, this jacket will keep you warm. Jesus, girl, you were shivering so much tonight, you made *me* feel cold."

"I'll throw in the gloves for free," said the cashier. She leaned over the counter and motioned for Becca to come closer. "You look pretty tough in that jacket," she whispered. "Seriously. If you don't want anyone to mess with you—just suit up."

Becca looked around for her father to get his opinion, but King had disappeared.

"Come on." Reno nudged her affectionately. "Become one of us."

Becca couldn't believe she was letting herself be talked into this, but she handed over her credit card.

"Hallelujah!" Reno exclaimed.

Becca downed her beer as though trying to dull the pain of her extravagant purchase. "Time for another," she said.

On their way to get drinks, Reno, Bull, and Becca paused outside a small tent advertising tattoos. "My diabolical plan to convert you from human being to biker chick is nearly complete!" Reno rippled the tips of his fingers together like a cartoon villain. "Tattoo to seal the deal?"

He was only joking but Becca looked him dead in the eye. "Fine," she said and pushed inside without looking back. She didn't want to lose her nerve.

Becca had a terrible fear of needles, but she wasn't going to back out now. She was so determined, she didn't even realize that she'd cut the line and planted herself in an empty chair. The bikers who'd been waiting were so amused that they only laughed.

"You sure you're old enough for this?" one of them said.

"Your mama know where you are?" said another.

"I thought this jacket was supposed to make me look tough," Becca complained, and the men laughed harder.

"Becca, you really want to do this?" Reno had made his way

through the crowd to her. It was the first time he'd used her actual name—called her something other than *girl*—and she understood that in a moment, she'd be changed for good. A jacket could come on and off; a tattoo was a commitment.

"What's it gonna be?" The tattoo artist looked utterly uninterested, like a diner waitress snapping her gum. *What's it gonna be?* But this was serious. Like the biker vets with their U.S. Marine Corps crests and American flags, Becca was taking a stand. She was making her own political statement. "What hurts the least?"

"It all hurts," Reno said.

"You want a soft area," her soon-to-be-tormentor advised. "But you don't seem to have any of those." She took her own tattooed hand and pinched Becca's upper arm. "Solid as a rock, this one. Unlike them." She nodded at the paunchy bikers. "How visible do you want it? If I do your back, you can hide it, but you'd have to sleep on your stomach for a while."

Becca did not want the tattoo anywhere near Ben's bruises.

"Inner wrist," Reno said, and Becca could tell he'd been giving the question serious thought. "It's visible but not too visible, but it'll hurt like a mother." Reno flashed his gold-toothed smile, and there he was—the Reno from King's kitchen, the man Becca despised, reveling in her discomfort. Which was all she needed to be convinced. She offered up her left arm. "I want it to say *King* in black. Cursive but not too fancy."

"No heart with an arrow through it?" Reno laughed. But Becca ignored him. The tattoo artist swabbed Becca's wrist with alcohol and already she felt like passing out. "You need to bite on something?" Reno said.

There was a pressure on her arm and she flinched. This time, it was only the woman making the outline. Reno shook his head. "You don't look so great." Now he seemed truly worried about her.

"This good?" the tattoo artist asked. Becca looked at her father's name, inked across her wrist, soon to be permanent.

Reno shook his head. "Your daddy isn't gonna like this one bit."

"You said to make an effort," Becca snapped. "Let's get this over with."

And then pain. Specific and brutal pain, the nature of which she'd never felt in her life; it was like a hive of hornets had landed on her arm or like a blunt knife was sawing her hand off.

"Well, look at you, Rebecca." This was Bull. He seemed to have materialized specifically to bait her, but then she saw that he was carrying another beer.

"No alcohol allowed in here," the tattoo artist said, barely looking up.

"Give it," Becca snarled. She grabbed the cup with her free hand and gulped it down like water. "Get me another one," she demanded.

The tattoo artist shook her head, but she kept on working.

"Get the girl a double shot of whiskey." Reno handed Bull some money. "You seen King out there?"

"He's over with Elaine. Should I . . . ?"

"Just get the poor woman her drink."

"Yes, sir." Bull saluted and ducked out of the tent.

"Who's Elaine?" Becca huffed, grimacing, feeling the urge to scream. But she was not going to let that happen. She was going to take this. She was going to suck it up.

"It's a good thing your daddy doesn't have a longer name," Reno said.

Becca forced a smile. She felt cold, then hot. She was going to vomit. Her head swam in a nauseated blackness. The minutes passed. Bull seemed to have forgotten about her drink. Reno stood by, chatting with a couple of vets. He hadn't told her who Elaine was, but who cared? How long had she been sitting here? How much longer was this going to last? Time seemed to have slowed; it was like entire minutes had been packed into seconds.

"What in the hell are you doing to my daughter?"

The whole tent seemed to look up at once. King stood in the doorway, as menacing as a madman. He pushed his way through the line, leaving the other bikers mumbling in his wake.

"Looks like Bull took a detour on the way to the bar." Reno laughed. "Hiya, King!" He gave an exaggerated wave.

"Get outta that chair!" King lumbered forward, and the tattoo artist held her hands up like there was a gun in her face.

"All of a sudden you care what I'm doing?" Becca snapped, puffing through the pain, which continued to bite through her arm even though the pen wasn't touching her.

"It's your name she's putting there," Reno said and Becca held her wrist up. The tattoo artist had finished only three letters, so the tattoo read KIN; next to it was the *g*, much fainter, in pen.

"King," Becca said. "It's going to say *King*."

King stopped his advance. His eyes were deep gray and glowering, like gathering clouds. His jowls quivered.

"You make that lady stop now," Reno said, "and people will look at your kid and think, *That's one lonely girl who's got to write* Kin *on her own arm*."

Reno was only trying to lighten the mood, but his words were like a kick in the chest. Becca *was* all on her own. She was all the family she had. "Finish it," she told the woman. "Please." The tattoo artist lowered the needle and Becca winced as the tip bit in. She kept her eyes fixed on King's reddened face, staring him down as her body screamed.

"Branded!" Reno announced. And they left the tent with Becca's wrist wrapped in a bandage.

King didn't look angry anymore. More like resigned.

"She chose your name for her body. And she doesn't take kindly to needles," Reno said.

"You're going to regret that, Becca," King said, shaking his head. "It's expensive to get those things removed."

"I'm not getting it removed." She turned from her father and beelined to the bar, wondering what in the hell she'd just done to herself.

Becca was drinking and watching the crowd dance to hair-band covers and rockabilly when a hand floated into her field of vision. She was confused at first—what was somebody's upturned palm doing so close to her nose? But then she saw that the hand was attached to a wrist and that the wrist was attached to a forearm and that the arm was connected to a shoulder. The man standing before her looked Hispanic, possibly Mexican. He was stocky and thick around the stomach, with a glossy head of black hair. He flashed a large, toothy smile. He nodded at his palm.

Becca looked around, confused. "He wants to dance with you!" somebody shouted. She looked dubiously at the stranger but decided to get up. The next moment, she was in the crush of bodies on the dance floor. Her partner—who was hardly taller than she was—twisted and turned her with ease. He was keeping his distance and Becca could tell he must be making a huge effort at politeness, because around them, almost all of the dancers were pressed together, their hands squeezing each other's asses. It was a baffling scene: gnarled bikers, many of them vets, so stiff and silent in their daily lives now out on the floor swinging their biker ladies easily by their waists.

Becca spotted Reno dancing with some townie with an exposed midriff and tight jeans. He looked downright elated, his gold caps flashing. A slow song came on and all the couples who weren't already pressed close collapsed together. Becca was suddenly pulled against her suitor.

"You're a good dancer," he said into her ear. He smelled of cologne, the kind that was advertised as having the power to make women lose control of their faculties.

"No, I'm not."

"Can't a guy give a pretty girl a compliment?"

She didn't answer. As uncomfortable as she felt in his meaty arms, she wanted to let the moment play out.

"You got a husband, huh," the man said. Becca could smell the beer on his breath, but it wasn't entirely unpleasant. She glanced down at her wedding band and the engagement ring with the small square ruby. She didn't answer this question either, which the man seemed to take as a good sign. He squeezed his hands tighter around her back and she noticed that the bruises were hurting less. They looked grotesque, were fading to a greeny yellow, but the ache was now a quiet pulse, much less painful than the frigid motorcycle wind or the sting of the tattoo needle.

It felt odd to have this stranger's hands on her. They were different than Ben's hands. Shorter, thicker fingers.

"You're sexy," the man said, and instead of feeling offended, Becca smiled. Why shouldn't a man call her sexy? The hands began a descent down her lower back and onto the back pockets of her jeans. She let them linger there for a moment, then changed her mind and moved them back up. "Don't push it," she said, and the man laughed.

They danced in silence for a second slow song and she let her partner pull her even closer, his belly ballooned against her torso. Moving in and out, his stomach and chest felt uncomfortably alive. How strange, she thought, to feel the inner workings of a person whose name you didn't know.

A fast rockabilly number came on and Reno cut in. She hesitated, but he just shook his head. "Come on, girl, you've had a couple beers, gotten a tattoo. You could do worse than dance with ol' Reno."

Every time he twirled her out, she felt like she was about to crash into the other couples, but just at the brink of disaster, he'd pull her back, safe.

"Watch the hand!" she shouted, worried that Reno was going to grab her wrist right over the fresh tattoo.

"I gotcha!" he called, as though she were dangling over a cliff, her feet kicking into the abyss. She thought she might throw up, but then Reno put one hand firmly on her back and they danced more calmly. Gradually, the world stopped spinning.

"I like you better like this," he said.

"Like what?"

"A little drunk and without a damn pole stuck—well, you know."

Reno was only slightly taller than Becca, and dancing with him, she could see his face up close in a way she hadn't before. His skin was burlap tan and the furrows around his quick eyes made him look older than he appeared from a distance. He couldn't have been much younger than her father.

"I like you better when you're not a total hard-ass," Becca said.

"That really is what you think about me," he said, turning her slowly.

"You never gave me reason to think otherwise."

"You know what I think, Becca?" She stiffened, her easy feeling fading. "I think you set your mind against most people and refuse to budge."

She started to protest, but Reno shook his head. "I get it, okay? I know why you do it."

He rocked them both, left, then right. He turned her in a slow circle, still swaying to the music.

"It's not true," she said.

Reno looked at her in a joshing way that said, *Lies – after all we've been through?* She looked back at him as though to say, *You may be right, but you'll never hear me admit it out loud.*

The song ended. "Thank you for the dance, Miss Becca," Reno said and gave a little bow.

Becca felt, suddenly, a swelling in her heart. It was sadness and uncertainty all mixed together. "Reno, what was in Kath's letter?" She knew she must have looked awfully weak to him right then, but she didn't care.

Reno fixed his eyes on hers, and Becca believed that he was finally going to tell her everything. But then his eyes shifted to something over her shoulder. "Brace yourself," he said.

Becca turned to see a tsunami of frosted bangs rushing at them, led by a bosom that looked ready to burst from its denim halter.

"Becca!" The woman squealed like a teenager. "I can't believe I'm finally meeting you!" Becca shrank back, afraid she'd be knocked over. Instead, the woman grabbed her shoulder and pulled her into an embrace. It felt more like a throttle. The bruises screamed.

"King, she's the cutest thing. I mean, she's perfection."

"Perfection," Reno mimicked.

Set free, Becca looked around for her father. He was hiding behind Bull as though cowering from this explosion of feminine excitement. Who was this person?

"Oh, I envy your shoulders, Becca," the woman said. "So narrow! Those are model shoulders."

Becca had never once thought about her shoulders. "Thanks?" she offered.

"I mean, just look at these hunks of flesh! I look like a linebacker."

"Elaine, you haven't even introduced yourself," Reno said.

"Oh!" The woman's eyes widened beneath eyelashes that looked coated in tar. "Well, I'm Elaine. Your daddy's woman."

King has a girlfriend? Becca was too stunned to feel hurt for being kept in the dark.

"You're about as dainty as they come," Bull assured Elaine, and Becca saw her father blush deeply. It wasn't exactly true —the woman's halter exposed skin that had clearly wrinkled beneath unnatural UV light. Her arms were more or less skinny for a woman in her fifties, though she'd deftly hidden her stomach paunch with high-waisted jeans. Her belt, Becca noticed, was stamped leather. Clearly, a present from King.

"We have so much to catch up on!" Elaine winked at Becca. "But first, your daddy's promised me a dance."

No way, Becca thought and then watched in astonishment as her father followed Elaine to the dance floor. He just *went,* like dancing was simply something you did at a party where a band was playing. Which it was — for normal people. To be fair, what King was doing now could not be called dancing, exactly. His body jerked and folded and stretched and there was this expression of intense concentration on his face, like the activity was extremely complicated. Periodically, Elaine took his hand and tried to pull him into a rhythm. It never worked. They'd fall out of step, trip over each other, and then separate until Elaine coaxed him back into line. She smiled and didn't seem to mind the mess that was King on the dance floor.

"Horrible, ain't he," Reno said. Becca nodded dumbly.

The song ended and Elaine returned. "Let's get to know each other," she said. "I've heard so much about you." *I've heard zip about you,* Becca thought but she followed Elaine anyway.

"Truthfully, it's good to have girlfriends to drink with, since, you know, I'd never drink with King," Elaine said as they walked toward the bar. "He says he doesn't mind, but I prefer not to have a beer when he's around. It doesn't seem fair. Don't you agree?"

For the next thirty minutes, while they sat at a picnic table drinking Coronas, Elaine talked about herself. She was a nail technician in town but was studying acupuncture. She'd been riding motorcycles for nearly twenty-five years, ever since her husband—now ex-husband—informed her that women "weren't fit" to ride. Elaine was living outside Flagstaff, Arizona, at the time, and the very next day, she'd gone to the DMV for her motorcycle license. Then she put her entire savings—all forty-two hundred dollars of it—toward a bike. "A beautiful bike," she said wistfully. Her husband had gone ballistic over the purchase. "He was a red-necked, dimwitted brute," she said and explained that the man had beaten her for years. Through all of this, Becca noticed that Elaine's voice sounded cheerful, as though she were discussing a great movie she'd seen and not the tragedy of her marriage. "Of course he tried to stop me," she said. "But things had changed. I had the bike!"

"You ran him over?" Becca asked, incredulous. She wasn't sure that she liked Elaine, but the woman was certainly impressive.

"No, nothing like that. I hit him with a lamp. But I felt like that motorcycle had given me special powers. The lamp, by the way, was an antique my mother had left me. The metal base must have weighed twenty pounds. He took it right in the chest. It was like a kick from a samurai or something—only it was a lamp!" Elaine shook her head, as if even now she couldn't believe it.

Elaine said she hadn't looked back, had just jumped on her bike and gotten the hell out of there. "I might have killed him for all I know," she said. This was over a decade ago. She'd met King at a motorcycle rally back in 2002. She was there with a motorcycle club called the Biker Bitches. "Biker Bitches!" she said gleefully. "I don't have my vest on tonight or I'd show you our patch. It's a motorcycle with pink headlights. Some of the gals think it's silly, but I love it. Anyway, I spotted your daddy in the crowd and I just had to talk to him. Everything he's been through, it boggles the mind. He wasn't sober yet, but he was trying. And I knew I could help him. I could be his rock." Elaine raised her beer to her lips only to discover that she'd already finished it.

"Wow" was all Becca could say. Beneath her astonishment at Elaine's story, she felt the itch of jealousy. Was she the only person on earth who didn't know anything about her father's life? She wanted to hate Elaine. The woman seemed less a rock than a swamp of emotion. But King was doing okay and if Elaine had played any role in helping him, then who was Becca to judge. Also, unlike Jeanine, Elaine gushed understanding.

"So what about you, honey? I bet you and I have plenty in common."

Becca wondered what Elaine knew. Did the woman hope to bond over their both having fled their men in the middle of the night?

"You know, I get this sense about you," Elaine continued. "You can take care of yourself. Not many women these days really do that. They don't have the—the wherewithal. Now, you don't have to thank me for the compliment," she added quickly. "I'm guessing that compliments make you uncomfortable. Same as your daddy."

Becca blushed. Maybe she was warming to Elaine. Or maybe the sudden tenderness she felt for her was from a more calculating impulse: Elaine could provide information about the enigma that was Kleos.

"Now, let me see what you've got under that bandage."

Becca hesitated. "I'm supposed to keep it covered."

"Oh, just a quick peek!"

Slowly, she unwrapped the gauze.

"Is that not the dearest thing!" Elaine turned Becca's wrist this way and that, evaluating the design like it was an intricate work of art. "I'm going to give your daddy a talking-to. He'd better understand how lucky he is to have a daughter like you." She pulled a tissue from her pocket and dabbed her eyes. "Sorry for the display. Menopause. Makes me batty. More beer?" She stood up and was back in a flurry with two more Coronas.

"Elaine," Becca said, after they'd sipped for a while. "I was wondering. My dad is so quiet. Not like . . ."

"Not like me." Elaine nodded. "Oh, don't I know it."

"But then how do you—I mean, does he show you—" Affection, emotion, love? Do the two of you *communicate?* These were the questions Becca wanted to ask.

"I love your daddy more than I've ever loved any man, Becca. And I know I love him so much because I'm still with him. We've had to work hard to get where we are."

"He was willing to work?" Becca said. *Willing with you,* she thought, *but not me.*

"I spotted him at that rally and I went to him, Becca. I almost always go to him. You know what I mean?"

Becca picked at the beer label. "And that doesn't bother you? Don't you want things to be equal?"

"Our relationship isn't about equality. Not for me, anyway."

"Then what's the point?"

"Love," Elaine said, as though this were obvious. "And perseverance. That's what your daddy and I are all about." Elaine laughed and added, "We also live a couple of states apart, which I guess helps us get along."

• • •

Later, Elaine took Becca back to the dance floor. Drunk, the woman turned belly dancer, all undulating hips and snaking arms, even during the hair-band songs. It was a strange way of moving, but Becca found it oddly beautiful. She wanted to try it, but even with the alcohol working through her, she felt shy. She did not like making a display of herself. But why not let loose a little? Why not try on someone else's way of doing things for a couple of hours?

She imitated Elaine, tentatively, and Elaine smiled wide; Becca understood that if a movement made her feel happy, it was perfect. Her head began to feel like a giant wineglass, with the wine swirling round and round. She had not been so drunk in a long while. At one point, she'd tried to calculate her alcohol intake. A bunch of beers before Elaine, a double shot of whiskey, then the beers Elaine bought her. A random biker had presented Becca with a hard lemonade, claiming to know what "girls" liked. Becca was about to throw it in his face when Elaine fixed her stare on the offending hunk of leather and said, "Girl? This here's a woman." At that, they'd both burst out laughing. Were there more drinks after that? Possibly. There were certainly more men. Generally, when Becca consumed this much alcohol, she'd planned ahead. Ate a big dinner, at least. But tonight there was no plan.

A man who was not King started dancing with Elaine, and the Mexican appeared again and started dancing with Becca. This time she let him pull her in so that they were pressed together and she could smell his beery breath and cologne and feel her hand warm in his hand and his other hand on her lower back, slipping lower to rest not quite on her ass. Then the Mexican moved away, as though the music were a rope pulling him backward. And there before her was Reno, dancing with her, smiling as if to say, *Fancy meeting you here.* He offered her his hand and she took it without really thinking too much, just noticing a faraway voice that said, *Be careful,* and she'd laughed at this voice because for the first time in weeks, she just didn't care.

Becca felt like she owned Motorcycle Mountain. She felt as though she were the Queen of these bikers, Queen of this music, Queen of her destiny.

The music slowed. Elaine was dancing with King, and Bull was grinding with some townie. But Becca wasn't on the floor anymore. She was leaning against a picnic table under the sky, and there was another beer in her hand, and a group of men and a couple of ladies, none of whom she knew, were standing around, and they were all laughing about something. Someone was pointing at the sky, which was bursting with stars. The music was close but also distant. And for a second, the tent was a big top, and King and Elaine and the other dancers were circus performers, and Becca was in the audience watching them. But that picture faded when she felt someone lift the beer from her hand. Then that someone took her hand in his own and she saw that it was Reno, and there was that voice again saying, *Careful now,* and her brain saying, *Shut up,* which she must have spoken out loud because Reno said, "Huh?"

"Nothing," Becca replied. So Reno led her to a patch of grass just a few yards away and now they were dancing to a slow song together. Nobody else was there and nobody came by to bother them and the music floated out of the tent and over them and it felt like they were in a small room made of sound. And then, out of nowhere, she was thinking about Ben and the wedding and how they'd stood at either end of the aisle listening to the fiddles play. The fiddles had formed a kind of invisible room around them the way the music did now, bringing them together, and neither of them could quit smiling.

Becca started to tear up, but she didn't want Reno to see, so she pushed the memory away. Reno turned her slowly and led her in this careful way, because they were both painfully drunk. He turned her out and then he pulled her to him with his hand firm on her back. The way Reno was hugging her felt strange. She felt a sense of needing in his hug, something basic, like he was afraid and she was this person he could cling to — maybe the only person. And so that's what he was doing, clinging. And Becca's heart was pounding, because she didn't really understand what was happening or why she was having this effect on Reno and she was starting to cry again. This time, she didn't know why.

Later, Becca followed Reno into the maze of tents. There were campfires and music but no fiddles. Becca imagined this place as an army encampment filled with soldiers readying for battle. But who were they fighting, and why? Becca and Reno arrived at a campfire where Elaine sat with some others, warming her hands. King was nowhere to be seen, but Bull was there. People were talking and drinking and watching the flames, women sitting in the laps of their men, their eyes glazed with firelight. And now anxiety began to penetrate the haze of Becca's intoxication. How would she find her way back to Reno's bike to get her tent? She felt a stab of panic when Elaine said good night and disappeared. But then Reno came over and sat down beside her. As he chatted with friends in the circle, he ran his hand from the top of her head to the nape of her neck and then back up. And she started to feel her worry slip away. His hand smelled like cigars and it felt so good and it was making her shiver and she thought about the two of them dancing earlier and her heart was beating rapidly again. Then Reno took his hand away and her neck felt cold.

Later, when the flames started dying out and almost everybody else had left, Reno stood. He hovered over her so that she was tucked inside his shadow. He offered his hand and she took it, let him pull her up. She followed him from the warmth of the fire into the thick of the tents until they reached his. And then Becca understood what was happening. She realized that she'd understood it for a long time now, even though Reno was almost King's age and she had hated him and possibly still hated him. But something between them had changed. And now this was going to happen, and it was all right.

Becca stood shivering in the dark as Reno unzipped the tent flap. He held it open and she climbed inside. She waited. Reno knelt down outside the tent door so that they were now face-to-face, Becca on the inside, Reno on the outside. He leaned forward and she closed her eyes.

Reno pressed his lips to her forehead, his touch so much softer than she would ever have expected. She leaned forward slightly, waiting for the next phase to begin, but nothing happened. She opened her eyes. Reno had vanished into the night. The ghost of his lips lingered on her forehead, like a blessing.

16

THAT NIGHT, CURLED inside Reno's sleeping bag, Becca dreamed about the Old Moon. She and Ben had been together a month, and he'd driven down from Fort Campbell to take her to the bar. It was to be her introduction to his coterie of fellow musicians. "These are my people," he'd told her. "They're going to love you."

"Even though I don't play an instrument?" she'd asked, and Ben frowned at her, like she should know better.

The bar was beery and dark and their shoes squelched against the sticky floors. As they looked for a free table, they passed a trio of musicians who attacked their instruments, oblivious to the fact that another band played on the stage just yards away. Meanwhile, people kept stopping Ben, giving him exaggerated salutes and making inside jokes. Becca trailed behind, a smile gelled on her face. It was too loud to catch people's names and nobody seemed particularly interested in her anyway.

As soon as they sat down, Ben stood up again. "Forgot the fiddle! Don't move!" He kissed Becca atop her head and then he was hurrying back through the bar. The band finished its set and music swelled from the floor, instruments appearing around bar tables as though from thin air. With nothing to hold but her beer, she felt strangely exposed.

"Hey there!" said a voice. "You must be Becca."

Becca looked up. The band's lead singer stood over her, holding a mandolin under her arm. She had Nashville hair and wore a mix of cotton, silk, and studs. Becca felt the plainness of her own T-shirt. "I'm Katie Jacobson," the singer said. "I'm with the Sexy Fiddles." She nodded at the others onstage. "We've all been eager to meet you. Where's Ben?" Katie sat down as though the table belonged to her.

"Getting his fiddle."

Katie nodded, though she didn't really seem to be listening. "Heeey!" she called loud and twangy to someone across the room.

Becca knew she should feel proud that Ben was talking her up to his friends, but she didn't like this woman in her showy outfit.

"There's my boy!" Katie exclaimed suddenly, bounding over to kiss Ben on the cheek.

"So you've made each other's acquaintance." Ben put his hand on Becca's shoulder. This made her feel moderately better, but the next moment, his hand was gone and unlatching the fiddle case.

"You're up in five, Benny." Katie winked and returned to the stage, her hair lashing whiplike against her back.

"An old friend?" Becca asked.

"A friend," Ben said.

"A girlfriend."

"Not exactly."

"What does that mean?"

"Are you jealous, Chicken?" He grinned. Becca didn't smile back. There was so much they still didn't know about each other, wide gulfs of information. All she wanted, she realized then, was to reach a point when they'd lived more of their lives together than apart.

Becca made to say something about this, but Ben was distracted, wiping down the fiddle's exterior with a white cloth, fastening on the shoulder rest, rosining the bow, and turning the pegs. The instrument seemed like a toy in his large hands.

Up on the stage, Katie Jacobson laughed with her banjo player, their voices like bright major chords and too loud. If only Ben would stay put through a round of drinks. He was supposed to be a Southern gentleman, and gentlemen should not hop up onstage with other women. But the other woman was calling.

"Here goes nothin'," Ben said and then Becca was alone again.

Hard-driving bluegrass burst out from the band. These weren't the quiet murder ballads and fiddle tunes that Ben had played on the college green. This was music that demanded to be the center of attention. His eyes were closed and he seemed far away. Where was he, Becca wondered, and how could she get there? *Could* she even get there? Katie had her eyes fixed on Ben as she stomped her foot in time. Did everyone see that stomp for what it was? A beat that shouted, *Mine, mine, mine!* Becca folded her arms across her chest in protest.

Then Ben took a solo. A few measures in, his fiddle began to pull at her, like it could physically pry her arms apart. And soon, her feeling toward the music shifted. The sounds seemed to lift the roof clear off the bar, laying out the world plainly before her, possibilities multiplying infinitely, like reflecting mirrors. *If you played, you could have all of this,* the music said. *But you don't, so you can't.*

Ben opened his eyes and looked directly at her; his expression caused a physical jolt. Becca felt herself lifted upward toward the gigantic hole where the roof of the Old Moon bar had been before the music blasted it away. She gazed at the Kentucky fields and far beyond them, the million lives she and Ben were going to live. She saw that she could take her time living those lives. She need not rush, because the slower she walked toward the future, the more time she and Ben would have together. This whole time, she realized, he'd been playing for her.

Dawn brought a terrible hangover. Becca unzipped the tent and turned her face to the air, letting its dampness soothe her aching head. She spotted Reno sitting on a nearby log, his head hunched over his knees. A thin line of smoke curled from his cigar into the air. Becca climbed out of the tent and sat down beside him.

"You've been here all night?" she said. "Keeping watch or something?"

It was a moment before Reno responded. "Keeping watch, sure." She opened her mouth to speak, but Reno preempted her. "I hope you're not upset with me." He turned his head to glance at her, briefly, then looked back at the ground.

"Not at all." It occurred to her that she should feel horribly embarrassed for mistaking the nature of Reno's affection. And for the fact that she'd been open to it, maybe even wanted it.

"You're . . ." He looked at her steadily and she saw that his eyes were ringed red. "Oh, Becca." He sighed her name in a long breath, almost like he was invoking the name of somebody years dead.

"Reno," she said. "The letter?" She hadn't intended to ask him about it just now, but the request barreled out of her.

"Quit bothering me about that," he snapped and stubbed out the cigar on his boot. Then he walked to his tent, climbed inside, and zipped the flap shut.

Becca dug her heels in the dirt. How stupid could she be? Thinking that she and Reno had come to a kind of understanding. Over and over, she was wrong about people. She had misread her father on so many levels. And Ben! The most colossal misreading of all. She turned her wrist over and unwrapped the bandages. She should have stopped after the letter *n*. She was her only kin.

17

FROM THE SCENIC overlook, Lucy had given Ben a single direction—"South"—so south he went. Almost instantly, he regretted his decision to bring her along. He didn't like having a child watching him while he drove, and Lucy's phone wouldn't quit ringing. After the eighth or ninth call, she made to throw it against the windshield. Ben flung his hand out to stop her. "Just turn it off!" he snapped.

Lucy obeyed and stuffed the phone into her pocket. She looked down at her lap and started sniffing—a sure sign of tears.

Ben cursed himself. "So, do you live around here?" he asked, trying to make things better.

Lucy shook her head and wiped her nose. "Window Rock. We came up here on the powwow circuit."

"You mean dances and feathers? Those things still happen?"

Lucy frowned and shook her head, like Ben was a hopeless case. "We're frybread champions, Ricky and me. We've won awards, been written up in the *Navajo Times*. We could do big things, you know? Open a restaurant. Have a TV show on the Food Network. But these last few years, all he wants to do is perform magic tricks with our money. He snaps his fingers and suddenly the cash turns into beer. But I guess you know all about that," Lucy continued and nodded at the Breathalyzer. "Seriously. I got into the car, saw that thing, and almost got right out again."

Ben had not expected Lucy to be such a talker, but maybe this was her defense mechanism. Like Becca's stubbornness. "I'm sober," he said.

"Sober people don't need Breathalyzers."

Ben focused on the road. He *was* sober. Stone-cold. And he wasn't going to get mad. He was going to stay calm. Like a normal human being. He glanced in the rearview. He wasn't sure he wanted the nephew listening to this conversation. But the kid was asleep, curled up in his silver jacket like a potato bug.

"But obviously you're trying," Lucy added. "That's more than I can say for Ricky."

"Are you always so chatty?" Ben asked.

"Are you always so antsy? You need to pee or something?" Lucy pointed at Ben's leg. He hadn't realized that he was bouncing it.

"I'm fine," he said.

Lucy pulled her phone out and powered it on. "Ricky left a voicemail," she said. "Let's see what he has to say." To Ben's surprise, she put the phone on speaker. The message was over a minute long and full of sniveling apologies. At the end of it, Ricky broke into full-on tears. He begged Lucy to come back, swore that he'd give her the gas money, that he'd quit drinking. Lucy cut the message off.

"Emotional guy," Ben said.

Lucy shook her head. "It's not him crying," she said. "It's the booze." She put the phone away. "So," she said, drumming her fingers on the armrest. "Who's the white woman you need to find so bad?"

Since Lucy had so easily and quickly exposed her private life to him, Ben decided that lying to her was a waste of energy.

"She's my wife's mother," he said. "I'm hoping she can tell me where my wife is."

"Oh, boy." Lucy shook her head. "Now I don't feel nearly so bad for myself."

After an hour, they left the mountains. The pine trees disappeared, and the air warmed. They entered a brittle, khaki-colored plain, all shrubs and dirt to the horizon. It reminded Ben of Iraq. But on these long, empty stretches without overpasses or buildings, he felt less of an impulse to scan for snipers. With few other cars, he didn't worry about other drivers. Going around Dry Hills or between Becca's house and Fort Campbell, Ben felt like a pot of water on a gas range; every time he cooled down, some idiot in the next lane started driving reckless, igniting a new flame under his ass.

"You're bouncing again," Lucy said.

Ben forced his knee to be still. "Sorry," he said.

"So you must work out a lot." Lucy nodded at his arm. "How much weight do you bench?"

"Two eighty."

She was clearly impressed. "Ricky's such a lazy shit."

"I realize it's none of my business," Ben said. "But why don't you break things off? You don't seem to like him very much. And I'm sure you deserve better."

"How do you know what I deserve?"

"You seem like a nice person, and he doesn't."

"Wouldn't it make you feel good to be the hero who took me away from my drunk, verbally abusive boyfriend?"

"That's not what's going on here. You asked *me* for the ride—"

Lucy ignored his protest. "My whole life's entwined with that man. We've been together for nearly a decade and the business doesn't exist without him. Sure I do most of the cooking and the finances. But he's the one who *sells*. He can talk people up like you wouldn't believe. Me, all I can do is talk."

Ben smiled. "I see that. But actually, I don't mind." He was surprised to feel this way, but it was true. Lucy's jabber made the car feel lighter, brighter somehow.

They stopped for lunch at Sonic. Lucy ordered a large iced drink in a shade of blue that Ben doubted was available in nature. The boy – his name was Jacob, Ben had learned – gobbled down his burger and went to play in a ball pit attached to the restaurant. Ben watched him go down the slide and land in the tub of plastic balls with a perfunctory thud. Each time, Jacob just sat there for a second, like he was waiting for something to happen. When nothing did, he scrambled around and went back down the slide. He repeated this process three or four times. He didn't look particularly enthusiastic.

"When I was little I begged my parents to take me to one of those ball pits," Lucy said. "But they suck, you know?" She slurped at her drink. Her lips had acquired a bluish tint. "You want some?" She offered Ben the massive plastic container. He shook his head. "So I noticed your Tennessee plates. Shouldn't you be on a base back east?"

Ben stared, but Lucy just continued slurping, sucking out the dregs.

"I know army muscles when I see them." She shrugged. "Or maybe they're marine muscles? But you don't seem macho enough for that."

Ben couldn't help but smile. "Do you have family in the service?"

"I've got cousins all over the Middle East. And in Asia. Every place American Indians have no business being, I've got family."

"I'd rather not talk politics," Ben said.

"Who said anything about politics?" Lucy waved her hand like she was shooing away a crow. "We're Indians. American wars abroad are none of our business. But everybody wants to be a warrior. I bet when you were a kid, you were obsessed with Hulk Hogan and GI Joe." Ben nodded. "Well, white boys dream of being all-American heroes, and Indian boys dream of being Geronimo and Crazy Horse. But the domestic-warrior jobs dried up a long time ago. Our kids might as well become professional wrestlers."

"I always thought the Indian guys signed up because they needed the money. Not for the patriotism."

"That's why you went? Because you're one of those America-kicks-butt people?"

"Not so much. My dad went."

"So, family expectations?"

Ben hesitated. "Yes."

Lucy raised her eyebrows, clearly waiting for Ben to explain himself—and his reluctance.

"He died when I was sixteen and things didn't end well between us. I said a bunch of stuff I shouldn't have said." Ben had never confessed even this much to Becca, but somehow it was easier to tell a stranger.

Lucy nodded. "So you enlisted as an apology?"

"That's one way of looking at it," he said. Yet after Ben had enlisted, thoughts of his father had largely faded into the background. The "why" of his service held little importance amid the daily responsibilities of soldiering. And in the end, the army had not been about the past at all. In the most roundabout of ways, it had given him his future—given him Becca.

"And you don't regret it?" Lucy asked. "Doing this huge thing for your dad without his ever knowing about it?"

"I don't regret it," Ben said. "Not for a second."

• • •

After lunch, they drove for another few hours and then stopped at the Four Corners because Jacob wanted to stand on the intersection of four states. "The Four Corners isn't really the Four Corners," he announced from the back seat as they pulled into the parking lot. "They told us in school. They got the measurement wrong."

"Then why do you want to stand there?" Lucy said.

"Because," Jacob said, as though his reasons were obvious.

"I think we'll have to take a picture of you every place you step," Lucy said. "Just in case you happen to land on the actual Four Corners."

In the rearview mirror, Ben saw Jacob screw up his mouth. "That's stupid," Jacob said and pushed his way out of the car.

Aunt and nephew got in line so Lucy could take a photo of Jacob in the spot that might have been the Four Corners but probably wasn't. Ben didn't follow. The landmark was circumscribed by a ring of vendor booths. The Indians inside them sold jewelry and blankets, but Ben instinctively saw each stall as an offensive position. The mere possibility of such exposure made his heart pound. *There are no snipers,* he told himself. But he skirted the circle anyway, tracing the outside perimeter until he reached the picnic area. It sat on a flat peninsula that stuck out like a thumb over the rocky hills. At the very tip was a single rust-crusted grill. *The grill at the end of the world,* Ben thought and stopped just short of the drop-off.

He dug his foot into the earth, kicking up a cloud that settled on his face and stung his eyes. The feeling was familiar. He felt the weight of his body armor, a heaviness like the doubling of gravity. Or maybe he was feeling the weight of his invisible load, the mysterious thing he'd been dragging through his dreams. Ben closed his eyes and saw Coleman's blasted Humvee. Part of him knew that nothing could have stopped that IED. But what if? What if he had been there? What if he'd spotted the device? What if Coleman were still around to give Majid his Corn Pops?

But in any alternative scenario, Ben would likely be the dead one. And so his desire to have gone out that day was pretty fucked up. If someone had said to him, *Who lives, you or Coleman,* would he really have picked Coleman? Would he have done that with Becca at home waiting for him?

The three other soldiers had been severely wounded and were flown to the Green Zone. They were lucky — luckier than Coleman — they'd been blasted out of the vehicle when the bomb detonated. But Coleman . . . well, Ben saw what had happened to Coleman when the vehicle was finally hauled back to the COP. He'd nearly puked at the sight, but he forced himself to keep his sick down. Relief? Ben deserved no such thing.

This is Coleman, he said to himself. *This is Coleman's hand. This is his foot.* He named every piece of Coleman's body that he could see as though he were capable of putting his friend back together. But there wasn't all that much. Most of what remained was a sticky black substance of organic matter and metal.

Ben demanded a mask, smock, and gloves. The sanitization team tried to send him away. "This isn't your job, Sergeant," they told him. But he got angry and refused to leave, and, finally, they relented. He got to work with the rest of the team, collecting what was left of Coleman so it could be placed in a coffin, covered in an American flag, and buried. He tried to focus on the task, but his mind kept drifting to Majid. What if the kid turned up? What was Ben going to tell him? *Your friend is dead. He wanted to help you and look what your people did to him!* But Ben wouldn't say those things. He'd say that Coleman went home to America. He'd say Coleman's tour was over. And he'd sneak Majid some Corn Pops, because that's what Coleman had asked him to do. *"Fuck!"* Ben shouted. Because here was Majid himself, standing not five feet away. Ben wanted to throttle the kid. He wished the kid were dead so he wouldn't have to carry out Coleman's last request. He moved forward, his hands flexing. But someone was in his way; someone's hands pushed against his chest.

"Hey, now!" Lucy said. She'd stepped in front of Jacob, was shielding him with her body. "What's the matter with you?"

Ben felt like he'd come out of a trance. The taste and smell of the Humvee remained in his mouth. Jacob cowered behind his aunt, shrinking into his puffy silver parka like a turtle hunching into its shell.

"You can't threaten a child like that!" Lucy chastised him. And before Ben could apologize, she led the boy away.

After the Four Corners, they continued west in strained silence. Ben wanted to blame Lucy for imposing herself and the boy on him. But it was his fault. He shouldn't have taken them along. He tightened his grip on the wheel. He could feel the engine of the car pumping hard like the heart of a galloping horse. He had to believe that he was getting closer to Becca. Maybe he wasn't on the most direct route, but he was moving forward. He couldn't entertain any other notion or he'd simply give in to despair. More than ever, he wanted a drink. Many drinks.

The speedometer climbed as the lumbering car charged the horizon. And the horizon — coward that it was — retreated.

December 13, 1978

Dear Willy,

A year ago, Durga led me here, to the river between two dead towns. The first town, near the road, is old, and the second town, on a slope across the river, is much, much older. They're both deserted, so I've made them my own personal kingdoms. There's plenty of fish and time to read. Now and then, when I get lonesome, I pick up odd jobs in the closest human outpost, about thirty miles away. I don't need to work. I'm growing and selling plenty of the hippies' hash and cultivating their incredible hallucinogen. It's over an hour to the nearest library, but I ride out every few weeks and come back with a bag of cash and a stack of books, mostly classical history and ancient religions. And, of course, I have your *Iliad*. I glued the book back together, so the sections are now as one. I read it nightly, like my own personal Bible.

All in all, I'd be happy if it weren't for the nightmares. I can't remember when they started. I think to myself: *Did I have them at the dairy farm or at the hippie commune or at the colleges?* I can't recall. Nor do I remember the last time I slept a full night.

A few months ago, unable to sleep, I swam across the river and began to walk through the older town. I passed the last deserted house and kept on climbing. And when I reached the top, I stood with my back to the river and faced the horizon. I saw a great mesa and, beyond it, a desert plain. It reminded me of that day we stood on the ridge overlooking Li Sing. And then I realized that Durga had willed me to come here. She brought me to this spot precisely to reveal a new future — to anoint me. "Anointed for what?" I shouted. But the empty land had no answer and Durga, too, was silent.

The very next night, a couple of teenagers showed up. In the year I'd been here, Willy, I'd never had a single visitor, and suddenly, two kids were poking around my kingdom.

I guess I was in the mood for company, so I made myself known. When they saw me standing on my porch with my bushy beard and my hippie clothes and a candle in each hand, they looked dumbstruck. They were so wasted, they didn't know their asses from their ears. "He came from thin air, man!" I heard one of them say. "He's a ghost."

"He's not a ghost," the other kid said, "he's a shaman."

"Are you a shaman?" the first kid said.

I led them inside and offered them drugs in exchange for a favor. "Anything, shaman," the boys said, close to hysterics.

"When you go home, you must find the soldiers. The ones who fought in the jungles. Tell them you've seen Durga's anointed. Tell them to find the wise man between the two dead towns and he will help them."

I didn't know what I was saying, Willy. I was halfway to the moon myself. But Durga was my voice. She became my words. And she must have said the right things, because sure enough, within the month, a young man arrived. He'd been a Huey pilot. His wife had left him. He had nowhere to go. He was skinny and had eyelashes just like yours, Willy. Dark and thick and long. And when I recognized your lashes on this man's face, I knew that Durga had brought him to me. I didn't know why yet, only that he was meant to stay.

Currahee!

CO Proudfoot

18

THE SUN ROSE bright and hot over Motorcycle Mountain. Carrying her new leather jacket, Becca found Elaine, King, Bull, and some others sitting at a picnic table beneath a tarp shelter, eating cereal from Styrofoam bowls. "How was your night?" Bull said, grinning his sharp-toothed smile. "You and Reno were getting cozy."

Becca sat down beside Elaine. She ransacked her mind for a picture of Bull on the dance floor or at the campfire or near Reno's tent. What had he seen? What did he *think* he'd seen? She poured herself cereal and turned her attention to the new men eating beside them. Some wore vests, some jackets, and many had their bandannas folded up like napkins beside their bowls. At least half had long hair intricately braided or bound, like they were warriors out of the Scottish Highlands. Others resembled modern-day cowboys or frontier-town sheriffs, their beards sculpted into muttonchops and Winnfields and Vandykes. A handful were clean-shaven, but most had stubble at least a few days old. It was an eclectic and colorful crew, almost like a pack of movie extras, except their clothes weren't nearly so pristine, and their faces showed the wear of age and weather. "Are they all coming with us?" Becca whispered to Elaine.

"The CO brought them together. Isn't that right, Dooley?"

Dooley was skinny with thick lips and sleepy blue eyes. He chewed his cereal like a cow chewed its cud. "Yes, ma'am," he said. "I had nobody until I met the CO."

Dooley struck Becca as kind enough. "Nobody?" she said.

"Fought together, came out alone," Dooley said. "Kinda like life, that way—go in alone, go out alone."

"Look who's the poet," said the next vet over. He looked half Hells Angel, half Viking warrior, and he had bright orange eyebrows and a black bandanna tied do-rag-style around his head. The patch sewn to the front of his vest depicted two flaming swords and a cross.

"Now we've done it," Dooley said to Becca in a stage whisper. "Everybody, hold on to your Bibles. Frank's about to evangelize the shit out of this breakfast."

A bunch of guys laughed and Frank's face colored. "You can't embarrass me before the Lord," he said. "We come into this world and walk back out of it beside the Son of God." He pointed his spoon at Becca. "That's the Truth."

"That's a capital *T* on *Truth*," Dooley said. "And don't you forget it."

Frank grew serious. "You gotta be careful around these non-believers—er, what's your name?"

"Becca."

"And you better be careful, Becca," Dooley said, "or Frank here'll make you join the CMA. Christian Motorcyclists Association."

Frank displayed his vest patch with pride. "And if *you're* not careful, Becca," Frank said, attempting to one-up his friend, "Dooley here will try to turn you against the sweetest piece of tail ever to grace the silver screen simply because he doesn't like her politics."

Becca noticed the patch on Dooley's vest pocket: *I'll forgive Jane Fonda when the Jews forgive Hitler.*

Now it was Dooley's face turning red. "She's a traitor and a b—"

"Hey!" snapped Frank. "There's a lady at the table."

"Enough of the bickering!" Elaine interrupted brightly. "Check out what King's daughter did last night!" She lifted Becca's arm by the elbow. "Come on, honey. Show off your new accessory."

Becca held out her wrist for inspection. The group was clearly impressed. King just shook his head, but he looked more amused than angry.

"Your girl loves you," Elaine said. King grunted and packed a plastic spoonful of corn flakes into his mouth.

After breakfast, the group suited up and loaded their bikes. Elaine climbed onto the passenger seat of King's Gold Wing. *So* that's *why he bought it,* Becca thought. She saw Elaine whisper something into King's ear and then heard King laugh heartily, his belly bouncing in small hiccups. She still felt conflicted about her father's relationship with Elaine, but she couldn't help smiling. He looked happy.

As Becca searched for Reno's Harley, she inspected their expanded group. Frank had a picture of Jesus spray-painted onto his gas tank—the Son of God as He might have looked if He were in an eighties hair band. Dooley tossed her his helmet for her inspection. "I've got thirty-one stickers!" he announced with the excitement of a little girl. Becca turned the object over in her hands: *God Created Adam and Eve, Not Adam and Steve; VFW: Veterans Fucked by Washington; Jane Fonda, American Traitor Bitch; Jesus Loves You—I Think You Are an Asshole; Politicians and Diapers Need to Be Changed Often and for the Same Reason; If You Can Read This, the Bitch Fell Off.*

"It's great?" she said, unsure of how else to respond. Not so politically correct, these men. Finally, she spotted Reno. He barely looked at her as she climbed on and zipped up her new jacket. "Lovely day, don't you think?" she said, thrusting a good dose of coldness into her tone. But at the same moment, Reno started the engine, and her voice was revved into nothing.

Now eighteen strong, the line of bikes snaked southwest, heading toward gray mountains that looked upholstered in elephant hide. They stopped for gas once in Colorado and again in New Mexico. At the second stop King handed his daughter a Snickers, a Slim Jim, and an energy drink. "We're riding through lunch," he said. "I didn't want you to go hungry."

This generosity was so unexpected that Becca felt her throat catch. "I have money, Dad. You don't have to—"

"You're my kid." King's expression was dead serious. "I won't have anybody saying I'm not looking out for you. Now, get your helmet on. For some reason, Reno's acting pissed as hell today."

Becca climbed on the Harley, perplexed by the dynamic in play. Apparently she couldn't be in favor with her father and Reno at the same time.

The landscape morphed through the next leg, going from small, scattered boulders dotting dehydrated grass to rocky hills to desert. Becca tried to eat the Snickers but the helmet's inner padding compressed her cheeks into a fish pucker, and the helmet's jutting chin piece made it nearly impossible to drink anything without spilling most of the liquid down her neck.

Late afternoon set upon them and then dusk, with streaks of pink and pale yellow crisscrossing the horizon. The color drained from a single point in the distance where a great structure—like a finger of rock—punctured the sky. Just before the last rays vanished, the full formation came into view. *Shiprock,* said a sign, though it looked less like a ship and more like something from *Close Encounters.*

The nearby town—also named Shiprock—was an ugly, utilitarian way station through which eighteen-wheelers thundered en route to more populated destinations. Becca climbed off Reno's bike and stretched her back and quads.

"That's not the Jane Fonda workout, is it?" Frank said as he walked past. "You better not let Dooley see you doing those exercises."

"I'm wearing leather, not spandex," Becca said.

"And it suits you." Frank gave her an avuncular nod.

The men headed across the parking lot toward a windowless building. *Hot Wheels Grill,* read the sign, though it looked more like a strip club. Becca had to pee something awful, but she shuddered at the thought of the Hot Wheels bathrooms. Instead, she hurried toward the closest storefront, the Indigenous Hair Salon.

A forty-something woman with ample padding on her chest and stomach sat in a chair as the hairdresser worked neon curlers into her hair. The stylist looked to be in her midtwenties, a little bit arty, a little bit punk. When Becca walked in and asked to use the bathroom, the women just stared. "We've been riding for*ever*," Becca added, worried her leather jacket was giving the wrong impression. Female biker-gang members surely didn't say things like for*ever.*

"Did you ride in here with those men?" the hairdresser asked, incredulous.

"I love myself a biker," said the busty woman in the chair. "Or two!" She jumped up, pulled off the salon smock, and scurried to the door, her hips shaking in too-small black pants.

"Cholene. Get your ass back here," the hairdresser ordered. But Cholene had slipped out the door. She strutted across the parking lot despite the fact that half her head was a junk heap of rollers. "Bathroom's back there," the hairdresser said. Becca thanked her and hurried in. "So who are those guys?" the hairdresser called to Becca through the door. "I don't want Cholene getting into any trouble."

Becca flushed and came out to wash her hands. "They're harmless."

At that moment Cholene reappeared, grinning, her breasts bobbing like buoys. "Some real cute ones, Vicky. And they're going to the casino after dinner!"

Becca turned toward the door. "Well, thanks," she said.

"Wait." Vicky stood with her hand on her hip, biting her lip. "They're eating in Hot Wheels? That's *not* your kind of place."

Before, Becca had worried that the jacket was giving these women the wrong impression. Now it wasn't doing its job. Wasn't it supposed to make her look at least a little intimidating?

"Really," Vicky said. "There was a knife fight in that place last week. Two people went to the hospital."

Cholene nodded. "Also, it's a total hepatitis trap. Even I wouldn't eat there."

Becca had known Cholene for all of two minutes, but it was clear that coming from her, the statement carried weight.

"We've got Cup o' Noodles!" Cholene added. "And you could have a trim." She put her hand up next to her mouth like she was sharing a secret. "Vicky here really needs the business."

"You sure you don't mind?" Becca asked, and the women nodded. "Okay," she said and allowed herself to smile a little. "What kind of noodles you got?"

"So where are you and all your men going?" Vicky asked as she put hot water in the Styrofoam cup and then handed it to Becca.

"They're not exactly my men," Becca said as she blew on the

soup. She hadn't had one of these since freshman year. She'd forgotten how delicious they could be when you were really hungry.

"Tell me about the one with the panther eyes," Cholene said.

"That's Bull. He's kind of an asshole."

"I like myself an ass," Cholene said and winked. And then, as though concerned she hadn't been clear enough, "A nice biker ass."

Vicky snorted. "So you were telling us where you're going?" she asked, deftly sectioning and pinning Cholene's hair.

When Becca told them about Utah, Cholene screwed up her face. "There's nothing to do in Utah."

"I'm sorry," Vicky said, "but Shiprock takes the prize for bumblefuck."

Becca thought about how far she'd come since leaving Dry Hills—even since Kath's cabin. She had jumped the dog fence, all right. And yet these women considered their own part of the country more boring and backward than anywhere else on earth. Did anyone not feel boxed in? Was anyone ever satisfied? New Yorkers, maybe. But no, because those were the people who visited Kath in Arkansas. And yet. There'd been a time with Ben when Becca hadn't wanted any more than exactly what she had.

"So, the place in Utah?" Cholene demanded with a child's impatience.

"Kleos," Becca said.

Vicky's hands went still. "No shit. That's a ghost town."

"Now you've got her started," Cholene mumbled. "You know why Vic here doesn't have a boyfriend? It's 'cause she wastes every weekend visiting rotting buildings and tetanus traps. Not as bad as hepatitis traps, but still!"

"Cholene doesn't appreciate history," Vicky said.

Cholene held up the *Us Weekly* she was paging through. "I'm more interested in current events." She winked at Becca a second time.

"My dad's friend lives there."

Vicky shook her head. "Doubtful. The closest town is Navajo Perch, about thirty miles away."

"What do you mean, 'ghost town'?" Becca asked.

"Kleos used to be Indian land," Vicky explained. "Then U.S. Marshals discovered the Indians making bullets from the silver they'd mined. Then, well, suddenly it wasn't Indian land anymore. After that came the prospectors. And after them, I think it was the Mormons. Then the silver ran out. Now it's empty."

"Why would anybody waste silver on bullets?" Cholene said.

Vicky wrapped up the final section of Cholene's hair. "Hair dryer," she said and pointed to a chair against the wall. Cholene pushed and prodded the rollers with a long, manicured nail. "Leave it alone," Vicky said.

"I need a cigarette." Cholene fished in her purse. "Get the history lesson over with while I'm gone."

"It's kind of awesome how these places keep trading hands," Vicky continued. "Proves that nothing really belongs to anybody. I know, that's not really the indigenous thing to say . . . but I love how the towns are like undiscovered planets or lost civilizations. I'm a sci-fi nerd. So."

Cholene returned after a few minutes and lowered herself into the chair beneath the dryer. She pointed and flexed her painted toes, admiring them like she was a movie starlet. "Did you say this ghost town was near Navajo Perch? 'Cause I just heard something about that."

"Did you now?" Vicky said and brought the plastic dryer down over Cholene's curlers. The woman looked like a stripper-astronaut. Becca tried not to laugh.

"I ran into Ella Gibson and Mindy Nez at the drugstore."

"Ella's and Mindy's husbands are medicine men," Vicky explained to Becca.

"They mentioned some Facebook rumor about strange ceremonies in the desert. Ritual fires," Cholene said.

"Ella's and Mindy's husbands are on Facebook?"

"Why can't medicine men be on Facebook?" Cholene demanded. "Anyway, they told their wives that people were being burned out there."

"That's Burning Man, Cho."

"I *know* Burning Man. That's not it."

"Cholene, do you have any idea how you sound to this girl? She's going to walk out of here thinking we're lunatics."

"Vic here is one of three atheists on the rez. You can't talk to her about anything spiritual. Now, how's my hair?"

"Are you kidding?" Vicky said. "We just put that thing on."

"I don't want to keep the biker men waiting." Cholene winked yet again at Becca.

The mention of the men reminded Becca that she'd been in the hair salon for a while. She peered through the store window and saw a group smoking outside the bar. She'd been meaning to search Reno's bike for Kath's letter, but she'd missed her chance. "I should probably get going," she said, disappointed to be leaving them so soon. "But maybe I'll see you later tonight at the casino?"

"You bet!" Cholene beamed.

"Be careful out there, okay?" said Vicky, and Becca understood that her new friends would not be joining her that evening.

"I'm sure things'll be fine," she said, hoping that her voice masked her apprehension. The talk of people burning in ritual fires was more than a little worrisome, but nobody was going to mess with the bikers. She was probably safer in their company than she'd ever been. She zipped up the leather jacket.

"You just pull that off the rack?" Vicky asked. "It looks brand-spanking-new. It's nice with your short hair too—sorry we didn't get in a trim."

"Oh, it's okay," Becca said, her hand on the door. "And I'm still deciding about the jacket."

"Yeah, leather's tough to break in," Vicky agreed. "But once you do, it's like a second skin."

"Have fun in Kleos!" Cholene called as Becca stepped into the night. "And when you get to a computer, make sure to write Vic here a good review on Yelp! She needs all the help she can get."

19

THE HOT WHEELS GRILL was a strip club minus the strippers. The waitress uniforms left little to the imagination, and the banquettes were predictably covered in purple velvet that was oddly similar to the velour on King's Gold Wing. They were also speckled with rough black patches that, if you were being generous about it, could be dried gum.

Reno slid into a booth at the back of the room and lit up a cigar. A waitress came to take his order and he asked for a chicken salad sandwich and a beer. His crew sat across the room, and Bull stood chatting up one of the waitresses, taking advantage of his relative youth among the bikers. He leaned against the jukebox, his hips thrust forward, redundantly broadcasting his intentions. Becca was nowhere to be seen.

Reno knew he was being juvenile, refusing to tell Becca what was in Kath's letter. At first, he just hadn't wanted to deal with it. But now his increasing proximity to Kleos filled him with dread. He needed to treat this situation like he would a Band-Aid: rip the protective cover off, get the pain of it over fast. Reno told plenty of war stories about his time in the service, but this was not one of them. Others were bloodier. Objectively speaking, they were more traumatic. But there wasn't a one-to-one correlation between the amount of violence in a story and the way it affected you. Telling *this* tale meant inviting in a complicated and unhappy set of emotions. He just didn't want to go there. And yet he had been, quite literally, speeding in that direction for the past five days.

Reno had not looked at Kath's letter once since the Love's parking lot. Now he pulled it from his jacket pocket and flattened it across the table.

Reno: Despite our differences, I know you've long strived to protect my brother. Well, now that burden is fully upon you. King believes in the CO like Jeanine believes in Jesus. This is not a joke for him, and it shouldn't be for us. The CO is crazy, even dangerous. So what happens when King goes through this ordeal, into which he's put every last hope, and realizes it's a sham? And the physical risk! I'm truly afraid for my brother, Reno.

Maybe it's foolish of me to think that Becca can make a difference. But since they reunited, I've noticed a change in King. Haven't you? She is the one part of him that hasn't been corrupted by the CO's nonsense. Maybe you can sneak her into Kleos, like the Trojan horse—or at least get her into my brother's head so she can show him how much goodness the outside world has to offer.

Now, as for Ben: Please take my girl as far from him as you possibly can. You say that Kleos is like the end of the earth? Well, that's where she needs to go if it will get her away from that man. I am heartbroken for her, Reno. Which is another reason why you cannot allow King to go through with this. Becca needs his support more than ever now. And he owes her. Bigtime.

I'm relying on you.

Katherine

When Reno first read Kath's letter, he'd thought only of King. If Kath believed that Becca could help protect his best friend, then Reno would bring the girl along. But that was before he'd gotten to know Becca. Now he felt an obligation to her too.

The day after they'd all left the cabin, Kath called Reno's cell to say that Ben had shown up, that he had no memory of hurting Becca, and that he was determined to find her. Kath wanted her niece to get an annulment. "Think how free Becca could be if she left that painful romance behind. She could be happy someday," Kath insisted.

But Reno was reluctant to write Ben off. He himself had come a long way since the early days after the war. Even King, with all of his troubles, had made changes over the years. So second chances were fair and right. Shouldn't Ben have the same opportunities and the same support? And Reno didn't believe Becca's claims about being through with her husband. She was wounded, sure. But sometimes, *only* the wounded could help each other. Reno knew that in the wrong hands—say, the CO's hands—this philosophy was dangerous. But there was truth in it if you didn't fancy yourself some kind of Colonel Kurtz demigod.

Reno was not going to lose King to the CO's insanity. If Becca's father locked himself up in Kleos—or if he gave up hope entirely—then Reno, like Becca, would be entirely alone.

Back outside Hot Wheels, Reno walked away from the highway and the rumble of heavy trucks. It was noble of Kath to want to protect her niece. But he had to follow his gut with this one. He pulled out his phone and called Ben.

20

BECCA HAD NEVER been inside a casino before; the one in Shiprock was like the lobby of a not-quite-luxury hotel fused with a video arcade. Everything looked tacky-fancy, from the bronze-colored carpets to the chandeliers dripping with faux crystal. Against the background cacophony of chimes and buzzers, slot-machine patrons stood zombie-eyed before screens, their bodies jerking reflexively like they were on drugs.

"Can you believe they don't serve drinks on the floor?" Reno appeared beside Becca. "What kind of casino doesn't serve drinks on the floor?"

"I guess you'll just have to power through sober," she said and walked away. Reno was still keeping her in the dark, so what reason did she have to be nice?

She spotted King at a slot machine in the corner. It was a touchscreen with panels of cartoonish icons—apples, diamonds, and cherries. Instead of inserting quarters, her father kept swiping a plastic card, like he was paying for groceries. He was on autopilot for failure, losing round after round. Yet he wore a hopeful expression, a boyish look that brightened every time he sat back to watch the symbols flicker across the screen.

"You like watching your old man lose?" he asked.

"Better luck next time?" Becca offered.

"Listen. I'm sorry about what happened at the gas station in Kansas — and back at Kath's. It's just that —"

"Don't worry about it." Becca sat down at the slot machine beside King's and swiveled to face him. Hearing his apology and seeing how sincere he looked, she dared to believe that the standoff between them was over. She wanted to somehow confirm this fact, to cement it. She had one card to play, so she laid it down. "Can I tell you a secret?" she asked.

"You're not pregnant?" King sat back, alarmed.

"No!"

"Well, I don't know what *secret* means." He looked confused, but in an endearing sort of way. He looked like such a *dad*.

"A few months ago, my college running coach got a call from the University of Oregon."

"I take it that's good?"

"U of O has the best running team in the country. People who run for them get sponsorships. They go to the Olympics."

"And they want you?"

She nodded.

"So you're going to transfer schools?"

"In the fall."

King scratched at his beard. "And Ben's okay with the two of you picking up and moving to Oregon?"

Becca's stomach dropped. She had not anticipated this question from her father, and, hearing it, she realized she had made a mistake. "I never told him," she said quietly. "Not that it matters now."

King was silent.

"Come on, Dad. You saw what he was like at your house. Ben and I are done."

King's mouth tightened, like a screw turned too many times. "You married this young man without telling him that you planned to uproot your lives?" His hands gripped the slot machine, the knuckles turning white. "When you marry somebody, Becca, it's not just about you anymore. It's about the two of you. There's no place for selfishness in a marriage."

King was right, but he didn't know that she had tried. She'd wanted to share the news with Ben in person — not through a screen. Not on a video chat. And when he finally came home, there hadn't been a good time. First, there'd been his post-tour protocol at the base, then his official release from active duty. Then they'd dived into late-game wedding preparations. For two weeks they ran on black coffee and adrenaline. And then they got married. During all this, including the week of blissful calm that followed the wedding, Becca refused to do or say anything that might disturb Ben. They needed this time together. Needed it so badly. And didn't they have the whole summer to talk things over?

But maybe she'd been expecting everything to fall apart. Maybe she'd kept the University of Oregon as her contingency plan. She didn't want to think of it this way, because that would mean she'd never really believed in Ben. It would mean that there was nobody on the planet that she had ever, in her whole life, been able to trust.

"Don't lecture me about selfishness," Becca spat. "For six years, you pretended I didn't exist. Then you come back and disrupt everything, but the second you decide I'm too much trouble, you push me away." The amusement-park clamor of the slot machines was overpowering and Becca had to raise her voice to compete. "You don't have the right to judge me. You don't even know me."

Becca rubbed her eyes, disoriented by the flashing lights. When she looked around a few seconds later, she didn't see her father anywhere. She rammed her fist against the video console. She was about to hit the thing again when Elaine sat down beside her. "So," she said. "What was that about?"

Becca looked away, afraid she'd start to cry. All of a sudden, like a punch in the stomach, she wanted her mother. "Did you ever wish you hadn't left your husband?" she asked.

"Not for a second. He was the worst of everything. And there was no fixing him."

Becca pictured Ben clutching the neck of the fiddle he'd just destroyed, completely ignorant of the fact that only moments before, he'd laid into her the same way. She remembered how empty his eyes had looked, like all the essential stuff had been sucked out of them. "Ben can't be fixed either."

"In my experience, honey, there are the men who hurt you and there are the men who try to hurt you. They are not the same breed."

"Ben knew he could hurt me. He knew it was possible. And he didn't do anything to stop it from happening. He drank and sulked. He barely gave his meds a try before dumping them. He gave up on me."

"He's been back only about two months, right?"

"So I'm just impatient? Are you saying that I should just stick this out for however long it takes him to admit that he's sick? *If* he ever admits it?"

"I think you need to decide what's more important to you, Becca, being with him and accepting the struggle, or being without him and riding free."

"Why do those have to be the only options? I want different options." Becca fought back the tears.

She felt Elaine shift toward her, her perfume like an invisible fog. A few strands of frosted hair brushed Becca's cheek. "Your father just mentioned something about a running scholarship. So why not get on with that? Leave this whole life behind and never look back." Becca looked up at Elaine, questioning. "I'm not telling you to do that. I'm just reminding you that you can."

Can, Becca thought, *and should.* King had left. Then Jeanine left. Why couldn't she also leave? Run straight out of this life and into another one. Wasn't that what she was doing anyway, at this very moment? *Momentum, rhythm, stride.* She was already enacting the plan.

Becca left the casino and picked Reno's Harley out of the pack. It looked a little sad among the larger, flashier vehicles. But Reno's bike was sturdy enough, Becca knew, having now sat on it for over one thousand miles.

Reno's saddlebags were not locked and Becca found his jacket folded up inside. Covering the back was an enormous embroidered map of Vietnam, Laos, and Cambodia. A defiant bald eagle was shackled by a chain to the landmass. Beneath it all ran the words *Leave No Man Behind.* King had once told his young daughter that many American soldiers went missing in Vietnam, and the army had never tried to find them. *They were abandoned by their country,* King had said. *Some of them are probably still out there.* It seemed to her now that this was the legacy of the war—of all wars. In the aftermath, back at home especially, it was every man for himself.

Becca found Kath's letter in the jacket pocket. She read it eagerly, trying—but largely failing—to parse the meaning. King was in some kind of danger, and Kath believed that Becca could protect him. Part of her wanted to run from her father as she had run from Ben. But then she'd be letting him off easy. Her father owed her and she was going to make him see that. She was going to demonstrate, beyond a doubt, that he was in her debt. It was backward, she knew—sticking her neck out for the debtor in order to collect what she was owed. But it made sense. A heart sense and a gut sense.

She turned her face to the vast, starlit sky. She knew Ben was probably searching for her, that somewhere inside, he knew exactly what he'd done to her. And if he really, truly did not know, then she could never tell him. She could never hurt him like that.

But she was no longer in his sights or on his team. She was part of *this* unit now, a member of these special forces that had set out across the heartland to save King.

PART III

Exposure Therapy

December 13, 1979

Dear Willy,

There are a dozen men here now, all of them wounded. They found their way to me through rumors, stories of a wise man living in the two dead towns. But in truth, Durga brought them to me. Because I am carrying her heart. Because I am anointed. The men call me their commanding officer.

There is a routine to our days. We wake early and exercise. Then we cook breakfast and eat together. Each afternoon we study the ancient warriors. Durga, the writings of Sun Tzu, the Stoics, and, of course, by your example, Homer. When I feel a man is ready, I teach him about the heart. And that's when the real work begins — the process of a soldier being reborn. There are many tasks and challenges to aid this process, but I ask all of my men to do what I have done: tell their stories, pour their pain into the earth, and mark the spot. Each week we do this and bury more of the dead.

But laying the dead to rest is not enough. We must honor each man's spirit, let him know that he earned his death fiercely and proudly. For this reason, I have decided to call this place Kleos, from the Greek word meaning "battle glory," a warrior's greatest achievement. *Kleos* is what the war gave to us and it is what I pass on to every man here. I give them *kleos,* bestowed as from a father to his son.

It is meaningful, don't you think, that the name Patroclus —which translates to "glory of the father"—holds the word *kleos* within itself? You should not think for a minute that I've forgotten that night, Willy, when you told me about Achilles's closest companion. I think of it always. I hold that memory inside of me as *Patroclus* holds *kleos*. Inside of my belly, the memory of that night writhes like a worm. I should have answered you when you asked me about Patroclus. I know that now. But I was a different man then. A lesser man. Can you understand? Will you ever forgive me for my silence?

I have a story for you, Willy, that I've been eager to share. A few weeks ago, a motorcycle pulled up. The driver did not dismount, but the passenger got off and walked with great purpose toward where I stood by the river. She planted herself in front of me. Her eyes were large and hungry-looking. Her ears poked elf-like through her brown hair. She was the first woman who had ever stepped foot on my land. I'd made no rules against this, but the men implicitly understood that if they were in need of companionship, it was best to seek it in town. I had unwittingly taken a vow of chastity. Durga, after all, is female. And her heart is inside of me, like a lover, but permanent.

Which is all to say that I found myself face to face with a woman I should have desired but didn't.

"That's my husband glued to that bike up there," the woman said. "We've been searching for you. And now that we've found you, I'm hoping you can help him." Here, her veneer cracked, and I saw tears in her eyes. "He's so angry. And he's in so much pain. Can you . . ."

I smiled and reached out my arm. The woman stepped forward until I could touch her shoulder. "I can try," I said.

"But you will have to leave. He needs to be here on his own."

"For how long?" She swallowed her emotion and fixed her face into a stoic mask.

"I don't have an answer for that," I said. But now the biker was approaching. I knew this man, I realized with shock. It was King Keller. His body was large but somehow wasted, as though his skeleton had grown in size as the flesh had shrunk away. He'd been twenty-two the last time I'd seen him, nine years before.

Silently, we took each other in. And then he began to cry. I'd never seen King cry. That wasn't something we did—certainly not in front of each other. But here he was, weeping. So I did something I'd never done before either: I hugged him.

It was at that moment, feeling King sob against my shoulder, that I truly understood what it meant to be Durga's anointed.

Currahee!
CO Proudfoot

21

HEY!" LUCY SNAPPED at her nephew. "Put your seat belt back on!"

Ben had driven the car into Monument Valley, where the rock formations resembled monstrous petrified cacti. Jacob was kneeling on the seat, his face pressed to the window, his open mouth fogging a circle of glass. He made a show of sitting down, but seconds later, he was back up, eager as a puppy. Lucy's orders were no match for the command of that extraordinary rock, its brown and orange and red washes of color flashing against the sky.

"All of this used to be underwater," Jacob announced as they passed between two enormous buttes. Ben considered the possibility that they were moving through some giant's decorative rock garden. At any moment, the car could be mistaken for an ant and squashed.

"Now, that can't be true," Lucy said, swiveling around to eye her nephew. "We're in the middle of the desert."

Jacob squeezed his lips like a fish and giggled.

"I'm pretty sure he's right," Ben said. "You can see the striations on the rock walls where water used to be. This was probably the bottom of an underwater canyon. Really, we're driving across the ocean floor." Ben glanced in the rearview. Jacob was smiling with triumph.

"Well, I don't like to think about that," Lucy said, folding her arms across her chest. "I can't swim. And this talk makes me think about flash floods. I'm a flash-flood-aphobic."

"The water left millions of years ago, Aunt Lucy," Jacob said.

"I know that," she answered testily and ended the conversation by turning on the CD player. David Grisman's "Wayfaring Stranger" rose from of the speakers. "Hick music!" Lucy announced. Though Jacob had easily recovered from Ben's fury back at the Four Corners, Lucy was taking longer to forgive him.

"You don't like it?" Ben asked.

"I like my music harder. I guess I got a lot of rage."

"Wouldn't you say that I've got more?"

Lucy nodded. "Headbanging as anger management. You need some Metallica or Anthrax."

"Maybe," Ben said and thought about Becca asking him—no, begging him—to play the fiddle. "It'll make you feel better," she'd assured him. "Like your old self." But he couldn't touch the thing. The mere thought of playing brought to mind that horrible vision: his dad standing on the street in Iraq, the smell of Coleman's Humvee, and "Sally in the Garden"—notes that seeped into him like some kind of poison gas. But wasn't music just sound? Invisible waves, no more real than the snipers and bombs he imagined surrounded him here in America.

"I used to play a lot," he told Lucy. "I performed, actually."

"Like on tours? Ooh, I bet you had groupies."

"That's generous of you."

The Death Star coughed and shuddered and the three riders fell quiet. The car had over a hundred thousand miles on it. For the first time, Ben was thankful that Miles had given it an inspection, even if the tune-up had come with a Breathalyzer. "I think we should give her a rest for the night," Ben said.

"We can stop in Kayenta," Lucy said. "But you have to promise me something."

"All right."

"Let me play your sponsor tonight."

"I'll be fine," Ben said. "I've been sober for four days." But even as he said it, he heard how ridiculous the number sounded.

"Which is wonderful," Lucy said. "But you're still bouncing, and back there at the Four Corners . . ."

"I said I was sorry," he snapped. Lucy just looked at him. Not judging him, or asking anything more, just waiting.

Ben breathed in and out a couple of times. "I'm sorry," he said. "You're right."

Kayenta was a Monument Valley outpost, a frontier town for tourists. Ben drove along the main strip, past cheap restaurants and chain motels and stretches of lumpy earth resembling soil that had been turned over but not yet replanted. They followed signs to the Diné Inn, a motel that looked like an overly long railway car. The only other vehicle there was a Nissan so dusty, it resembled a tumbleweed. The place was a lot more *Psycho* than Ben would have liked.

After dinner, they inspected the map, tilting their heads together over the diner table. Ben could smell the sweetness of Lucy's shampoo and Jacob's soap-scrubbed, faintly chocolate scent. The proximity of these bodies—their warmth and life—put Ben on an odd type of alert. He felt as though his heart were pumping too close to the skin. Like it might burst out of him and sit there, pumping on the table. It was not a pleasant feeling and yet he wanted to freeze this moment. He wanted to sit right here, as part of this trio, absorbing the human-ness of his companions.

"So where are we going?" Ben asked, hoping that he had managed to gain Lucy's trust despite the incident at the Four Corners.

"You've got Internet on your cell phone? The place we're going isn't on this map."

Ben handed over his phone and waited. Lucy looked from the phone to the map on the table and back again. Finally, she pursed her lips and glanced out the window.

"I can't find the place," she said quietly. "I assumed it would be here somewhere, but it isn't." Lucy shrank back as though afraid that Ben might scream at her. But Ben felt none of the stringent anger or panic from earlier. He felt neither disembodied nor detached from himself. If anything, he felt too present. And so he was able to see the situation for what it was: a problem that needed to be solved.

"It's okay," he said and looked at Jacob, who was also following his aunt's lead and cowering into the booth. "We're doing the best we can, right?"

Lucy relaxed a little. "My sister told me the church was on a mission to someplace named Kleos. It's supposed to be near Navajo Perch, Utah. That's all I know."

This information was all Ben needed. It had been all he'd needed for the past two days. He felt relief, edifying and energizing. "Okay," he said and folded his hands on the table. "Here's the plan."

He'd been such a good soldier precisely because he could recognize the appropriate course of action in any given moment and then execute. Right now, what was required was a show of confidence.

"We'll get up early tomorrow, drive to Navajo Perch, and ask around. I'm sure somebody local can direct us. We will find your sister — and your mom," he said, nodding at Jacob. "Everything will be fine."

"And you'll be fine too?" Lucy said, clearly thinking about the afternoon.

It was not a moment for hesitation. "Absolutely," he said.

The Diné Inn faced a lot of nothing. There were no streetlights outside of town, just the motel's neon VACANCY sign fizzing at the roadside. Not so far away, the darkness dissolved into a small bubble of light: fast-food franchises through which residents of Kayenta eked out a living, and hotels with names that attempted to evoke luxurious getaways, Hamptons and Holidays.

"So, Utah," Ben said. "Is your sister trying to convert some Mormons?" They were sitting on the plastic chairs outside their adjacent rooms; Jacob was inside, glued to the TV.

"Not exactly," Lucy said. She did not seem enthusiastic about this line of questioning. "Listen," she said a moment later. "I'm sorry for being such a hard-ass about our destination. But I couldn't risk you stranding us at some gas station." Ben gave her a quizzical look. "I know you didn't want us along."

Ben saw how sincerely she believed this—that he might have abandoned them, without a second thought. "I wouldn't do that," he said.

Lucy glanced at the motel window. The curtain was pulled shut, but you could tell there was a television flickering inside. "I try to look out for him as best I can, but I'm on the road all summer. He deserves better than what he's got."

Ben could not even imagine what it was like to be a kid like Jacob: poor, with a mother who put her religious convictions before her child, and no father to speak of. But that nearly described Becca. "Can I ask you something?" he said.

Lucy nodded.

"How would you feel if Ricky came looking for you?"

"He won't. I know him."

"But for the sake of argument. What if he did?"

"Hard to answer that question. I guess I'd be angry. Once I'd gotten up the courage to leave, I wouldn't want anything interfering with the decision. A clean split — that's important."

"You've never left him before?"

Lucy laughed. "I leave him at least twice a year . . . and I always go back. It's because I'm an optimist and, also, a pushover."

"Pushover — you?"

"I took some business classes when we were just starting up the frybread operation, and I'll never forget, they talked about this thing called sunk costs. You know what that is?"

Ben shook his head.

"Basically, it means that no matter how much money you've invested in something, if the venture is failing, the best thing to do is get out."

"You mean cut your losses?"

"Exactly. You pretend that you're coming into the situation for the first time. If you wouldn't fork out the money right then, knowing everything that you do in the present moment, then you should get out, pronto."

"And this has to do with what exactly?"

"Well, sometimes I think the same principle should apply to relationships. I mean, just 'cause I've been with Ricky for so long and built so much of my life with him, that doesn't mean I should stay, right? If I met him now, would I get into a relationship?"

"Would you?"

"I'm an optimist and a pushover, but I'm not an idiot."

"That sounds pretty sensible to me," Ben said.

"For business, it makes tons of sense. But for love? The heart is a bottomless pit, Ben. You can sink the pain of a lifetime into it — all the love too — and it will never feel full. It will always want more. And more. But I don't need to explain any of this to you."

Ben looked at his feet.

"How long have you been married?"

"Six weeks."

Lucy whistled. "Want to talk about what happened?"

Ben shook his head. He twisted his wedding ring. He liked the smoothness of the gold against his skin, how easily he could make it spin. It was probably a little too loose, but in a way that was good; it reminded him that he was wearing it.

"We'd been together for about five months when they announced the surge," he said. Even now, the word brought to mind an enormous wave rushing toward a small beach. Hurtling toward the sand but never crashing. It was an infuriating image, like an unresolved musical stanza. "No way was I just going to leave her behind."

"You wanted to lock things down?"

Ben smiled. "It wasn't a trust thing. I just wanted us bonded. You know, more strongly than we would have been otherwise."

Ben remembered the moment so clearly. He'd gone to one of her races and waited for her at the finish line. It was a frigid February morning, but Ben didn't have to wait long. Becca was ahead of the others, as usual, but she ran those last yards as though the competition were neck and neck. It seemed like she was trying to reach him as quickly as possible, because their days together were dwindling. Over the finish line, she jogged past the cheering crowd, finally slowing to a walk. She must have had sweat in her eyes, because she nearly tripped over him.

She didn't understand why he was kneeling on the ground and demanded to know what he was doing. So Ben said, "Proposing." She still didn't get it, so he tugged on her calf, until she knelt down with him. Then he said that he wanted to spend the rest of his life with her and nobody else.

The next thing he knew, she'd jumped on him, which pushed them both onto the ground. In the process, he dropped the ring. It took them fifteen minutes crawling around in the grass to find it.

"Five months isn't a long time to know somebody," Lucy said.

"Yeah, that's what everybody told me. My parents. My friends." *It's not 1914, or 1939,* Katie Jacobson had told him. *And this is your life, Benny, not some Hollywood movie. I swear, if you knock her up before you leave and then go off and die . . .* Katie could be flippant like that, and at the time, Ben laughed her off. Remembering the conversation now, he felt angry.

"Getting engaged then was right. I knew it and she knew it. It felt like—" He paused, thought a moment. "This is going to sound strange, but it was kind of like that bread you make."

Lucy snorted.

"No, hear me out. See, when I came back from Iraq the first time, nothing tasted quite right. I don't know what happened. I was near a couple of explosions. Something fucked with my taste wiring or smell wiring. But that frybread woke up every taste bud in my mouth. And it went beyond that. It was ten times better than anything I'd ever tasted before. It was a feeling I'd never known existed."

"So you're telling me," Lucy said, "that your wife was like a flavor explosion in your life."

"Cut me some slack. I came up with this on the fly."

"Ben, do you have any idea what the calorie content in a single slice of frybread is? I realize I sell it for a living, but that stuff's like crack. It will *kill* you."

"Let's not take this metaphor to its logical conclusion," Ben said.

Lucy bit her cheek. "I didn't mean to make fun. I get it. Your wife was a powerful force in your life. She had healing abilities. And she was unexpected, which made everything about her feel that much more exciting."

"Yes," Ben said.

"I felt that way about Ricky," Lucy said. "Sometimes I still do. In glimpses."

Ben was about to respond when a sudden buzzing erupted in his pocket. He jumped from the chair, fumbling to get the phone off his person, like it had stung him. The object clattered onto the ground, where it continued to skitter like a roach. Lucy had also jumped to her feet, afraid that something truly dangerous was going on. But then she recognized Ben's response for what it was and returned to her chair. "So there's another thing you're not allowed to do around the kid—get a phone call. Big deal."

Ben called the missed number and, to his astonishment, Reno picked up. "I know what you did," said the older vet, not even bothering with hello. "I know you weren't trying to hurt her, which is why I'm calling you. I also know you're still to blame, which is why I am extremely ambivalent about it. Where are you?"

"Kayenta."

Reno whistled into the phone. "Jesus, you're close."

"To you? To Becca?"

Reno barreled onward. "Here's the deal. Tomorrow, you will drive out to Navajo Perch. From there, take BIA road fifty-two going west toward Kanab. After about thirty-five miles you'll come up on an old post office. You'll know it 'cause the roof's missing. Walk down to the river. I'll try to have somebody meet you and give you directions. There's an old mining tunnel you can take in, but it's too complicated for me to explain over the phone."

"Take in where? Where are you sending me? Will Becca be there?"

"To Kleos."

"No shit," Ben said. "That's where I'm headed!"

"Well, don't sound so excited, Sergeant. That place is the fucking heart of darkness."

22

THE NEXT AFTERNOON, they climbed into a plateau of boulders spotted with moss like balding heads. Soon a glinting river appeared and, not long after, a house. It was mostly a carcass, a building gnawed to the bone, and it sagged on the slope across the river. "We're getting close," Ben said. Sure enough, the full town appeared around the next bend. Crumbling concrete buildings were scattered alongside the road. Across the river were more disintegrating houses.

When Ben spotted a couple of motorcycles and a van parked beside a caved-in cinder-block building, his heart leaped into his throat. The structure was as Reno had said: a mouth of broken teeth yawning at the sky. Affixed over the doorway were two signs. One read *U.S. Post Office.* The second read *Kleos.*

Jacob picked his way around the trash, busted tires and rusted bedsprings, until he reached the first cabin. A plastic chair missing one leg lay overturned on the sagging porch and half of the roof was gone, like a giant had come along and taken a bite out of it. "Curtains!" he called to the adults. "Do you think this is somebody's house?"

"Come back here," Lucy ordered. But Jacob wandered over to the next cabin and disappeared from view.

"Want me to get him?" Ben asked.

"Nah. Let him poke around," she said. "You stay in earshot!" she yelled.

The wind knocked the post office's barely hinged door against the frame. This place was creepy and far too reminiscent of bombed-out neighborhoods in Iraq—places that looked dead but often were not. Standing out here, Ben felt exposed, certain he was being watched.

Jacob reappeared down by the river. He chose a stone from the bank and skipped it across the water. He did not seem unnerved by his surroundings. How blissful to feel that kind of ease, Ben thought. To carry out a simple activity without psychological or emotional interruptions. To let the world fall away. Playing the fiddle, laughing with Becca, even some parts of soldiering had once provided him a similar release.

Ben turned from the boy only to hear Jacob shouting. The kid had found someone.

A man descended slowly between the busted shacks and stopped just above the mess of seep willow and arrow weed that grew along the opposite bank. Ben and Lucy joined the child at the water's edge.

"You Reno's guy?" the man called out, cupping his hands around his mouth to amplify his voice. He looked to be in his sixties and had a stubbly white beard. He wore jeans and a black biker vest.

"Yeah!" Ben shouted back. "He said you could give us directions to the mining tunnel?"

"He would," the man replied and Ben realized that Reno's name was not exactly an open sesame. "Tell me your division, rank, and number of tours," he called out, "and we'll talk."

"This some kind of interview?" Lucy murmured.

Ben answered the questions.

"Active duty?" the man shouted.

Having finished his contracted service, Ben was now Individual Ready Reserve. Theoretically, the army could still call him up, but as long as recruiters like himself continued to peddle their wares successfully, the chances of that were slim. "IRR," Ben answered.

"You better be telling the truth about that," the man called back. "If you're AWOL and the CO finds out about it, you'll be very sorry that you lied."

Ben didn't understand what any of this meant, but first things first. "We've got our car up on the road," he shouted. "Where's the overpass?"

The man laughed. "No overpass."

"You got a boat then?" Lucy said.

"Soldier, if you want to get here, you're gonna have to swim." He turned around and started back up the rise.

"We've got a child with us," Ben said.

"And I can't swim," Lucy added.

The man looked over his shoulder. "Your friends aren't my concern. You, soldier, can swim. Or build yourself a raft. Or a goddamn bridge, for all I care." The man resumed his retreat.

"Hey!" Ben yelled. "Do you know a woman named Jeanine Keller?" But the man had disappeared over the rise.

"There's got to be a bridge." Lucy scanned up and down the river. "Or we can look for that mining tunnel your friend Reno mentioned."

They drove twenty miles in each direction, without luck. Nor did the river appear to narrow at any point. Back at the defunct post office, they pulled in beside the motorcycles and van.

"Who the hell do these vehicles belong to?" Ben demanded.

"Mom!" Jacob exclaimed from the back seat.

"What nonsense are you talking?" Lucy said.

"That's Mom's van." Jacob scrambled out and pointed to a decal in one of the van's windows: a Jesus fish surrounding a hand. "Hands of God! I want to swim across with Ben."

"Nobody's swimming," Ben said. "We'll find another way."

But in a flash the boy took off, a silver bullet flying toward the river.

"Come back here!" Lucy bolted after him. But the boy did not stop. He plunged into the water, lost his balance, and slipped under. Almost immediately, the current began to pull him downstream.

Lucy was in the river up to her knees, screaming, pleading for Ben to do something. Jacob's head popped back up, but the river sucked him farther and farther away. Ben dove in; his body spasmed with cold, but he fought the numbness and swam out, using the current as a boost. Jacob was flailing and crying, pulling himself under with his own hysterics.

"Float!" Ben called out. "Turn on your back!" He swam harder, pushing his arms through the water like it was a heavy blanket that he was trying to shove off his body. Finally, he came within reach of the boy. He grabbed at Jacob but managed to catch only a fistful of jacket. "Fuck." He spat out a mouthful of dark water. He grabbed again. This time, he caught Jacob's arm. Holding the boy to him, Ben scissored his legs and pushed at the water with his free arm, maneuvering both of them out of the current. When they reached a muddy pocket of bank on the far side, Ben hauled the kid out. Gasping, he grabbed Jacob and pulled the child in tight. It was all he could do to keep from bursting into tears.

"Ben? Are you okay?" Jacob whimpered.

But Ben couldn't let go. He pressed Jacob's drenched, dark head and frail body to his chest. He needed to be sure that the child in his arms was real. Real and still alive. And in this moment, he felt sure that he was holding on to Majid, which, somehow, was the same thing as holding on to Coleman. "You're okay," Ben whispered. "You're all right."

Jacob squirmed in Ben's tight embrace. "Ben!" he cried. "Ben! Aunt Lucy?"

Ben let go and felt the bodies of Majid and Coleman evaporate. "Let's go," he said, steeling himself against a loss that felt far too visceral. He helped Jacob out of his coat and wrung out the water. Then they climbed up the slippery bank. They'd traveled farther downstream than Ben had realized and the desert willows grew thick enough to obscure the opposite bank. Trudging along, Ben felt like he was on a mission with his platoon. His adrenaline was still pumping from the rescue, and he felt oddly exhilarated, energized in a way he hadn't been in weeks.

"Lucy!" Ben shouted, thinking they must be fairly close to their starting point. There was no response. Jacob looked at him, worried. Ben forced a smile. "We're almost back. See, it clears up over there, and those are the shacks we saw driving in."

Jacob took off again, scrambling ahead. Ben hurried to catch up. He emerged from the willow thicket to find Jacob standing in the exact place where the old man had stood.

"Aunt Lucy!" Jacob screamed. "Lucy!" He looked at Ben, panicked. And Ben immediately understood why. As far as he could see in both directions, the opposite bank was empty. Lucy was gone.

23

AFTER LEAVING THE Shiprock casino, the bikers set up camp on the property of a local Gulf War vet and waited for the stragglers to arrive. In the civilian world, the men were loners, but out here, prowling the highways of the American Southwest, they were a united pack, traveling as one.

After their fight at the casino, King was back to ignoring Becca, but she felt oddly cared for by the others. The next day at lunch, the men made space for her. They gave her sunscreen and told her to use it. They showered her with snacks. Unprompted, Dooley offered her a clean towel, and Frank gave her a pocket Bible with the subheading *Hope for the Highway.* Becca knew that they'd been talking about her situation; the men believed she was a battered wife, which was not at all how she thought of herself. She was running toward a new future. And yet, standing on solid ground, without the road to distract her, she found that Ben easily crept into her thoughts.

Late in the afternoon, she sat on the steps of the Gulf War vet's trailer and watched his young daughters chase their dog. The poor animal resembled a stray more than a pet, and it reminded her of a story from Ben's first tour. He'd been in a firefight, taking cover in an alleyway, when a feral mutt had wandered by.

"The dog was clearly starving," Ben had told her. "It was as much a veteran of the war as any of us, just out foraging for scraps. And right there in front of me, while I was returning fire, it got hit."

Ben knew that he was supposed to ignore the dog. He was supposed to keep shooting. "I'd been trained to block out distractions," he explained. "And a dog dying slowly not three feet away — well, that was a distraction." But he couldn't keep shooting. The animal yowled. It was bleeding from the neck. And Ben couldn't focus, so he crouched down and leaned into the alley to pull the dog out of the street. In that brief, unprotected moment, a bullet whizzed by his ear. Millimeters from his brain, he said. Because of a dog! Ben was so terrified, so furious with himself, that without another thought, he shot the dog between the eyes.

"You did it a favor," Becca had said. "You put it out of its misery."

"I know, Chicken. But I didn't kill the dog to ease its pain. I killed the dog because it was preventing me from doing my job."

Ben said this like he was expecting her to be disgusted, like he wanted her to call him a brute. But she found his truth-telling brave. What had happened to that honesty? When they'd met, she could ask him anything about his first tour, and he never made her feel embarrassed or regretful or stupid. Even in the first months of his second deployment, Ben eagerly told her detailed stories. On the video chat, he seemed like flesh instead of a set of pixels. But then the stories dried up, and he became two-dimensional, a clone. She'd gone on the research binge because she was desperate to retrieve the flesh-and-blood version of Ben. The real Ben.

When she told her father that Ben had become reluctant to talk, King told her not to take it personally. *It's hard to explain to somebody back here what's going on over there,* he'd said. *You don't want to make things harder for him.*

But what about me? She couldn't stop herself from wondering, even though she knew that civilians had no right to ask such a question. The soldiers in danger — their needs came first. But she couldn't wholly commit to this code of conduct. She needed parity; she couldn't help it. King, meanwhile, seemed to sense that she was struggling, so he gave her a gift — well, it was more like a loan.

There are other ways to understand what he's going through, King said and handed Becca his copy of *The Iliad.* Becca would come to understand that her father had an affinity for this particular book, but at the moment, she was dumbstruck. Epic poetry? *Her* father? Still, she devoured *The Iliad,* followed by other books and articles and movies. She felt prepared for Ben's return — at least, as prepared as she could be with only secondary sources at her disposal. When Ben was finally home, he spent hours clicking through the photographs he'd taken overseas. He avoided her, left home for hours at a time, and snapped at her when she so much as opened her mouth. He refused to touch her. He was acting, she realized, exactly like a spurned lover. Except that the other woman happened to be the war.

Now, sitting on the trailer steps, Becca thought about Reno's motorcycle jacket and the eagle shackled to Southeast Asia. All these vets were still trying to get over that destructive, codependent relationship.

"Hey. Mind if I join you?"

Becca looked up to see Reno standing before her. She made room for him on the steps of the trailer, and he pulled a cigar from his pocket and lit it up.

"Why do you smoke those things? They're nasty."

"What's got your knickers in a twist?"

"You."

"Fair enough." He nodded. "I've been an ass." Reno sucked on the cigar, blew smoke, then sucked again. Becca could tell that he wasn't savoring the thing. He was medicating. He scratched at the thinning hair on the crown of his head. "I've been holding off explaining things because I can't figure out what in God's name we're gonna do when we get to where it is we're going."

"What we're going to do about *what?*" Becca said, exasperated.

Reno breathed deeply. "You seen your father anywhere?"

"He's been in his tent all afternoon."

"Sulking like Achilles. How fitting."

"What are you *talking* about?" she demanded.

Reno looked around. He seemed nervous. "All right, then, Becca. Let's talk." He cleared his throat but didn't say anything further. She waited, but his hesitance was almost visible, thick as cigar smoke. Reno really didn't want to share this story, Becca realized. He was afraid of it. And so, what she'd been asking of him — to tell it — that was no simple thing.

24

BEN SWAM BACK across the river, but Lucy wasn't there, so he returned to the opposite bank. Dusk had begun to fall. "Let's go find that man," he said. Jacob nodded, sullen. "It was very brave of you to jump in the river like that," Ben added. "And also really stupid." He squeezed Jacob's shoulder and finally the boy smiled a little.

They climbed the hill and stood at the top of the rise, shivering in their wet clothes. A vast desert sprawled out below. About a hundred yards out, an encampment of low-slung buildings glowed among sparse trees. The camp was tucked into the shadow of an enormous mesa and illuminated by tall floodlights. It looked like a military installation.

"Look there!" Jacob tugged on Ben's arm. In the distance pulsed a bright bubble of light. A large fire.

"What is it?" Jacob asked, transfixed.

"Trash? In Iraq, people were always burning trash."

"But why all the way out there?"

The kid had a point. Why dispose of something in the middle of the desert unless you wanted to keep it hidden?

By the time they'd picked their way down the rocky slope, it was completely dark, and Ben wished for his night-vision goggles.

They passed through a stile, then stopped short. Before them stretched a vast graveyard: row upon row of wooden crosses. Ben knelt down in front of one. Hanging from the neck of the cross was a pair of dog tags with *Pvt. Pablo Rodriguez* stamped into the metal.

"Ben?" Jacob's voice was small and scared.

Ben let the dog tags fall back against the wood. "Come on," he said, and he took Jacob's hand. "Let's go find your mom."

Jacob was shaking with cold, so Ben lifted the child onto his back. The kid weighed about the same as Ben's armor, the difference being that now Ben was protecting the load attached to him instead of the other way around.

The crosses led Ben straight up to the compound's entrance. Standing beneath the floodlights was the old man from earlier. "Took you long enough," the man said. Ben eyed the guy's liver-spotted face and sunken cheeks. He eyed the hunting rifle strapped to his back. "Name's Arne," said the man. "Welcome to Kleos."

Yeah, Ben thought. *Warm welcome.*

"Can I see your tags?" Arne asked. "I need to verify your identity. For security purposes."

Ben always wore his tags, but he wasn't eager to show them.

"We can keep standing here staring at each other," said Arne, clearly impatient, "or we can get going." Ben pulled the tags from his shirt and held them out. Arne nodded and headed into the camp. His black motorcycle vest had a single large patch sewn on the back: an ancient Greek battle helmet with blackness where there should have been a face.

As they walked, Arne pointed out the trailers and hogans and concrete buildings that contained sleeping quarters and the mess. He pointed to the barns and said, "You'll probably start out with shovel detail, but if you stick around and the CO sees you progressing, he'll move you to something more dignified."

Ben ignored all of this. "Where's the woman who was with us earlier?"

"She was driven in. Through that mining tunnel Reno told you about—the tunnel he should not have mentioned in the first place. That man's got no respect for us."

"And we need to find this boy's mother," Ben said eagerly. "She's with the Hands of God Church?"

Arne didn't answer, but he motioned Ben into the laundry building. Ben helped Jacob into overly large sweatpants, a man's T-shirt, and a hoodie that came down to the boy's knees. Then he changed quickly into a pair of khakis and work boots. After this, Arne took them to a cinder-block building. "You may not speak with the civilians inside," Arne said. "If you do, there will be consequences."

Jacob squeezed Ben's hand and Ben returned the pressure. He forced a smile and urged the boy inside. There, on cheap dormitory furniture, sat a cluster of Indian women. Immediately, one of them jumped up and ran to Jacob. "My baby!" she cried, rocking the boy madly. Ben felt a wave of relief that intensified upon seeing Lucy safe and sound. Ben opened his mouth, but Lucy's finger flew to her lips, her eyes imploring him to keep quiet. But Ben had lost his words anyway, because there, beside Lucy, he saw a pale figure; gaunt, with an angular face and sharp, critical eyes. The woman wore a short-sleeved cotton dress and a gold cross. She looked very little like her daughter.

"Jeanine!" Ben said. "Are Reno and King here yet? Is Becca with them?"

Arne walked toward Ben holding a small object in his hand. "I told you to keep quiet," he said.

Jeanine gave Ben a you-asked-for-it smirk as Arne lifted his arm. A crackling sound escaped from his hand and Ben felt live wires tightening around his abdomen. He fell to his knees in agony. When he opened his eyes, Arne stood over him, pointing the Taser at his face. Jacob was crying. Lucy's eyes were averted, her expression slack and helpless. Nobody tried to help him.

"Get up, soldier!" Arne ordered. "The CO is waiting to see you."

"Does anybody want to tell me what's going on?" Ben demanded, pulling himself up. "Any of you? Jeanine?" Jeanine's face was stiff.

Arne nudged Ben with the flat head of the Taser. "Let's go," he said and prodded Ben out the door.

They continued through the camp for a good twenty minutes before entering a slug-shaped building. They climbed down a metal staircase and into a fluorescent-lit bunker. The hallway was narrow and punctuated by rooms harboring hydroponic plants. Somewhere a generator hummed. After a while, they reached a second metal staircase and climbed up and out into a white-walled garden. The perimeter was lined with sprouting basil, cottony sage, and thick bouquets of mint. The air smelled of sweet smoke. Above them loomed a massive, darkly hulking form, like a giant suspended wave. *The surge,* Ben thought and pushed the thought away. This must be the mesa, and its orientation suggested that they had just gophered their way beneath it.

"Wash," Arne said and pointed at a burbling fountain.

Keeping his eye on the old man, Ben walked over and rinsed his face and hands. "Is it safe to drink?" he asked. Arne nodded. Ben gulped down a couple of mouthfuls, buying time. Was he going to be imprisoned here? Could he manage to take Arne down? Was there any way to scale the walls?

"Come," Arne said and led Ben toward a wooden door across the garden. Ben hesitated, but Arne pushed the Taser against Ben's back. Ben wasn't sure what he'd expected to find behind the door, but it wasn't this: a perfectly square room with a wall of windows and a golden statue the size of a small child. The statue was a woman astride a tiger. She clutched weapons in her multiple arms. Could this be Durga, the mythical heroine from Becca's childhood?

But Ben's attention was diverted from this question by the room's other centerpiece: a man. He was a giant of a human being. His bare upper body had the heft and pallor of a concrete block. His eyes bulged with eggy whites and blue irises that had a crystalline, marble-like quality. Quite possibly, one eye was glass, but the man observed Ben with an expression that seemed almost clairvoyant.

"Welcome," said the man in deep, rumbling voice. "I am CO Proudfoot, your commanding officer at Kleos. Have a seat, soldier." The CO nodded at a small wooden chair, but Ben didn't move.

"I'll be just outside if you need me," Arne said and gave Ben a look of warning before exiting the room.

"Arne's a hoplite," the CO said, nodding as the door closed. "He is one of a dozen guardians of Kleos, named for the citizen-soldiers of ancient Greece. They are the oldest, most loyal inhabitants of this place."

"Your man Arne Tased me," Ben said.

"Because you spoke with a civilian, which is forbidden. I agreed to let those women in out of respect for Jeanine for first bringing King to me. But they have agreed to follow my rules."

"I'm looking for King." Ben pressed on. "And his daughter, Becca. Just tell me where they are and I'll leave."

"Well, I don't know about the girl, but King is on his way."

Ben's heart paused. "When will he get here?" he asked.

The CO looked toward the windows. In profile, the man's face was classically handsome. It conjured up images of gladiators and swords. "It seems," he said, still absorbed in the darkness beyond the glass, "that you now have a reason to stay with us awhile."

Ben shook his head. "I'll go back across the river and wait for her."

"Son." The CO sighed and looked squarely at Ben. "Will you please do me the courtesy of sitting down? You're making me nervous."

Cautiously, Ben pulled up the wooden chair and sat with his body arched over his knees. A ready position. He wanted to be ready — to run or to attack. Whatever was necessary.

"Nobody comes here by accident," the CO said.

"I told you why I came."

The CO smiled, exposing large gray teeth. "Becca." He nodded. "Yes, but that is merely the surface reason. The deeper reason is that you are sick. Your mind is a prison. You are desperate for rest and can find none. The people closest to you are strangers. Your Becca, perhaps?" The CO scanned Ben's face. Ben tried to remain impassive despite feeling increasingly uncomfortable. "Deep down, soldier, you know that you cannot function out there anymore." The CO looked at the center of Ben's forehead, as though tunneling directly into his brain. "You are here, son, because you have nowhere else to go."

"You don't know me," Ben said.

"It's true. And *you* don't know *me* either, which is why we should get acquainted. I was King's staff sergeant in Vietnam, as you may know. I started this place in order to help my brothers . . . and" — the CO nodded — "my sons."

I'm not your son, Ben thought. He said, "I don't want your help."

"Of course not." There was the gray smile again. "Soldiers help themselves. But left to your own devices, you're a threat to yourself and those close to you. The pain comes out, eventually. And if that energy isn't released properly, people get hurt. Loved ones, for example."

Ben felt his face redden. "You're just saying all of this because you know where I spent the last fifteen months." Ben sat up straight now and folded his arms across his chest. This was Becca's favorite defensive stance, and it made him miss her even more.

"Well, I'm *guessing* you've tried the army's remedies and they've done nothing for you," the CO said, losing some of his composure. "How many meds did they prescribe you? How many shrinks passed you around, playing hot potato with your head?"

Ben felt a burning in his chest. So what if the CO knew these things? His situation wasn't exactly unique.

"Out here, son, we're not interested in therapists and pills. You may not be aware, but the Greek generals did not fail their soldiers the way ours failed us. They did not see grief as shameful. They respected the unspeakable pain of warriors for their dead. What is the funeral pyre if not a public confession that where there is death, there is agony?"

Now the CO was just babbling nonsense. He was off the deep end. And since Ben was feeling fairly secure in his physical safety, he wanted to be alone. He needed to think through his strategy for Becca's arrival—and for how to get her home.

Home. He'd hated that place since he'd been back: the too-soft bed, the new pajamas she'd bought him, her attempts to make him comfortable, as if comfort were a sensation he could still access. But it was time to get on with his life. To be normal again.

The CO pulled a bag of weed from his pocket and packed a pipe. He offered the pipe to his guest. Ben had always enjoyed a couple of hits during late-night picking circles. There was nothing quite like playing old-timey fiddle tunes — those glorious musical merry-go-rounds — on a high. But since Ben didn't trust the CO, he certainly didn't trust the CO's drugs. Now, as the CO pulled and exhaled, the room began to fill with smoke. It filled quickly, with great billows. The smoke did not smell like marijuana, and Ben thought about the hydroponic plants growing underground. What in the hell had he stumbled into?

Through the haze, the CO's beard seemed to be composed of smoke itself, the tendrils curling from his face into the air. Ben's lungs felt warm and there was a soft ringing in his ears. He began to relax back into the chair, but something nagged at him. Becca, he remembered. Becca was coming. He sat up, opening his eyes wide against the fog, but his eyelids felt heavy.

The CO said, "I'd like to tell you a story about how I came to be here and why I think you should stay with us."

Becca, Ben thought, and tried to speak her name. But his tongue was numb. He could not even open his mouth. The CO leaned forward, and for a moment, Ben saw the man's neck and chest as a snake's body, a shimmering cobra that stretched through the air and hissed.

"Relax," said the CO as his forked tongue flicked Ben's cheek. "It's going to be a little while before your girl arrives, and anyhow, what do you have to lose?"

December 13, 1980

Dear Willy,

We sat on the plateau overlooking the decimated village of Li Sing for hours. Reno was still passed out. You and Lai talked and the sound of her language was like a screeching jungle bird. I pulled a can of peaches from my pack and ate them, facing Li Sing. It was the one pleasure I'd allowed myself on the trip. Instead of our usual C rations, we'd been sent out with long-range rations, or long rats, the kind of lightweight, just-add-water slop that Special Forces guys carried. But that was where the similarities between us and the real Special Forces ended. They were men trained for months before being sent out on this kind of mission. And us? King was twenty-one. Reno was only nineteen. And though I'd been in longer and had more experience, I was secretly petrified. All of you depended on me.

A dull pink color washed over the rubble and made Durga glow, as though the statue pulsed with an internal light. I had the strange thought that if I touched the gray stone, it would feel warm, even alive. I felt unaccountably sad, like I missed things I couldn't name and people I'd never met. I carried my peaches over to you and asked what you were talking about. You said Lai was explaining Durga's prophecy.

"The statue's prophetic?" I asked.

"It's not a statue, Proudfoot. It's a goddess."

"You mean a statue of a goddess," I said. "So what does this goddess prophesize? Can she tell me the next time I'm gonna get laid?" This crack sounded juvenile even to my own ears, and you pretended not to have heard.

"Lai says that Durga foretold Li Sing's destruction."

"And according to her, who or what was responsible?"

"The forces of the universe."

"She can't be any more specific?" I licked the last of the peach juice off my spoon and put the can back into my pack.

Some guys would just throw it into the jungle, but I wasn't convinced there weren't VC hanging around, and I didn't want to leave behind traces.

"According to the prophecy," you continued, "when the village was destroyed, only a single person would survive. And that person would become the Carrier — I think that's how it translates — the one who emerges unscathed to carry forward Durga's legacy. To embody her."

"You're saying that Lai here thinks she's a goddess?"

"More like a steward."

The light was fading and the pink glow had disappeared from Durga's hard skin. "That's a hunk of stone," I said. "It's not a prophet or a goddess. And neither is she."

"He's right," King said, looking up from the letter he was writing. "If the bombs missed the statue, it's only because the air force's got shitty aim."

Lai spoke quickly to you, her eyes wild. She seized your arm, and her touch sent a visible tremor through your bony frame. "She's the Carrier! It's the truth. You have to believe, Proudfoot!" You were pleading with us.

"Willy! Hey!" I said. "Snap out of it. She's out of her mind. Anyone can see that."

But Lai was talking faster now, digging her nails into your arm. This woman wasn't just crazy, I thought. She was Fucking Nam Crazy.

"If she's the Carrier," King said, "then what's she carrying?"

"Durga's heart."

"And how did she get it?" I demanded. "Did she scale the statue? Pull out some hunk of stone from inside Durga's chest?"

"She says it's a real heart."

"A muscle full of blood? I'd like to see it."

You said something to Lai, but she shook her head. "You can't," he said.

"Why not?"

"Because she put Durga's heart in her stomach."

Before this statement could register with any of us, Lai pulled up her tunic. To the left of her bellybutton was a patch of shiny pink flesh. Running through the center of the damaged skin was a scar. It was scraggly and white, about five inches long. It looked as though someone had dragged a blunt knife across her belly.

"Jesus," King whispered.

I squatted down for a closer look. Suddenly, Lai grabbed my wrist. She pressed my palm flat over the scar, held it there with an iron grip. I was frozen and speechless. I couldn't do a thing. Because I felt something. Something alive, pulsing inside of her. I pulled my hand back.

"What is it?" you whispered, your face close to mine. "What did you feel?"

I stood up and backed away. "Soon as Reno wakes up, we're out of here."

"You felt something," you called behind me. "You felt the heart."

I turned to see you putting your hand flat against Lai's stomach, gently touching around the scar like a doctor listening with his stethoscope.

"You felt something," you said, frantic. "You did!"

"Those cheek bits you got splattered with really messed you up, Willy," King said.

You stared at King like you didn't understand what he was talking about. You seemed not to notice that Lai had gently removed your hand from her abdomen.

"You don't belong out here," King snapped, angry out of nowhere. "The army never should have sent you."

"Proudfoot felt something!"

Fuck this, I thought and walked into the trees.

That night, I lay in the dark, staring at the sky through

a net of overhanging leaves. Out in the jungle, the cicadas screamed. The sky was very black; the stars no more than pinpricks. Reno slept beside me, snoring, which I took to be a good sign. A few hours before, he'd finally woken up and groggily had some water. Then he'd passed out again. Lai mixed a new batch of paste, forced some of it down his throat, and spread the rest over his body. Then she disappeared inside her shelter. "We'll take turns guarding her for the night," I said. "First thing tomorrow, we're moving out."

Unable to sleep, lying on my roll, I prayed for something to take me far away from this place, from myself. I'd done this simple thing—touched a woman's belly—and it had filled my body with so much fear, I thought I might explode. And how could I explain that? How could I let in confusion and fear when my life and the lives of my men depended on just the opposite? I thought about borrowing a section of your *Iliad*. Maybe a story could help me relax.

But I must have fallen asleep eventually, because when I opened my eyes again, it was morning.

I rolled over to see Reno shaking King, asking why the fuck he was covered in mud. King groaned and sat up.

"You feel okay?" I said.

"I feel like shit."

King offered the canteen to Reno, and Reno drank without trouble.

"What's out there?" Reno asked, nodding toward the ridge. Fog hung thick in the gully, obscuring the village. I could just make out Durga's head through the mist, floating as though disembodied.

King explained about Lai and her mad-ass prophecy. He told Reno about the woman's scar. He conveniently left out the part about Lai seizing my hand.

"I missed all that?" Reno shook his head. "Sounds like the most fun we've had in weeks."

"Let's get Willy and get out of here," I said.

"Willy!" Reno shouted. "Wake the fuck up!"

"Willy's sleeping?" King and I were on our feet in a flash and running over to where you lay by Lai's hut. Sure enough, you were curled up in a fetal position, cradling your gun like it was a baby. "Hey, kid!" Reno called out. "You dead?" Reno jabbed at you with the toe of his boot and you bolted upright. "Who's dead?"

Reno let out a deep-bellied laugh. "You are, kid. See out there?" Reno pointed to the fog. "That's heaven."

I pulled a couple of branches off Lai's shelter. It was empty. "Willy, you were supposed to wake me for the next watch!" But even as I said it, I knew it wasn't your fault. I should have stayed awake. It wasn't the kind of mistake I'd ever made, and I burned with shame.

"She probably went to get her gook friends," Reno spat. "Wanted 'em to slit our throats while we slept."

"She didn't go to get anybody," you whimpered. "She's alone out here. Her village is gone."

"We're moving out," I said. "To hell with this mission."

"She's all alone out here," you repeated. "We can't just leave her."

"Come on, Willy," King said. "It's okay."

King, the squad mother. I knew it wasn't a role he wanted to play, but he couldn't help it. He was just too decent a person.

"Hey!" Reno shouted and we all turned. Lai stood at the edge of the tree line, maybe fifteen yards away. She held something in her hands. Reno cocked his gun.

"Don't shoot her!" you yelled.

King and I jumped to attention and scanned the wall of jungle. There was a dead stillness. Not even the wind rustled the leaves.

"What's she got there?" Reno said. "Ask her, Willy."

You moved forward, speaking to Lai. She rattled back a response, her strange language grating against our ears. I moved up behind you, motioning for Reno and King to follow.

"She's scared," Willy hissed. "You're scaring her."

"That's a grenade," Reno said from my left.

"No!" you pleaded. "She says it's a bowl with more medicine."

"My ass it is."

"She'll show you, Reno." You spoke quickly to Lai and she began to raise her arm.

"No, Willy—" King started to protest.

And then Lai was gone. Vanished into thin air. But it wasn't magic. She'd merely fallen to the ground. You looked at Reno, your face wrenched in shock. But it wasn't Reno who'd fired the shot. It was me.

King and Reno just stood there, staring at Lai's body. Then you realized what had happened. "No!" you screamed and ran to her. "You killed her!" you cried. You moved your hands over her body, searching for something—some switch—that might let her get up again. "She wasn't going to hurt us!" You were sobbing.

"She had a grenade," Reno said. "Why don't you bring it over for show-and-tell?"

"She wasn't going to hurt us." You kicked the object that had fallen from Lai's hands. It rolled over to me and stopped just shy of my boots: a metal bowl filled with a foul-smelling paste. Medicine.

Reno spat and turned away. King sighed. "Come on, Willy," he said. "Let's go."

But you seemed not to hear. You were looking up at me, your eyes glazed, almost like Lai's eyes had been. Then you pulled a knife from your belt and pushed up Lai's shirt. In my head, I was screaming at you to stop, but the words wouldn't come out. King and Reno shouted your name. But it was too late. You'd pushed the knife into Lai's belly and, in one quick motion, sliced her open.

We gaped in disbelief as you tossed the bloodied knife aside and pushed your hand into the seam. You got your fingers in good, moving them around like you were mixing batter with your hand. Blood ran out of the gash and down the sides of Lai's body. You released a whooping cry. "I told you it was real!" You pulled your hand, red and glistening, from the gash and held it in the air. You seemed to be holding something, but we were too far away to see it clearly. "It's real." You cackled, pulling your fist to your chest and cradling it there. "You didn't believe her, but it's real."

I turned away. After all these bloody months, seeing a woman mutilated was something I still couldn't stomach. But I also knew that approaching you now would be like triggering a mine. I'd seen men go berserk before; I worried that what you'd done to Lai was only the beginning.

"I'm taking the heart now," you announced. "Do you hear me, Proudfoot? I'm going to carry it. You felt it. But you were afraid. You were afraid of the heart, so you killed her." You stood up and walked a few steps forward. Blood ran down your arm in long streaks. "I'm the Carrier from now on. I'm not afraid of anything." You held up your fist. Your hands had stopped shaking.

Reno chuckled. "Looks like he's been washed in the blood of the Lai."

"Jesus Christ, Reno," I snapped. And without another look at the village of Li Sing or Lai's body, I hoisted my pack and marched into the jungle. King and Reno followed, and behind us all, walking steady at last, you.

Back at the CIDG camp, I gave my report to the major. I said the village was bombed out and deserted. I said we'd encountered no one.

"Anything happen to Private McKenzie out there?" the major asked. "He looks a little bit off in the eyes."

"He's not fit for this," I said.

"He says he wants to stay," the major said. "After the mess HQ made, I don't really know why. But his skills could come in useful. And your squad's short a few men."

For the next couple of weeks, Willy, you kept to yourself. You ate alone. Mornings, you were up early, helping the villagers haul water from the well. You learned your way around the tools fast and took over construction of the local school. You'd changed. Everyone could see it. Your pale skin burned, then peeled, then tanned. You were still skinny, but you looked stronger now, your arms less spindly. Even your acne started to clear up. And you'd hung a drawstring pouch from your neck like a piece of jewelry. You never took it off; not in the afternoons, when the soggy heat forced us out of our shirts, not in the shower, not even to sleep. At night you tucked the pouch into your armpit for extra protection. A couple of times Reno tried to steal it, to see what you were carrying around with you—because it wasn't actually a heart. We all knew that much.

Everyone whispered about the pouch. They called you Pretty Willy. When they passed you in the camp, they asked if you had lipstick and a compact in your little purse and whether you could recommend any nice Vietnamese boys from the village. Reno was the worst offender—*faggot* this, *poof* that—and I got sick of it. I didn't like to hear them talk that way. So I told Reno, "You better let him be and tell everybody I said so."

Later, I heard Reno grumbling to King about how I must have felt guilty for killing that woman and that maybe I was going soft.

"Proudfoot knows he did the right thing," King said.

"So then why's he protecting Willy's faggy ass? The kid's not one of us, King. And he's crazy. I'm telling you, one day I'm going to rip that little purse off his neck."

"Willy's pulling his weight," King said. "Just leave him alone."

I, on the other hand, was not pulling my weight. I didn't let on, of course. But ever since Li Sing, I'd had this recurring nightmare in which our planes were dropping bombs on the ancient village, the rounds falling over the huts, showering Durga like hail. When the smoke cleared, I saw Lai standing amid the destruction. Blood gushed like a fountain from her belly, ran down her legs, and seeped into the ground. And that's when the truly scary part of the dream started. Because when the blood hit the ground, it burst into flame and shot off in a straight line, like fire following a gasoline trail. I watched this trail of fire rush through the jungle, over mountains and hills, heading for our camp. I saw it snake toward our barracks. And just before the fire was about to burst upon me, I'd wake up. The dream was like a plague — like a punishment. The remains of Li Sing were out there. Lai's body was out there. We hadn't buried her. We'd left plenty of people on the ground like that, but we should have buried her. That stupid bowl looked like a grenade. I didn't have a choice. But she'd helped Reno. She deserved a grave, at least.

A couple of weeks later, we started training for a new mission. We ran drills, studied maps, learned each other's signals. It was now expected that you'd eat with us. And because you ate with us, it was expected that you'd drink with us. Nobody mentioned the pouch anymore. And then one day, you left the first hundred pages of *The Iliad* on my cot.

"I don't want this," I said.

"It'll help you with the nightmares," you said. I wondered how you knew, but by that point, I was so desperate, I'd try anything. Soon enough, you and I started getting into these long discussions about the meddling Greek gods and whether the Trojan War had been worth fighting. Reno looked askance when he saw us debating the motives of Thetis and the defilement of Hector's body. I paid him no mind. Every day, I couldn't wait to get through the training so I could get back to the book—and to our discussions. I hated the fact that I liked talking to you so much. But I couldn't help myself. I needed your approval. I needed to know that you believed in me. Because of what I'd done. Because of what I'd felt beating beneath Lai's skin.

Currahee!

CO Proudfoot

25

THE TALE EMERGED from Reno like an endless string of scarves yanked from a magician's mouth. Every time he seemed ready to wrap things up, another impossible detail flew out. Never had Becca heard a story more riveting, more bizarre, or more bogus. And yet, it explained the origin of King's tattoo. It explained this CO Proudfoot they were all going to see. But it explained nothing about Kleos or what kind of danger her father was facing.

"Story's not over yet," Reno said. He wheezed like a runner whose lungs were on the verge of collapse.

"We can take a break," Becca offered. But he only shook his head. He needed to power through.

"Our next mission, again in Cambodia, was to surveil a North Vietnamese army weapons supply. We were supposed to assess the size and strength of the outfit and make a report about whether to send in the big guns. But everything was different now. Willy walked like an Indian. He didn't make so much as a peep. There was no sign of Charlie on the first day. But that night, something strange happened.

"See, Willy and the CO had been spending a lot of time together, always involved in these intense conversations about one of Willy's books. It bothered me, you know, 'cause the CO was a no-bullshit guy. And Willy was nutty, wearing that so-called heart in a sack around his neck. I was starting to question whether the CO was really in *his* right mind, whether killing that woman had caused him to snap. But after they thought King and I were asleep, I overheard the two of them talking. My ears really pricked up when I heard Willy say that he never wanted to go home again, because of course, that's *all* we wanted. To get the fuck out of the jungle. The CO asked Willy how Vietnam was in any way preferable to his cushy university. And Willy told this story about how he'd fallen in love with somebody back at school and gotten caught and *that's* why the university had been so happy to get rid of him when the army came calling."

"You mean he slept with a teacher?" Becca asked.

"That's what the CO wanted to know."

"And what did Willy say?"

"He made advances toward his adviser." Reno raised his eyebrows at her. "His male adviser."

"Oh," she said.

"So then Willy said, 'I don't think I ever felt like myself until I came here. For the first time in my life, I have a purpose.'

"'But even if that thing in the pouch is what you say it is, Willy,' the CO said, 'Durga's not your god. And Li Sing wasn't your village.'

"'They are now. Proudfoot, life back home—it was intolerable. It wasn't really life at all. But here! This is the only place that I've ever felt true to myself. That trouble with my adviser—'

"'Don't tell me about that, Willy,' the CO said. 'I don't want to hear about it.'

"'But you're—'

"'I'm a soldier! I'm the leader of this squad. I'm responsible for completing the mission and getting us home. That's who I am.'

"And then things turned strange," Reno said. "I couldn't see either of them, but I could feel the awkwardness, thick and sticky-like.

" 'Why is it, Proudfoot,' asked Willy, 'that you and I never talk about Achilles and Patroclus?'

" 'We talk about them,' said the CO.

" 'Their relationship,' Willy said. 'That part of it, we don't discuss.'

" 'You want to talk about them? Fine. They were like brothers to each other.'

" 'Brothers?' Willy repeated.

" 'What do you want from me, Willy?' the CO asked.

" 'The way Patroclus puts on Achilles's armor and rushes into battle. The way that Achilles grieves over him, pouring dust over his head and face and lying down in the dirt. Achilles says he'd die rather than live in a world without Patroclus. And you call that the love between brothers.'

"Willy stopped talking then, like he was waiting for the CO to refute him. But the CO was silent. After a little while, I heard Willy speak the CO's name. And then, in a voice that sounded so pitiful it made my insides hurt, Willy said, 'Proudfoot, if I die, how will you grieve for me?' "

"And then what happened?" Becca asked, hunching over her legs so that her head and Reno's were side by side.

"Nothing," Reno said. "The CO never answered."

Hearing this, Becca's heart opened into sadness; she wanted to say something or do something to ease Willy's pain. Where, she wondered, was Willy now?

"Anyway, the next day, we resumed the march. At some point, Willy calls out for us to give a wide berth to this particular bush.

Only your dad wasn't paying attention, and he just kept coming. And fast as a whip, Willy sticks the neck of his rifle into your father's chest, halting him in his tracks. And we all look down and there, on the ground, inches from your father's feet, is this bouncing Betty, just sitting pretty in a pool of sunlight, like the thing was fucking tanning itself. Had Willy not been there, that mine woulda jumped belly high and disemboweled your father. And as for you and me? Not sitting here right now. That's for sure."

Becca shivered, thinking about the close call and how Willy had likely saved her father's life. She wanted to ask more questions, but Reno hurried on with the story. "We stopped at dusk, ate long rats for dinner, sharpened our knives, and got our gear in order. The plan was to march forward as a group and then split into pairs. King and I would circle the perimeter of the weapons supply to get a sense of its size, and Willy and the CO would assess the route in and out. We'd meet back at our base camp and call in the report. Depending on what we found, the major might send in the gunships. It was supposed to be a non-contact mission. 'If you get in the shit,' the CO said, 'throw some smoke flares. But don't get in the shit.' He and Willy split off and disappeared into the jungle.

"The weapons hub was like a hive. King and I found coils of barbed wire strung between the trees, and the brush haphazardly thinned. Shadows moved between firelight. Then, suddenly, we heard shouting, followed by a quick pop of gunfire. Sparks flared and vanished as bullets sprayed into the black. One of us had tripped up, and the NVA thought they were getting ambushed. King waved me forward and we made our way to the far side of the camp. If the CO and Willy were in trouble, we had to help them. We saw a group of five NVA up ahead. We shot one down, but then the remaining four morphed into seven or eight, their bodies doubling like a string of paper men. The last one to step out raised an RPG to his shoulder. We dropped flat, pushed ourselves into the undergrowth. The rocket missed us but sent a wave of heat and smoke over our backs. Something sharp bit into my neck. King was cupping his ear and there was blood on his face. I was bleeding, half frozen with shock. Your dad pulled two smoke grenades from his belt and threw them. Then the world exploded into yellow and cherry-colored clouds. We struggled up, sprayed a round of fire to cover ourselves, and ran.

"At our base camp, King called in the pickup coordinates and the grid coordinates of the weapons hub. We gathered up everybody's packs and headed toward the pickup spot. King helped me bandage up my neck. And then a second later the CO came crashing out of the trees, followed by tracer fire, shouting 'Move!' He had Willy's pouch around his neck.

"The Huey was just coming down, whipping up a cyclone of hot wind. The three of us shot back into the trees, then cut through the long, stinging grasses and threw ourselves into the bird. Then we were in the air, swinging up and away as the gunships flew in and let loose over the weapons hub. Fire flowers bloomed from the ground. It was gorgeous. I am not ashamed to admit that it was the most beautiful thing I've ever seen."

Reno paused. Becca waited for him to continue, but he didn't. He just sat there, silent. Finally, she asked, "What happened to Willy?"

"I don't know. The CO wouldn't tell us."

"And that's it?"

"No," Reno said. "There's one more thing. A few months later, the CO came back from leave in Saigon. He didn't have the pouch anymore and when we asked where it was, he said he'd had an operation and now the heart was safe. I didn't have a fucking clue what that meant, so I asked for an explanation."

"Okay." Becca's heart was pounding. Maybe she wasn't ready

for this after all. Maybe she wanted to stay on the outside of things, where people lived normal, nonpsychotic lives.

"In Saigon, the CO found a doctor who'd agreed to slice his stomach open. He had the doctor insert Durga's heart. Then he got his belly sewed back up."

26

BEN WAS SWEATING and chilled through. He couldn't remember the last time he'd eaten anything and he had no idea what time it was. He'd somehow left the CO's desert study and given up his personals to Arne. Now he stood in this empty spot at the edge of Kleos beneath scattered trees. One of the hoplites had told Ben to dig himself a foxhole or sleep on the ground.

Soldiers took care of themselves, the CO had said, which was apparently why Ben had been forced to swim across the river. If he wanted a place to sleep for the night, he'd dig it. And he might as well do something to pass the time, even something useless. Becca was coming, and he needed a physical activity to channel his anticipation. He felt so keyed up, it was a wonder his body did not glow with hot, red light.

Ben dug in, shoveled, and threw dirt. Dug in, shoveled, threw dirt. A satisfying hole opened beside him. Meanwhile, he was starting to recall details from the CO's story: the soldier named Willy Owen McKenzie, the destroyed village, the woman with Durga's heart in her stomach. Then there'd been a mission; Willy had not come back. But the CO had come out with the heart — or whatever was inside the pouch. The CO had told Ben that he was going to die soon. More than four decades ago, he'd been exposed to chemicals sprayed down by his own government to defoliate the jungles. He'd been sick for a while, he said. And now it was time — time to pass the heart to a new guardian. The chosen recipient would be healed, fully and wholly, and in return, this man would assume responsibility for carrying on Durga's legacy and healing others.

Even through the haze of the drugs, Ben remembered thinking, *This story is bullshit.* And the CO must have seen that on his face, because he'd said, "I was once a skeptic like you, but I changed when I saw Durga's heart at work. It saved Willy. It saved me and gave me the power to save other men."

"Is that why King is coming out here, to be saved?" Ben had asked. He realized there was a pipe in his hand. He did not recall accepting the CO's drugs.

The CO frowned through the smoke. "King's not exactly a model of commitment."

"Because he left his family," Ben mumbled. He was now too high to enunciate clearly.

"Because one day he puts his faith in Durga and the ancient warriors and the next he runs back to Tennessee. The world beyond" — the CO had waved his hand at the window and the black, unseen desert — "is like a drug for that man. Dangerous and addictive. But King is strong. He always manages to pull himself back here and continue our work. He could be a prime contender for the heart."

Later there was more smoke and more talk, and, strangely, Ben had the needling sense that *he'd* been the one speaking. He felt empty, like only scraps of thoughts remained: a soccer ball, a charred metal cage, the sad, slow melody of "Sally in the Garden," the steady, ominous beat of a heart monitor. Not being able to remember how all of these details fit together should have been a blessing. Instead, Ben felt more uncertain, more vulnerable. He didn't like the idea of his memories slipping around in the shadows, hiding from him. He should never have smoked the CO's drugs.

Dig in, shovel, throw dirt. Ben put his whole body into the motions.

"You should compete for the heart," the CO had said. This Ben remembered clearly. The CO's blue eyes cut tunnels through the smoke. "You could be the next Carrier, the one to carry on Durga's legacy, the anointed! Do you want to know how?"

Had Ben nodded? The CO kept talking.

"The Greeks believed in catharsis, the purging of grief and fear after tragedy. You and I and King are all tragic heroes, and to heal we must attain catharsis. But catharsis doesn't just happen, Sergeant Thompson. The emotions and memories must be drawn out of the mind and re-created in the physical world. To that end, this interview has been quite helpful, should the opportunity for your catharsis present itself."

The smoke seemed to part then, so Ben had a good look at the CO, the old man's massive face and the chalky hue of his skin.

"I'm not interested in your voodoo," Ben said. "I'm getting my wife and we're going home."

"After what you did to Becca? You really think so?"

How did the CO know what he'd done to Becca?

Ben plunged the shovel into the ground. What he'd dug was not a foxhole at all but a pit. *We will go home,* Ben thought. *I will make things right. I love her, and I will do anything to prove it.* He worked on through the night until the moon began to sink and the stars winked out. *Becca,* he thought finally, lying down beneath the bruise-purple sky. *Forgive me.*

27

IT WAS THEIR last morning on the road. For Becca, it had been a full eight days since she'd left home, though it felt much longer. Rags appeared and motorcycles were cleaned of their grime, the chrome shined up and the leather brushed down, as though the men were preparing for some sort of mechanical horse show. These preparations were made quietly, almost solemnly, as though this day had been pronounced holy.

After breakfast, a medicine man in a bolo tie and jeans assembled the bikers into a circle. They stood in reverent silence as the man knelt over a small fire with a clay bowl, smoking with leaves. A complex series of smells — shades of sweet and bitter — filled the air. Then the medicine man began to move around the circle, wafting smoke over each man with a feather. In turn, the men cupped their hands and brought more smoke toward their faces, as though dousing themselves.

"Smudging ceremony," Reno whispered to Becca as the medicine man made his way around.

When he reached her, he stopped. "You are the daughter?" he asked. "The one who requires special prayers?"

Hyperaware of so many eyes on her, Becca looked nervously at Reno. Reno nodded. "I'm Becca," she said. The medicine man motioned for her to step forward. She looked at Reno again; again he nodded encouragingly.

"Close your eyes," said the medicine man. Becca did and was aware of his voice, low and melodious. She could almost feel the smoke, like a translucent ribbon of silk, brushing her face. When she opened her eyes, she saw that the men were fixated on her. They not only believed in this ceremony, she understood, but were lending their conscious support to it—to this protective blessing over her.

She stepped back into the circle, feeling unexpectedly re-energized. Now Frank stepped forward and bowed his head. The entire circle, including the medicine man, bowed their heads too. Reno rolled his eyes at Becca, but he, too, bent his head. "Dear God," Frank said. "We thank You for providing us the road, our sustenance. We pray to You for clear skies, mild temperatures, and safe passage into Utah. In Jesus's name, amen."

"Amen," the men said in unison. All at once, the circle disbanded.

"You ready?" Reno asked.

"I'm ready," Becca said.

As she and Reno traveled deeper into the desert, Becca mulled over the rest of Reno's story. After losing Willy, Proudfoot became obsessed with Li Sing and Durga. He'd somehow accumulated a wealth of obscure knowledge about the village and the goddess, so Reno could only conclude that either his squad leader had been taken in by Willy's crazy or he had gone a little nuts himself when the kid didn't make it out. Meanwhile, Proudfoot never spoke about the mission or what had happened at the weapons hub. It was like Willy had never existed.

After Saigon, Proudfoot seemed to be his old self again, silent and stalwart as ever. Other than that one-time mention of the operation, he did not talk about Li Sing and Durga anymore. Maybe, Reno thought, Proudfoot was putting one over on them. Maybe it was just a big, fucked-up joke. But one night, Reno finally decided to ask about Willy. In response, the squad leader lifted his shirt and revealed the scar on his stomach. Reno was so disturbed that he told King about it the very next day. And from that moment, nothing was ever the same between the three men. King and Reno could not cross the gulf between their sanity and Proudfoot's madness. And it hurt them, Reno said, to realize that they could no longer depend on their leader — the man in whom they had once put total trust.

After the war, Reno settled in the Tennessee Smokies, found work as a mechanic, and eventually took over the shop. King didn't do nearly so well. After his parents kicked him out, he'd landed a tannery job in Dry Hills. He held it for a while, but Reno watched him descend deeper and deeper into alcoholism and depression. "Your daddy plummeted through all the circles of hell, and when he hit bottom, he just broke on through and kept going," Reno said. At one point, King was barred from every bar in town as well as half the businesses. He was fired from the tannery. Barely twenty-five, King lived on charity in a busted trailer.

Now and then, Reno would ride over and drag King to AA meetings. He encouraged King to get a motorcycle, even loaning him the money for a down payment. Sometimes, King made an effort and spent a couple of months sober. In those good times, he and Reno would ride together on the weekends and participate in motorcycle runs with other vets who had also claimed their hard-fought-for piece of America — their open road — with Hondas and Kawasakis and, mostly, Harley-Davidsons.

It was on one of these sober stretches that King met Jeanine. "Your mother was a miracle," Reno said. Amazed, he watched

King go four months, then six months, without a drink or an arrest. He watched King hold on to steady employment at a small company that made custom-order saddles. He saw the two of them even buy a small house together.

"Your daddy was in love," Reno said. "And who could blame him? Your mother was beautiful. And she was tough. I thought, *If anyone can save him, it's going to be Jeanine.*"

But even Jeanine, sturdy as she was, couldn't accomplish that feat. A few years into their marriage, King crashed. After many brutal months, Jeanine dug up some rumors about a vet out in Utah who was healing soldiers from Nam. Nobody knew exactly who the vet was or what he did that worked so well, but everyone seemed to know a guy who knew a guy who'd gone to this place in Utah and was saved. Never mind that there were plenty of men who entered this mysterious place and never came out again, like it was a black hole. King, for his part, didn't believe it existed, but he was always happy to ride. So he indulged his pleading wife, and off they went.

Three weeks later, Jeanine came back to Dry Hills via Greyhound. King stayed in Utah for nearly a year. When he finally returned to Dry Hills, he arrived sober and with a picture of Durga tattooed on his arm. He told Reno that he'd met Proudfoot in Utah. Only he wasn't Proudfoot anymore, King said. He no longer responded to that name. Now, he was just the CO. The commanding officer of Kleos.

King claimed to be better, but Reno wasn't so sure. True, his friend wasn't drinking. But he was smoking some kind of strange hash. He was sluggish and enervated, but most troubling was King's new and unshakable belief in Durga's heart. Jeanine told Reno that King spent long nights on the phone with the CO, often not talking at all but listening to the man ramble on about prophecies and deities and ancient wars. When Jeanine confronted King about these conversations, he became defensive, angrier than he'd been in a long time. The shadow of his rage began to creep back into their marriage. Only when Jeanine stopped asking about the phone calls did the shadow slink back into hiding.

From then on, Reno said, King would make the trip to Utah about once a year. It was like he needed periodic infusions of whatever was there to maintain his sobriety and his sanity. Jeanine put up with it, even though King would leave for months at a time, just take off without warning, eventually reappearing out of the blue and saying that he missed her and loved her and would never leave her again. And then, shortly after King came back from one of his long trips, Jeanine got pregnant. Now she made King promise that he wouldn't leave again. She made him promise to stop smoking the drugs he'd brought home. She forced him to quit the overnight phone calls.

King did as she asked. But after Becca was born, he slipped back into his old ways: drinking and raging, with scattered moments of calm. Those moments had been Becca's rare glimpses of King as a father instead of a monster. Finally, her mother had had enough with King's drinking and rage, so she kicked him out. He retreated to Utah, the only place he knew to go.

Reno had been out to Utah a couple of times to see Kleos with his own eyes. His worst suspicions were confirmed. "The CO's certifiably insane," he told Becca. Even though there was no alcohol allowed in the compound, the drugs were concerning in their own way. He added that King was also going to AA on a regular basis. Clearly it was this, and not the CO's craziness, that was keeping King on the wagon.

Becca wanted to know why King had run from Kleos this last time.

"Well, his leatherworking, which he's been doing on and off for years, is still in demand and he'd gotten some new opportunities. But more than that, Kath swooped in with her usual handiwork."

"What does that mean?"

"Please don't tell her that I spilled the beans . . . but she asked King to come home for you. She saw how you were in need of some fathering, what with your mother AWOL and your fiancé overseas. So your father came."

All this time, Becca had assumed that she was taking care of King, not the other way around. That's how Kath had put it to her back in October: "Why not see your father? He's all on his own and could use a little help around the house." But the idea that King would have left Kleos even partly because of her left her dumbstruck. He'd left behind his safe haven for her; in his mind, he'd already done so much to help. Becca felt relieved that she hadn't known. If she had, she probably would have let her father off the hook.

"The business side of things was going well," Reno continued. "And the daughter side of things seemed to be coming along?"

Becca nodded.

"But then the CO announced that he was passing on Durga's heart to a new leader, and that upended everything."

"There's not actually anything inside the CO's belly," Becca said. "Right?"

"Fuck if I know. But Proudfoot is billing this thing as a tournament, like we're all fucking knights about to joust with each other."

"And the competition for the heart involves what, exactly?"

"No clue. But your aunt and I are in agreement that whatever the man has concocted, it could physically and emotionally do your daddy in. I don't mean to be callous, but there it is."

• • •

And now here Becca was, sitting on the back of Reno's bike, heading for the mysterious place her father called his refuge. How was she going to stop King from competing in the CO's tournament? His belief went back decades. She couldn't exactly walk up to him and say, *I'm pretty sure you're involved in a cult, and I think you should come home.*

At a gas station in Arizona, Becca asked Reno why he and Kath thought she could help. Reno slid his credit card into the machine and snapped the tank shut. "Because you're the only thing rooting King in the present," he said. "In the now."

"What about Elaine?"

Reno scoffed. "You didn't notice Elaine's lips stained red with Kool-Aid?"

So then it's just us, Becca thought. *Like you said before, back when I refused to listen.*

For days, Reno had been riding near the front of the pack, always a short distance behind King. Now, when the group growled off down the highway, he turned in the opposite direction. After a few miles, he swung abruptly onto a dirt road that led into the heart of the desert. The land opened up around them, expanding like lungs. The sun was a pulsing white spot overhead. Out in these dusty plains, the only markers of civilization were power lines strung between the broad-shouldered metal Goliaths that straddled the desert floor.

Soon mesas came into view, and rock formations that arched dramatically into the air like ship prows. Rivulets of sweat ran down Becca's back, and sand slipped through the helmet's face guard and settled in her mouth. Her bruises, though fading, hurt. But at this speed — Reno must have been going upward of eighty miles per hour — she felt drunk. The desert itself was a kind of drug.

They came upon a heap of smoldering logs piled with bones.

For a brief moment, Becca felt real dread, but Reno sped by so fast, she doubted what she'd seen.

The road wound the bike around a mesa and brought them in sight of an encampment between scattered cottonwoods. The camp was bounded on the east by the enormous rock formation, on the south and west by open desert, and on the north, as far as the eye could see, by a steeply rising incline full of boulders and cacti. Reno slowed and then stopped.

"Is that Kleos?" Becca asked, pointing at the buildings ahead of them. "It doesn't really look like a ghost town."

"The ghost town is on the other side of that rise. It's where the CO lived when he first moved here. He called it Kleos. Then he built this place."

"And where are the others?"

"There are three ways into Kleos. A mining tunnel takes you through that rise on the north horizon, but the CO's men are liable to see us coming from that direction, and if they did, they'd stop us and make us swim."

Becca raised her eyebrows, questioning.

"It's part of the CO's shtick. All vets that come have gotta swim. The route we just took, I discovered a long time ago."

Becca did not believe that her father would agree to put a body of water between himself and his motorcycle. She certainly couldn't imagine him swimming. She said as much to Reno, who only shook his head. "It's a strong hold the CO's got," he said. "An iron grip."

In some parts, Kleos resembled a little village, almost quaint, with the hogans scattered among scrubby trees and cows lowing in their pens. In other parts, it was like the industrial farms that Becca knew from Tennessee: mazes of metal gates and corrugated pens that led animals to slaughter. Reno said Kleos ran on solar power. The men produced their own food and their own medicinal herbs, and they had a warehouse full of hallucinogen-producing hydroponic plants that the CO had cultivated. "It's not as ramshackle as it looks," he said. "Proudfoot is nutso, but he and his followers have enough practical know-how—not to mention drug money—to have built quite an operation."

Becca asked how many people lived here. The camp felt huge to her, like a person could wander around for days, yet so far they'd seen no one.

"There's about a hundred, but people tend to come and go. I'd say half are permanent." Reno snorted. "A god needs devotees. He can't lead if nobody's following. But a lot of these guys—your father included—weren't meant to live here, on some stage set." Reno nodded at the ridge and sky. "King was meant to ride. To love his woman. To be a father to his daughter."

"Then why does he keep coming back here?" Becca stopped walking, made Reno look at her. She was on the cusp of understanding something vital about her father.

"Because as fucked up as this place can be, it's a lot easier for a man like King to be in here than out there."

"I can't imagine my dad giving up his motorcycle for any amount of time."

Reno nodded gravely. "You know that thing vets always say: freedom isn't free. But the problem is, when you pay for freedom with blood, like we did, it changes you. Makes it so that freedom—sustained, prolonged—is hard to come by. The bike helps, sure. But you can't ride a motorcycle twenty-four/seven. The men here, they're like convicts who can't make it outside the prison."

Men liked Kleos, Reno said, because it reminded them of the military. Proudfoot had them follow strict daily regimens based on their spiritual progress and healing. Most of it was repetitive physical work. "Mr. Miyagi bullshit," Reno said. "And some of it's seriously twisted."

"Is Proudfoot a shrink or something?"

"Who needs to be a medical professional when he can be a demagogue?"

"And people can just wander in?"

"We're in the middle of nowhere. It's pretty impossible to drop by accidentally. But Proudfoot knows better than to put the compound on lockdown. Nothing draws attention from the outside world more than a big old fence."

"So it's not really a cult. I mean, if you can leave whenever you want."

"Ah," Reno said, his eyes brightening, "but that's the old man's genius. Proudfoot claims to be healing them, but really, he's just brainwashing them and drugging them and making them dependent. He puts the choice to stay or go—to be healed or not—on them. Those are powerful chains, psychologically speaking. But like I said, your dad keeps shaking off the shackles. That *really* gets the CO's goat. King was there when all of this began. But if the man who saw Li Sing with his own eyes and watched Lai die isn't a true believer, then who could ever be?"

"And somehow, you steered clear."

"Not everybody who went to war comes back a total mess, Becca. I was able to compartmentalize, to more or less keep the worst of the war locked away. Your father was unlucky. But for whatever reason, I'm not fucked up enough to need this place. CO knows I'm a waste of his time."

Hearing this, Becca felt awash in sadness and pride for her father. He must possess incredible strength to keep breaking free, especially when that freedom was so difficult. And yet King did not seem to recognize his own power. Becca wished that she could show him. She wished that he could see himself standing out in the world, on his own legs. He had a strong heart already. He didn't need another one.

"Look," Reno said. "We found them." Picking up the pace, he led Becca through a group of hogans and trailers and into a clearing. On one side stood sixty or seventy vets, all of them wearing black biker vests that displayed a gold helmet in the military style of ancient Greece. Across from them, a cluster of Native American women swayed in prayer, their hands pressed to their hearts, their eyes shut tight. Between them stood a line of men holding rifles. Becca glanced at Reno; the guards and praying women – what was going on? But Reno's eyes had drifted to a wooden platform high above the crowd. There stood a man imposing and still as a cement block. Gray hair cascaded from his cheeks and chin, and his large blue eyes glowed like neon. He wore a gray robe, like a monk's, that reached his feet. So this was Proudfoot, the fabled CO.

The look he gave to Reno was inscrutable, but the one he turned on Becca was clear enough. It said, *Welcome, but you really shouldn't be here. Perhaps I'll have the nice men with the guns show you out.*

And maybe he would have, if it weren't for the bikers approaching the CO from behind. The men were soaking, their legs muddy. At once Becca saw that her father was in pain; his meaty face was flushed red. His ponytail hung down his back like wet rope. She ran toward him, but halfway across the arena, hands caught her. Almost robotically, the guards separated into three groups. One pushed the Native American women back, one kept the bikers at bay, and the final coterie pointed their weapons at her.

"Oh, let her go," the CO said and waved his hand dismissively, as though he considered Becca nothing more than a nuisance. The guard holding her released his grip, and she ran to her father.

"Go back to Reno," King huffed. He was shivering in the sopping clothes. Becca thought of his lumbering body swimming the river, his cheeks puffing as he struggled to keep the water out of his mouth. She thought about his heart beating so much harder than it was used to. She felt a swell of anger toward Proudfoot.

"Friends and comrades!" the CO announced with a tooth-filled grin. "Welcome to Kleos. You have come a long way to be here. You have crossed the killing fields, humped through the jungles, weathered the assault of unending slurs. You have wandered through alleyways strewn with needles and broken glass, battled bureaucracies, swallowed too many pills. You have struggled through marriages with women who never knew you—and who could never know you. You have disappointed friends and family, abandoned children and been abandoned by them. And now you have arrived here to compete for the heart of Durga. After all of these trials, you have come to find your peace."

The men were rapt. The only sound was the faint mumbling of the women in their prayer. Even King, who was clearly hurting, kept his eyes locked on the CO. And then, all of a sudden, the CO threw off his robe. His belly loomed over the crowd like a moon, bald and pale. It was bisected by a Milky Way of shiny skin—the scar. The lesion was grotesque, but Becca was unable to look away. A cry rose up from the men. Except for King. He'd been reduced to a wide-eyed child.

One by one, the CO called out to each man, addressing him by his name and military rank. "Do you agree of your own free will to compete for Durga's heart, accepting the physical and spiritual sacrifices therein?" Becca watched each one step forward and give his assent. Meanwhile, her father wasn't doing well. His breathing was labored, and the color had drained from his face.

Suddenly, his legs buckled and he collapsed.

"Dad!" Becca screamed and dropped to her knees. The CO halted his roll call and shouted for medics. Two of the guards rushed over, joined by Reno and Elaine. Elaine was also soaking. Her shirt clung to her breasts, and mascara ran down her face.

"A hospital!" Becca pleaded.

Reno shook his head. "Ain't no hospital anywhere close."

"I'm fine!" King gasped. "Just the angina."

"His nitroglycerin pills," Becca cried. "Check his pockets." But the pills must have been in his saddlebags. Across the river.

"He's in no shape to compete," Reno said.

"No!" King coughed. "I have to."

"And have a heart attack?" Becca demanded.

"I have to compete! I have to!" King craned his neck toward the platform. Everyone did. And Becca realized something: the CO could prevent her father from competing. With one word, he could send King home.

"He's sick." Becca stood up. "Just look at him!"

"It's my business," King said, wheezing, still on the ground. "You don't know. You're not even supposed to be here. Tell her! Elaine, tell her!"

"Honey . . ." Elaine reached for Becca's arm, but she jerked away. Everyone looked up to the CO, awaiting his verdict.

"I'm sorry, King," the CO said finally. "I can't allow it. Not in your condition."

King exploded. "You can't take this away from me. You won't, you son of a bitch!" The exertion caused him to double over again but then he struggled to sit up. His face prickled with sweat. "I've waited too long for this chance," he cried. "I deserve this chance!"

"I'll compete for him!" The familiar voice made Becca's heart slam into her spine. "Let me take his place," the voice said. "If I win Durga's heart, he can have it."

Becca turned. Surely she was imagining this – Ben, standing not ten feet away.

"Let me do this for you, Chicken. Please."

"Ben." She did not recognize the sound of her voice speaking his name. She did not understand what was happening. She heard herself chant: "Momentum, rhythm, stride." Only she wasn't running anymore. Her feet were fused to the earth.

"All right," the CO said. He looked intrigued – almost delighted – by the sudden turn of events. "But King must be present to complete the final challenge, provided Sergeant Thompson makes it that far."

Reno looked at Becca and his expression indicated that things were spinning wildly out of control. "Wait!" she yelled. "Ben!" But nobody was listening.

"Do you, Sergeant Benjamin Thompson, agree of your own free will to compete for Durga's heart, accepting the physical and spiritual sacrifices therein?"

"I do," Ben said.

"No!" Becca shook her head madly. "Ben, no."

"Specialist King Keller, do you agree to let this man take your place?"

King did not hesitate. "I do," he said.

"Very well. Arne, take King to the infirmary."

"Ben!" Becca cried again. But the CO's voice boomed through the clearing. "There will be no further conversing with civilians." One of the guards slung King's arm around his own shoulder and walked him into the trees. The others led the vets in the opposite direction. Just as Ben was about to leave the arena, he turned. At the wedding they had stood apart and faced each other in just this way. "Ben, no." Becca shook her head, tears budding in her eyes. But the guards prodded him with their guns and he turned away.

A rough hand touched her shoulder, startling her. It was Reno. "Listen to me," he said. "I'm going with them. I'll keep an eye on your boy. Okay?"

Becca nodded dumbly, not really understanding.

"Keep your wits about you. We'll figure this out." Then he jogged off after the group.

The Native American women began to file out in an orderly fashion, like congregants exiting church pews. And that's when Becca saw the face, white like a patch of sun-faded stone in a brown canyon wall. Her mother.

28

"YOU'RE NOT GOING to give your mother a hug?" Jeanine said.

Becca couldn't move. The shock of seeing Ben had not yet worn off, and now here was her mother, who was supposed to be a few hundred miles to the northeast gardening organic vegetables in the name of Jesus.

"Are you a hunk of rock?" Jeanine asked. Becca put her arms around her mother, but the older woman's hands on her were feathery and noncommittal. "What in God's name are you doing here?" She pulled away from her daughter.

Becca was saved from having to explain herself by Elaine, who emerged from the departing crowd. The middle-aged women eyed each other, one buxom, one lean, and both equally guarded. The air was charged, crackling, as if two opposing forces were about to collide.

"So you're Jeanine," Elaine said with none of her typical good nature. Her mouth was cinched tight.

"Who are you?" Jeanine looked Elaine up and down with unchristian disdain.

Elaine seemed shocked. She and Becca exchanged glances. "That's Elaine, Dad's girlfriend," Becca said.

"Girlfriend?" Jeanine snickered. She pulled a pack of cigarettes from her dress pocket, poorly affecting nonchalance.

"Of five years," Elaine said, smiling.

As her mother lit up, Becca did the math. Five years meant that King had taken up with Elaine shortly after her mother had kicked him out. Jeanine must have realized the same thing just then, because a small fissure of hurt cracked open in her face.

"So that was Ben," Elaine said, her eyes softening. "He's handsome."

"I suppose you're in support of all this," Jeanine said to Elaine, picking up on a conversation they hadn't been having.

"I'm in support of King finding peace of mind," Elaine said. "However he needs to."

"Despite it being a huge mistake."

"You're here to bring him to Jesus, is that right?" Elaine shook her head. "King said you might show up and try to save some souls."

"My sisters and I came here to save him, it's true," Jeanine said. "But that has nothing to do with Jesus."

"Says the missionary."

"I don't need to explain myself to you. I know my own purpose."

Maybe it was because Becca had not seen her mother in a long while, but suddenly she recognized herself in Jeanine's stance, heard her own voice in her mother's combative tone.

How much Jeanine had taught her, Becca realized now. How unfortunately alike they were.

"I know I never cared much for your husband, Becca—"

"You've never even met him!"

"But," Jeanine went on, ignoring her daughter's protest, "at least he had the selflessness to take King's place." And then

Becca heard her mother murmur something that sounded like *Better your man than mine.* But that didn't seem right.

"You heard the CO," Elaine said to Jeanine. "King has to complete the final test on his own. He's going to participate and he's going to win."

"We'll see about that." Jeanine threw her half-smoked cigarette on the ground and crushed it with her shoe.

King was the infirmary's only occupant. Laid out on one of the narrow beds, he looked like a giant in a child's room. Jeanine sat beside him in a wooden chair, hunched over, her face close to his. Becca stood alone in the doorway, failing to make sense of the scene before her. Jeanine had been so relieved to get rid of King all those years ago. So why was she now smoothing his blanket and running her fingers across his forehead? What was she doing here, watching over him?

Over the years, Becca had periodically asked her mother about King's leaving. What had finally caused the breakup?

It's not about any single thing that happened, Jeanine would say. *It's about who your father is and what he is—and is not—willing to do for us. It's about where his allegiances lie.*

Now that Reno had filled in many of the gaps in Becca's parents' history, the question of allegiance took on new meaning. Perhaps the trouble between her mother and father was more about this place than the army. But Jeanine had known that King would run straight to Kleos when the marriage fell apart. So why, all these years later, was she suddenly trying to pull King back out?

29

ABOUT A QUARTER of the men at Kleos had arrived with King and were still wet from their swim across the river. The rest had been at the compound for some time and obviously considered themselves superior. Ben, meanwhile, was the FNG, the Fucking New Guy, the kid who showed up green to the infantry unit and was hated because he didn't know how not to get them all killed. He was no better than the hapless Willy Owen from the CO's story. Not even Reno, who'd somehow latched onto the mass of them like a parasite, was looked at with such obvious disdain.

But none of this mattered. In Iraq, Ben had fought for his men. Every single day, he'd risked his life for them and them alone. When King collapsed, Ben realized that he'd been given new orders. He would do for Becca—for their future—exactly what he'd done for his soldiers. This was his pledge to her.

As the hoplites led the vets through Kleos, Ben evaluated the CO's guard force. They were all like Arne: old and beaten. Their hair was gray and their stomachs were soft, but they had real weapons and they'd been trained to use them.

After giving the competitors new clothes, the hoplites led the men toward the forest at the base of the great mesa. The group passed a couple of camouflaged guardhouses and headed along a dirt path into the gloom. It was hotter now, as though the cottonwoods' canopy had trapped the heat. Long mess tables were set up beneath tarps. Something in the air smelled delicious, but all the hoplites gave them were bowls of steaming broth and slices of tough, tasteless bread.

Reno slid in beside Ben, so he shifted over, unhappily. He was eager to take a swing at the guy, but clearly this wasn't the right time. One of the men who'd come with King's group landed heavily on the bench across the table. He was tall with overly long arms, pockmarked skin, and cheekbones so high and sharp they looked capable of drawing blood.

"Why are you looking at me like that?" the man demanded of Ben.

"Like what?"

"Like I'm pissing you off."

Ben wasn't sure whether this guy was picking a fight or merely responding to Ben's eyes. They frowned at the corners, made people think he was angry even when he wasn't. "I don't have a problem with you," Ben said.

"Yeah, you do," the man said.

"Bull, for Christ's sake," Reno hissed. "Just drink your soup."

"I want to know how some stranger can just show up all of a sudden and take King's place."

"You're just pissy 'cause the kid's younger than you are and in better shape," Reno said. "You thought you were a sure thing and now you're not."

"This 'kid,' as you call him, has done some pretty awful things." Bull held his eyes on Ben's face. Ben let him look.

"Sergeant Thompson has been on this earth half as long as you and a third as long as me," Reno said. "He hasn't had the time to rack up enough bad behavior to come within shouting distance of either one of us."

"Why the hell are you defending him?" Bull spat. Frankly, Ben wondered the same thing.

"Everybody, just drink your soup." Reno scowled.

Ben lifted his bowl to his lips. He dipped some bread into the watery liquid. It tasted okay. It just wasn't substantial. At least the hoplites had given him a decent breakfast: fresh eggs and bacon from Kleos's animals, strong coffee.

After lunch the hoplites led the men into a large hogan deeper in the woods.

The single room was dim, lit by a wood-burning stove, and the walls were lined with a kind of white canvas. A network of lights and speakers hung overhead. The CO entered and arranged himself yogi-like on a pile of blankets. The men sat cross-legged on the ground before him, like schoolchildren.

"From this moment, the competition officially begins," the CO said. His resonant voice seemed to emanate from everywhere. "Twenty-four hours from now, one of you will be selected to carry on Durga's legacy. You will take my place as leader of Kleos and become the new CO. This is both a privilege and a burden. And it is the reason we compete. You must have enough strength to shoulder the responsibility."

The CO unfolded his heavy body and stood up. Ben glanced to his left and right. All eyes were straight ahead.

"To prove that you are fully committed, you must be bound irrevocably to the service of Durga. Your willingness to do this is your first test."

The CO walked to the wood-burning stove and pulled out a metal poker. The tip was the size of a child's fist and had been fashioned into the shape of a Greek military helmet. Ben deflated. So these were the trials the CO had in store? Ben thought about how King had begged the CO for this opportunity to be branded with a hot iron.

"Stand," the CO commanded, "and remove your shirts."

Ben's entire body tensed, but he could hardly think about himself, because the branding had begun. The men stuffed their T-shirts into their mouths and tried to stifle their cries. Their faces contorted. A few of the older vets fainted. A few ran from the hogan before it was too late. The poker approached.

"She doesn't want you to do this," Reno hissed between his teeth. "Drop out, for Christ's sake."

"You won't get me disqualified," Ben hissed back, certain that Reno wanted him kicked out.

"We can get out of here," Reno said with new urgency.

We? Ben thought. But then he remembered his black eye and Reno dumping him on the roadside. "I don't trust you."

"Like husband, like wife," Reno said and shook his head. But before either one of them could say more, the CO arrived. He held the poker like a monarch's staff. The tip was so hot, it glowed white.

"This pain is for all the men you failed to save," the CO intoned. "For all the brothers you disappointed. We receive our pain together, because only we know what it feels like to have entered the crucible of war and returned."

"Thank God you did it too," Reno said, forcing joviality into his voice. "Otherwise I'd feel like a sucker."

The CO looked down at his own chest, which bore a similar brand, long healed. He nodded, completely missing Reno's sarcasm. "This marks us forever as separate. No one outside understands what you have been through, Reno. Hear the words of Achilles: 'My heart bids me shun the society of men.'" And then the CO pushed the iron into Reno's chest. Tears poured out of Reno's eyes and his face contorted, but he did not cry out.

"Say it!" the CO commanded.

Reno struggled to speak against the pain. "'My heart . . . bids me . . . shun . . .'"

A loud voice in Ben's head agreed with Reno: This *was* crazy. This was wrong. But Ben silenced the voice. It was his turn.

More men failed the CO's first test. Some fought the pronouncement of their defeat, and once or twice a Taser was used to subdue them. There was something brutal about the Tasers. They degraded the men, turning them into soulless, sniveling creatures.

Ben sat on the hogan floor with the other victors, breathing through his pain. On two tours in Iraq, he'd received no substantial injuries. Nothing worse than sunburn, blisters, and some damaged olfactory nerves. He had no right to complain about this.

"Who among you burns with pain?" the CO asked.

"Not I!" Bull shouted. He staggered to his feet. "Not I, sir."

"Who here burns with pain?" the CO repeated.

"Not I!" Ben jumped to his feet. If Bull was going to be his main competition, it seemed advantageous to follow the man's lead. But no sooner had Ben spoken than hoplites seized the both of them and dragged them to the CO.

"Not you?" the CO asked, breathing heavily into their faces.

"Not I, sir," Bull said, though Ben held back. If they'd given the correct answer the first time, the CO wouldn't keep asking. It seemed that Bull had forgotten the unwritten rules of facing a drill sergeant.

"Not you?" the CO spat at Bull. "'When Hector saw great-hearted Patroclus fall back after being wounded with sharp bronze, he went down through the ranks, up close, and struck him with a spear-thrust to the belly, drove the point straight through . . . Now vultures will devour you here, poor wretch'!" The CO made a stabbing motion into the air that caused both Ben and Bull to flinch. The CO smiled. "You feel no pain?" he said, still directing his ire toward Bull. "How about you, Sergeant Thompson?"

"I feel pain, sir." He did not understand why this was the correct answer, only that it was.

The CO nodded. "You lie to me and to yourself," he said to Bull. "*All* you feel is pain. And if you ever hope to achieve catharsis, you must give yourself over to it. Do you understand?"

Bull nodded vigorously.

"Do you understand, Sergeant Thompson?"

"Yes, sir." Ben nodded and the movement made him horribly dizzy. He squeezed his eyes shut, willing himself not to faint. His chest burned. It throbbed. He felt pain, all right.

"You are blind, all of you," said the CO. "But within the day, every single one of you will be made to see."

30

BECCA LEFT HER mother at the infirmary and began to explore Kleos. She peeked inside the hogans and found the most basic of living quarters. She used one of the composting toilets. Then she visited the animal pens. She bypassed the cows and pigs and stood for a while at the chicken coop watching the birds pecking around and the roosting poles crowded with hens. Ben's uncle in Kentucky kept chickens, and she and Ben sometimes drove over for fresh eggs. On their first visit, the animals had flocked around Becca's ankles like she was one of their own. They were like dogs or cats, the way they rubbed their plump bodies against her legs. Had anyone ever known chickens to act this way? "Did you rub your jeans with feed?" Ben joked. Unfamiliar with the ways of livestock, Becca was afraid the birds would start pecking her, so she stood there, paralyzed, in the center of the chicken swarm as Ben laughed and laughed. From that moment on, Becca was his chicken. *I love you, Chicken. Don't worry, Chicken. What's the matter, Chicken? Let me compete for your father, Chicken.*

Becca left the birds and wandered toward the camp's northern edge. Then she stopped, her mouth open wide. Before her, a massive graveyard of wooden crosses stretched beneath the hot sun like a field of desiccated crops. Could these crosses actually mark bodies? And whose bodies? But the crosses were so close together. Maybe they marked remains? King said there were people who searched the jungles for remains to make sure the men missing and killed in action — the MIAs and KIAs — received proper burials. Even a strand of hair deserved a burial, he said. But would those men have ended up here?

She turned from the graveyard and walked toward the mesa on Kleos's eastern boundary. A broad stretch of matted grass tapered off around a forest of cottonwoods. No sounds came from the woods, although, as she approached, a guard materialized. Only then did she pick out the guard stations, camouflaged among the trees. He shouted at her to stop. She resisted the urge to raise her hands above her head.

"I'm just taking a walk," she said.

"You'd best get back to the guest quarters," the guard said.

"Sure." Becca turned around. She felt his eyes on her. Whatever was happening, she thought, was happening in those woods. Whatever it was, it could not be good.

31

FROM THE HOGAN, the CO led the men deeper into the woods and stopped in a small clearing. "'They carried woodcutting axes and stout ropes, and the mules went before them. Far they traveled, uphill, downhill, sideways and aslant, until they reached the shoulder of Mount Ida of the many springs,'" the CO recited. "'And there they set in haste to felling towering oaks with their long-pointed bronze. With a great crash the trees came down. These the Achaeans split and tied behind the mules, which measured the earth with their feet in striving through dense brush to reach the plain. All the woodcutters carried logs . . . and cast them down in a row upon the shore, where Achilles planned a great funeral mound for Patroclus and himself.'"

When the CO fell silent, Arne stood before the group. "Form teams of two and then chop up the trunks according to these specifications." The hoplites held up long logs. "You will not stop for any reason."

"You're with me," Reno said to Ben and picked up the saw without giving him the chance to argue.

The implements were long and heavy, with wooden handles on each end. Ben and Reno dragged the metal teeth across the tree trunk; it took upward of an hour to take even a small bite out of the wood. The wound in Ben's chest throbbed, then burned, then grew numb, then throbbed again. He imagined that the alternating feelings of numbness and pain would never end. He felt like that man who pushed the boulder up the hill each day only to have it roll back down at night. Or did the man never reach the hilltop in the first place? Ben couldn't remember. But he understood the moral: how the false promise of healing made the pain that much worse.

For hours, the woods echoed with the sound of saws. The CO had said nothing about a time limit or what quantity of lumber he expected, but the men implicitly understood that they were vying for something. He and Reno kept on until their tree fell. Theirs was the second to go, behind Bull and his partner's. As soon as the trunk was down, they took up axes. The sounds gradually shifted from sawing to chopping. The older, frailer men were lagging. A few had already dropped their saws and been escorted away.

One old man sat on a log; he looked faint.

"You're out," one of the guards said. "Go to the truck."

"I just need to rest a moment," the man said, panting. "I'm going right back to work." He stood up.

"You're finished."

"Please," the man begged.

"Truck," the guard said. "Now." He held out the Taser, and the man slunk away.

"That's not fair!" his partner said. "I can't do this by myself."

"Then give up," said the guard.

At this comment, the man charged, but he didn't get far before a Taser hit him in the chest. The man convulsed and fell. Two hoplites picked him up and laid him in a truck like he was a piece of lumber. Ben kept chopping.

32

AFTER HER RUN-IN with the guard, Becca found the guest quarters. The Indian women, along with Jeanine, sat in a circle of folding metal chairs. Their eyes were closed and their bodies swayed back and forth like seaweed in a current.

"Lord Jesus, protect these men from their unbelief!" chanted a heavyset woman with black hair that fell nearly to the floor.

"Lord Jesus, protect these men from their unbelief!" the others repeated.

"Save them from these pagan gods and devil spirits!"

"Save them from these pagan gods and devil spirits!"

"Protect King in his illness. Guard his soul from despair!"

"Protect King in his illness. Guard his soul from despair!"

"Oh Lord Jesus!"

"Oh Lord Jesus!"

Becca had never seen praying quite like this. She half expected somebody to speak in tongues. No one did, but their ranks grew more frenzied, all of them squeezing one another's hands so tightly, their knuckles turned white. Their bodies moved faster, more erratically.

"Please, Lord Jesus!"

"Please, Lord Jesus!"

It seemed to Becca that she wasn't watching twelve women but a single organism, all of their throats straining as a single voice. When Jeanine jumped from her chair quite suddenly, the circle shuddered in response to its severed limb. The two empty hands on either side fluttered and flailed violently, the ten fingers like sinews.

Jeanine crouched on her knees, her hands clasped in what struck Becca as a parody of prayer. She shook them at the ceiling, like she was calling on God to knock His heavenly fist through the roof. She grabbed her dress and twisted it as her body writhed. Watching her mother's contortions made Becca feel a little sick. How could Jeanine, so stalwart and disciplined, appear so out of control? What would drive her to this?

Becca couldn't think, nor could she bear to watch, so she ran from the guest quarters and made her way to the edge of Kleos. At the graveyard, she looked around frantically and then, not knowing where else to go, ran straight through the tangle of crosses. Her legs knocked the posts, but she did not stop. She ran toward the rocky slope that stood between the graveyard and the ghost towns. She stopped at the foot of the rise, panting. The sound of her blood whooshed in her ears. She turned to the north and looked up at the great mesa. After all these years, could her mother still be in love with her father? It seemed impossible.

"Hey!"

Becca whirled around to see a woman approaching, brown-skinned like the Indians but dressed more in Becca's own style, in faded jeans and a T-shirt. Beside her walked an oversize ball of tinfoil with a head and legs.

"You're Becca," the woman said. She had a broad forehead and large, dark eyes. A guarded face. Not mean, but not welcoming either. "I saw you run out this way," she continued. She looked down at the ball of tinfoil. "This is Jacob. I'm Lucy. Are you all right?"

"I'm fine." But Becca did not feel fine and she suspected that she did not look fine either.

"You're Ben's wife," Lucy said. "He brought us out here."

Becca looked at the woman and child, incredulous. Ben had picked up a couple of strangers?

"We sold him frybread!" the boy said gleefully, as though this clarified everything.

"Ben went up to Hands of God to find your mother," Lucy explained. "He found us instead. And now we're all here."

"Ben saved my life!" the boy exclaimed.

"I'm sorry?" Becca was confused and feeling frantic.

"My nephew was dumb enough to think he could swim that river over there." Lucy nodded at the rise. "Ben dove right in. Didn't hesitate for a second." She tousled the boy's hair roughly. "Though I will tell you, your husband's got the worst mood swings I've ever seen. Worse than when my grandma went off her Prozac. And she was loony tunes . . ." Lucy pointed her finger at her temple and twirled it around. After a moment, her face fell. "Hey," she said. "I was just trying to lighten things up. I didn't mean to make fun."

Becca wiped at the wetness on her cheeks. She turned away, hiding her face. But maybe it was funny—to call Ben's problem "mood swings." To liken him to somebody's batty relative. Maybe she needed to laugh at all of this, just a little.

"He bought me a milk shake," Jacob said. "He took me to the ball pit at Sonic."

"He did?" Somehow, these details seemed even more extraordinary to her than what Lucy had said about the river.

Jacob nodded, his head rocking exaggeratedly up and down, like it was about to roll right off his neck. He was so earnest

— he seemed so enamored of Ben — that Becca couldn't help but smile through her tears. And soon enough she was laughing. She laughed at the absurdity of Ben and King and Jeanine and herself all showing up here at the same time. She laughed at her fucked-up life, the kind of life she'd struggled so hard to avoid. She laughed and cried, because none of this was very funny and because she had no control over any of it.

"You okay now?" Lucy asked when Becca had calmed some. Becca nodded. "Good. Now, let's get down to work." She told Becca that while Ben was swimming after Jacob, she'd been picked up by one of the guards and blindfolded. She'd been terrified, but when the car stopped and the guard let her free, Lucy realized that she was inside Kleos. She told Becca about how one of the guards had Tased Ben for trying to talk to Jeanine. Then she put her hands over Jacob's ears. He squirmed, but she didn't let go. "My sister says the men here have a ritual. They build these huge pyres in the desert." She dropped her voice to a whisper. "They're burning people out there." She looked at the sky as though she expected a shadow to descend. "I want to get out of here," she said, finally releasing Jacob. "But not without his mother."

The wind had blown the tears dry on Becca's face and now her skin was tight with salt and dust. She shivered despite the heat. Two different sources had now told her about fires in the desert — about burning. This very morning, there'd been the pile of smoldering bones.

"We're going to help you," Lucy said, squeezing Becca's shoulder. "We'll help you get Ben and then we'll all get out of here. We've got a big black beast of a car. It's parked over the rise."

The Death Star! Becca swallowed hard. "And my dad," she said. "I can't leave without my dad."

Lucy stroked Jacob's dark head with such tenderness that

Becca thought, *Why aren't you his mother? You should be his mother.* She thought about how her own mother had selfishly dragged all these women out here, putting them in harm's way. And then she thought of Ben, who'd come out here following *her.* The moment she ran from Dry Hills, she might as well have written a summons to him across the sky. He'd hurt her too badly and loved her too much to stay put.

33

LUCY AND BECCA wanted to hurry back to Kleos, but Jacob lingered among the graves like a dog sniffing out a hidden prize. Soon enough, he brought the women a leather pouch the size and shape of an envelope. "Let me see that." Lucy took the object and extracted from it a dirty piece of paper.

September 15, 1991

Dear Harvey,

To be honest, it never would have occurred to me to write you a letter, but that's one of the things we do here. Every week, we write to somebody who didn't make it back, and we bury the letter in a kind of grave with a cross. Letters come from the outside too. Bags of them, like it's almost Christmas and we're at the North Pole. People send dog tags and photographs. Sometimes money. I don't know how the CO convinced anybody to send these letters here. I often wonder where the senders think their letters are going. But they come by the bagful and the CO has us read them and then bury them too. Personally, I think there're plenty of sad stories in my head; I don't need to read other people's. But the CO says it's good for us. He says he's written letters too, that his were the first to be buried in this earth. He says all of these stories must be read and then put to rest. He says we — and no one else — must be the ones to do it.

You've never seen anything quite like the graveyard of letters, Harvey, and it grows larger by the week. Sometimes, I think it'll fill up the entire desert.

I told the CO about you, Harvey, and that's why I'm writing. Before I met the CO, nobody knew about you, but he's got this way of bringing things out. We have private sessions with him — he calls them Purgings. Even when I don't want to talk, I end up talking. And somehow, I do feel better. At least some of the time.

Your friend,
Roger

Lucy folded up the letter and put it back in the leather envelope. "Return this to where you found it," she said sternly. "And leave the others alone. This is not our place."

Back at the camp, in the infirmary, Becca found King sitting up in his cot and Jeanine in the corner of the room, her arms folded across her chest. Clearly, Becca had walked into a standoff. "How are you feeling, Dad?" she asked.

"Fine." The word dropped with a thud. Becca had hoped that some sympathy and deference might ease her father into communication, but clearly it did not.

"What's going on with you guys?" she asked. She kept her voice gentle, her expression open, as though to say, *You can tell me. I won't judge.* But neither of her parents spoke. They wouldn't even look at her. They wanted her to leave, that was obvious. But Becca had come too far and endured too much to walk away. She could feel a fireball gather strength in her stomach and she had no desire to hold it back. "What the *fuck?*" she demanded.

King looked taken aback. Jeanine, who was not taken aback by much, stiffened.

"I'm here. You can't keep pretending that I don't exist. It's obvious I should never have expected anything from you. But I don't know . . ." Becca shook her head and opened her palms as though truly surprised by how empty they were. "Aren't parents supposed to love their kids unconditionally? Was I so naive, so stupid, to want that? To think my parents might give me the one thing in life that's totally free?"

Jeanine slowly shook her head. "Ungrateful child." Becca opened her mouth to protest, but her mother said, "I sent away the man I loved because it was my responsibility—as your *mother*—to give you a normal life. I mean, Jesus, if it wasn't King's raging and wrestling, it was those ridiculous, cultish stories about Durga." Her mother sucked in a breath. "You were absorbing every part of that man. If you went on being his daughter, do you really think you'd be in college right now? Would you ever have stopped fighting off the whole goddamned world? I sacrificed my marriage for you, child, so don't you dare lecture me on love."

Becca gaped. She'd never once considered that Jeanine's critical and distant mothering was born from resentment. Jeanine was probably right—by sending King away, she'd changed the entire trajectory of Becca's life. Or maybe her mother had succeeded only in sending her on a brief detour. Because now, hadn't Becca ended up exactly where she'd started? Worse off, even?

She could still feel Ben's hands on her, beating her awake. Disoriented from sleep, she'd thrashed and screamed, tried to push him away, but he'd only doubled his efforts. As his strength waned, she'd nearly submitted, then decided to play dead until he stopped. She finally managed to roll away from him and onto the floor. By the time she stood up, he'd left the bedroom. She discovered him in the next room, slamming the fiddle against the shelf.

"Maybe you made the wrong sacrifice, Mom," she fumed. "And maybe *you,*" Becca said, turning to King, "shouldn't have been so quick to run away when she showed you the exit."

Becca knew her parents thought they'd done the right thing, and maybe they couldn't have predicted the fallout—Jeanine coming to resent her daughter, King seeking his salvation out here instead of with his family. But it made her so angry to think that they'd just given up on each other and on her.

Jeanine and King looked at each other like they were both waiting for the other one to claim responsibility for the insolent creature accosting them. Becca had never yelled at them both like this. But that was mostly because she'd never had the chance. They hadn't all been in the same room together in six years.

"Your mother did the right thing," King said quietly. "I wasn't fit to be a father. You know that. And look at you now. The first Keller to go to college. A running star! See how you've turned out?"

"You're right, Dad," she said. "But let's show Mom, because she hasn't seen it yet. Here's how I've turned out." Becca pulled up her shirt. The bruises were now greenish yellow, like muddy grass stains. She stared at Jeanine, watching the shock register on her mother's face. It was grief, the purest form of sorrow. King had already gotten a look at his daughter's bruises, but he seemed to be seeing this all for the first time. He hung his head.

It was cruel, what she'd just done, and childish. But Becca felt a numb sense of justice when she left her parents in their stunned silence and walked out of the infirmary. King was right. Life with him *was* awful. But the fact that her parents had been in contact for so long, lying to her, living half their lives behind her back, even sneaking around at her own wedding, made her feel insignificant to the point of worthless. She was baggage to them, dead weight.

Becca stood outside the infirmary, not knowing where to go. It had grown dark. And now a flatbed truck headed her way. A bunch of men sat in the back, hunched over their knees. The losers, Becca realized, and she strained to see whether they were injured. Whether Ben was among them. Mostly, they looked exhausted. And, of course, Ben was not there.

34

THE MEN PILED most of the chopped wood on the truck beds and then walked toward the mesa in a single-file line, each person dragging a log behind him. They followed the rock-face for a short time before turning eastward and heading out of the trees. In front and behind them, the hoplites kept watch. Ben found this procession — the heat, and sand, and steady march — all too familiar, and he looked at the night sky to try to remove himself. What was Becca doing? He longed to be with her. His need felt as large and vast as the desert.

The hoplites stopped the men in the middle of nowhere. Here were the trucks, piled high with wood, and a Wrangler Jeep in which the CO stood, waiting.

"Achilles decided funeral games would be held for Patroclus," he bellowed. "And so the men entered the ring, 'and grasped each other with their mighty arms . . . The sweat streamed down while many a blood-red, swollen bruise appeared on their ribs and shoulders. And they were eager for victory.' " The CO surveyed the men. Their number had shrunk to just under forty.

The hoplites split the men into teams, and a series of competitions began. There were races, and wrestling matches, and javelin contests. Winners and losers were sorted and paired and pitted against one another. Ben felt uncomfortable watching these old men fight, watching the way they grunted under the strain, how sweat poured down their faces, how their bellies heaved.

Left and right, men were relegated to the sidelines. At first, Ben assumed these losers had been cut from the competition, but sometimes the CO would send a defeated man back into the ring. Sometimes he had the hoplites lead winners into the trucks. When the first truck was full, it headed back to camp. The remaining men paused to watch, their faces glowing in the headlights with vindication and relief.

"But maybe they're the ones advancing," somebody said, and Ben felt the group deflate. He didn't want to think about the other men. He needed to win this thing, needed to be the last one, so that he could help King reach the final challenge, whatever it was. Then he needed to get Becca into the Death Star and get them home.

Ben was called to wrestle Reno.

"This isn't the way to get her back," Reno said when they stood face to face. The whistle blew. Reno was more agile than Ben had expected, his movements slippery, but when Ben did manage to get a hold of him, it was easy to pin Reno to the ground. Reno smiled up at him, and Ben wondered if he'd lost on purpose. Then Reno winced. Ben had his elbow pressed on the poker burn. He could have Reno kicked out right now. He needed only press a little harder, dig his elbow in deeper. But for some reason, he couldn't. He let up slightly.

"I promised her I'd help you," Reno said, wheezing. The whistle blew and two hoplites yanked them apart.

Ben hoped Reno's loss meant that he'd be taken away in the truck, but that didn't happen. Instead, the hoplites lined up the remaining twelve contenders and began patrolling the ranks, drill sergeant–style. When they'd reached the far end of the line, Bull nudged Ben. "Your girl spent the night with Reno," he said through clenched teeth. "You know that, right?"

It took a massive amount of self-control for Ben not to grab Bull by the shoulders, but he couldn't keep from turning to look at him.

"Eyes ahead!" snarled one of the hoplites, prodding Ben with the Taser.

"You don't believe me?" Bull whispered. "They danced all night, pressed up close, like. It's disgusting. Reno and King're the same age."

Reno was at the end of the line and Ben couldn't get a good look at his face without moving. It couldn't be true. Bull was messing with him. But who knew what had happened on the road? Becca was angry and hurt. She might have done something to try to hurt him back. He shook his head as though to physically shake off his doubt. It was hard. So goddamned hard. He wanted to throttle Bull, and Reno, and the CO. He was succumbing to the stress of things, to the unreality, the uncertainty, the exhaustion. It was so much like the war.

That realization snapped Ben back to attention. The CO knew that every vet here was vulnerable to these feelings. He was using this knowledge to manipulate them. It was as brilliant as it was terrifying.

Two hoplites unrolled a set of building plans on the hood of one of the flatbeds. The CO stood up in the open Jeep and cleared his throat. "Build it!" he pronounced.

The men looked at the CO dumbly, awaiting further instructions.

"I said, build it!"

Ben jumped into action. The CO was looking for a leader and that's what Ben would be. He proposed a plan to divide up the work. The men shifted, obviously irritated by Ben's sudden decisiveness. But the CO was still watching, and under his gaze, Ben knew, the men could not protest. Their reflexes hadn't been quick enough; they'd lost this part of the challenge and the most they could do now was prove themselves to be strong, efficient workers.

The teams followed the plans until a coffin-shaped structure began to rise from the ground. Soon it was waist-high, then chest-high. The hoplites pulled ladders from the trucks, and the men kept on building. All the while, the CO watched. It was too dark to make out his face, but his shadowed figure was as large and imposing as a mountain. All of this was part of the CO's plan, Ben kept thinking. But what that plan was – what they were building for him – he couldn't begin to know.

35

BECCA HAD MADE up her mind to find Ben on her own. She needed a better view of those woods, so she headed back through the graveyard and up the ridge. It was steep and she spent half an hour navigating dense thistle bushes and avoiding shaky rocks. Her hands were covered in scrapes and dust by the time she reached the top, and she turned her stinging palms to the wind for relief. Kleos was spread out below in the floodlights' glare. The woods where the guard had stopped her a few hours before were dark. The ghost town sagged on the opposite slope, as though at any moment the whole hillside and everything on it would slide into the river and be swept away.

Becca squinted across the water, trying to make out the Death Star, but it was too dark. Her instincts urged her to run: skid down the ridge, swim the river, jump into her car, and be gone. She thought of how the driver's seat had molded to her body. She felt her foot against the gas, the car's heavy motor at her command. It would be so easy. To run. Right now. Finish this evacuation before things got worse. Except Ben had her keys.

She looked back the way she'd come. It was always a mistake, looking back. Races were won by going forward.

Something scraped in the brush. Some desert rodent—or

maybe a snake? Becca had not considered the possibility of snakes. She'd been so worried about tripping over the flora that she hadn't even considered the fauna. A dozen yards below her, a weak spot of light punctured the darkness. Had one of the guards followed her? Was a Taser headed her way, or, worse, a rifle? Heart throbbing, she crouched down and tried to be still. The light snapped off, and now the scraping sound grew louder. And then, suddenly, a silvery trunk sprouted before her, like a tree growing in time-lapse film.

"Jesus, Jacob!" Becca stood up and picked her way toward the boy. "Does Lucy know where you are?"

"She thinks I'm with Mom."

"And your mom?"

"She thinks I'm with Lucy."

"Jesus," she repeated. "So you're following me for fun?"

"No. I found them," he said. "Your friends." His lips spread into a triumphant smile. His eyes flashed silver, just like his ridiculous jacket.

"Do you ever take that thing off?" she asked and Jacob shook his head. He looked at her imploringly. "All right," she said with a final glance at the ghost town. "Show me the way."

Halfway back to Kleos, Jacob turned left and headed to the woods. They'd been moving quickly, but now Jacob slowed. Soon he stopped walking entirely.

"What's the matter?" Becca asked. He did not answer, and when she repeated the question, his face was tight with fear. At once she understood. The child hadn't found some secret route through the woods. He was leading them blind.

"I wanted to help you," he murmured, hunching into the protective shell of his jacket. "I wanted to find Ben."

"I know," she said and looked around, trying to get a sense of where they might be. "You like Ben, huh?"

Jacob nodded. "He gets mad sometimes, but he doesn't mean it."

The words of an abused wife. But it was also comforting to hear. It meant Ben had been likable. And he'd saved the boy from the river, which meant he'd been selfless. She allowed herself to feel the faint warmth of hope.

They started walking again, creeping carefully in case guards were patrolling the trees.

"Becca?" Jacob's voice was a mere peep. He looked very small beside her, like an armadillo in his silver jacket. But an armadillo had a hard shell. Becca shuddered to think of the boy on the receiving end of a Taser or bullet. "Why did you run away from Ben?" he whispered. Becca hesitated before she answered and kept walking.

"We had a fight."

"A bad fight?"

"Yes."

"He misses you."

"I know," she said. And then, "You said Ben got mad sometimes?" She felt crummy using a child for this type of reconnaissance, but she needed to know.

"Yes . . . but he told Aunt Lucy that he was going to get better, no matter what."

Jacob sounded so hopeful. It made her sad. It made her own hopeful feelings seem naive.

"Listen," he whispered and tugged her hand. Voices and lights filtered through the trees. They crept forward, pausing to listen after each step.

At first, when Becca heard the scream, she thought they'd been spotted. When the second scream cut through the trees like a terrible birdcall, she knew it had nothing to do with them. They hurried forward. *You're going the wrong way,* she thought. *You're going toward the trouble.* But she kept moving nonetheless. The clearing came up so quickly that she almost ran straight into it. She caught herself and pressed against a tree trunk, pushing Jacob behind her. Before them sat a large hogan with two guards stationed at the door. A truck was just pulling up. Becca motioned for Jacob to stay put and crept closer.

"Dropped them off," the driver was saying to the guards. "How many are left?"

"Not many," replied one.

The driver nodded. "So I wait?"

Another horrible scream cut through the trees, and the guards stiffened. The three men glanced at one another nervously, as though to say, *It'll all be over soon.*

36

THEY'D BEEN IN the hogan for hours now, the same one where they'd been branded. They were naked, but the wood-burning stove had turned the room into a furnace. At first, Ben had found the nakedness jarring. He tried not to gawk at the bellies that drooped like half-full flour sacks over pubic bones, at the sagging buttocks, stretch marks, wrinkles, and liver spots. He felt hyperaware of his own muscular body, his youth. Not that he was faring much better than the others in the heat. After each trial, a hoplite stoked the fire, and the flames would lick the stove's open mouth. Ben's hair was matted to his head, and his eyes stung. The hogan stank of vomit. He'd shut his eyes during the last trial—the poor vet crawling on the ground trying to find his way out—but the CO had ordered Ben to look.

After completing the wooden structure, the twelve remaining men had been marched back to the hogan. And the final round of contests began. Early on, Ben had set his thoughts on Becca as a way to ignore the heat and his aching body and the extreme tiredness he felt from so much physical exertion and almost no food. And as he stood in that sweltering room—because they were not allowed to sit down—and watched each man pass through the particular crucible that the CO had constructed for him, Ben tried to picture Becca's face. He tried to feel her like cool air, to lose himself in the sound of her voice. But even she had faded away under the stress and noise and awful things that transpired here. In some ways, this part of the competition was the most like Iraq, only without Iraq's boredom. This was Iraq distilled and it was pure poison. Tears slipped down Ben's face as he watched the other men struggle and scream. Or maybe it was just sweat. Maybe, watching grown men be reduced in this way, he was too embarrassed even to cry.

There weren't many left now. Twelve had been whittled down to three: Bull, Reno, and himself. It was Reno's turn and as he approached the CO, he glanced at Ben. What message was he trying to send? Reno looked sad, almost apologetic. As though he were saying, *I did my best to help you, but now you're on your own.* It struck Ben that he and Reno together might be able to take the CO and Bull. They might even be able to wrestle the guns away from the guards outside. But this realization — and his acceptance of Reno's help — had come too late. Because Reno was now drinking from the cup of dark liquid that the CO had given to each of the previous vets.

"Keep it down," the CO ordered. "You must keep it down. Or maybe a nonbeliever like yourself lacks the stomach for this?" Reno swallowed and the CO nodded approvingly. "I don't know why you've chosen to come into the fold after all these years, but I give you credit for making it this far." Reno mumbled something that might have been *Fuck you*. Then, for a few minutes, nothing occurred. Reno sat back, his face calm, almost serene. It had happened exactly this way with each man. The reprieve didn't last. Sure enough, Reno clutched his stomach and moaned. He staggered and moaned again. He fell to his knees, and suddenly, he was vomiting into a bucket, liquid spewing out of him like a faucet. Ben and Bull looked away.

"You must bear witness to this man as he purges his pain," the CO ordered. "This is the start of his catharsis. He will be asked to confront the terror that lives inside of him and expel it — if he is strong enough to do so."

Ben forced himself to look at Reno, who continued to retch. "Get up," the CO said, and Reno staggered to his feet. The room began to fill with sounds, faint at first, but steadily growing. Ben heard feet crashing through brush and a man's heavy breath. He heard branches and leaves snap and a machete hacking through foliage. The breathing grew more insistent, became peppered with grunts. This was the sound of a man running from something. His own heart began to pound, as it had during the other trials. His body tensed with dread. *This isn't for you,* he reminded himself. *This is for Reno.* And in fact, Reno was stumbling around as if he were trying to escape the noise. He pushed at invisible walls, swatted invisible insects. And then the hogan was full of color. Images of dense jungle burst to life in 360 degrees. The more Reno thrashed, the more the movie images jerked, almost like the pictures were responding to his movements. Ben felt as though he were watching the scene through Reno's eyes, sharing his frantic, drug-induced delirium.

Meanwhile, the CO had donned a mask: the visage of a woman with slit-like eyes and blood-red lips. He removed his robe, revealing his belly, white in the firelight. As he walked to Reno, Reno backed into the wall. The jungle images played over his naked body. "Whaddya want?" Reno whimpered and pushed his hands out in front of him in a pathetic attempt to protect himself. The CO walked closer. He held an M16 and touched Reno three times with the weapon: on his chest, shoulder, and side.

"Do you know this gun?" he asked, his voice slightly muffled inside the mask. "Do you recognize it?"

Reno shook his head.

"It's not your gun?" the CO said.

Reno leaned forward as though to inspect the weapon.

"It's your gun, isn't it," the CO said, and this time Reno nodded. "And do you remember what you did with this gun, Reno?"

The walls flashed with explosions. There were men on the ground, groaning. A soldier with a severed leg crawled around the perimeter of the hogan as a Vietnamese aggressor stalked him with a knife. Reno watched, gasping as the distance closed between the two men. He turned and turned until he collapsed from dizziness and confusion. The CO placed the gun on the floor, and Reno grabbed it. The sound of recorded gunfire exploded throughout the hogan, and Reno began to slither across the hut, holding the gun in his armpit. When he'd reached the opposite wall he stood and pointed the weapon first at Ben, then at Bull. Both men ducked. The CO shouted at them to stand straight and still. They obeyed, holding their breath. And then Reno pointed the gun at the CO.

"Who did you kill with this weapon?" the CO asked as he crossed the room.

"Nobody." The gun shook in Reno's hands.

"Don't lie to me, Reno. I was there. I saw you do it with my own eyes."

The image of the wounded soldier moved across Reno's body, followed by the stalking Vietnamese.

"Was it a woman?" the CO asked. He stepped up to Reno. "Did she have eyes like these?" He pointed to the mask. "Did you shoot her in the eye?"

Reno cocked the gun and the CO stepped back just a few feet, almost like he was encouraging Reno to fire it.

"Who was the woman, Reno?"

"She was just a girl."

"No, she wasn't, Reno. She was a fucking gook. She was a

gook breeder. She bred the sons that killed your friends. She made *him!*" The CO pointed to the picture of the Vietnamese soldier. "Shoot her, Reno. Blow her fucking brains out." The CO knelt down before Reno as though in supplication. Reno shook, frantic as a trapped mouse.

"Shoot me, Reno!" the CO ordered. "Blow my gook brains out!"

Reno pointed the gun at the CO's forehead.

"All the horror you've been carrying. For forty years. Let it out, Reno. Embrace it and purge it. Now!"

None of the nine other vets had gotten so far into the CO's charade—at least, none of them had been handed a weapon. They'd all collapsed much sooner or gone mad or given up and passed out. And now Ben needed to do something. He wasn't going to let this happen. He began edging toward the two men.

"Do it!" the CO demanded. "Don't fail me, Reno."

But Reno dropped the gun. He fell to his knees and sobbed into his hands.

"Coward," the CO whispered.

And then, all at once, the video snapped off and the sounds disappeared. The CO threw off the mask. "Take him!" he snarled, furious, and two hoplites entered. They lifted Reno by the arms and carried him out the door. Now Ben, Bull, and the CO were alone.

"My sons," the CO said, motioning for each of the men to drink from the vat of dark liquid and then kneel before him.

37

BECCA WATCHED THE guards carry a man from the hogan. She shuddered at the sight of the body whimpering and twitching, but when she realized it was Reno, she nearly cried out. The guards laid Reno on the truck bed, where he writhed, mumbling nonsense. Then he fell still. One of the guards took his pulse. "He's not great," the guard said to the driver. "You should take him to the infirmary."

"Ask the CO," the driver said. "And ask when he wants me to bring King."

But the guard's answer was unexpected. "He doesn't want King anymore."

"What do you mean?" the driver protested.

"It's what he told us," the second guard said, but he went into the hogan anyway. When he came back out, he opened the door wide. It was the briefest moment, but in that window, Becca's body went cold. Inside the room were two naked men on their knees. One of them was Ben.

Becca thought fleetingly of Jacob and prayed that he would stay hidden. Then she bolted toward the hut. The guards looked genuinely startled to see her, but they weren't going to let her through. In unison — almost in slow motion, it seemed to Becca — their arms extended. And then a beast bit into her stomach.

Its jaws ripped through her skin and sank into the muscle. She spasmed and collapsed, clutching her belly. All she could think was that she hadn't even made it to the doorway. She hadn't come close. Meanwhile, the beast had discovered her breasts and shoulders and was gnawing upward toward her eyes.

"You want me to get her out of here?" someone asked.

"No," replied a voice, deep and slow. "Bring her in."

Hands grabbed her shoulders and lifted her like she was nothing more than a sack of bones. They carried her forward and dropped her inside the sweltering hogan. She heard the door shut. Then hands covered her shoulders. Large, familiar hands. She looked up into Ben's face. He was waxen and drenched, but she saw that he was all right. He pulled her close, soaking her shirt with his sweat. "It's okay," he whispered into her ear. "I'm okay."

"What's happening?" she cried. She felt nauseated, partly from the pain and partly from the stench of vomit. Her eyes flickered around the hogan, searching for the next threat. The room was empty except for Bull and the CO, who sat placidly on a pile of blankets. He looked like he was sleeping with his eyes open.

"We're the only two left." Ben nodded at Bull. Bull appeared to be in worse shape than Ben. His head lolled on his neck like he was drunk. "I'm gonna be sick," he said and rushed to a bucket in the corner. A moment later, Ben heaved and rushed to a second bucket. Becca followed and knelt beside her husband, stroking the damp hair on his head. It was when Ben sat up that she noticed the wound on his chest: the Greek helmet, pink and oozing. "What is this?" she cried. She held her fingers above the spot and Ben winced as though she'd actually touched him. "What did you do to him?" she screamed at the CO.

"You aren't going to deny the sergeant his chance to win the heart? Surely not so close to the end," the CO replied calmly.

"I drank that stuff." Ben nodded at the dark liquid. "He drank it too." Ben motioned to Bull, who was on his knees, gripping the sides of the bucket. "It's a drug."

Ben looked like he wanted to say something else but then he threw up again. In between expulsions, he looked at her. "I'll be fine." He panted. "Go outside and wait for me, Becca."

She shook her head.

"I don't want you to see this."

"I'm not leaving," she said.

"Please," Ben pleaded, his eyes frantic.

"I think she should bear witness," the CO mused, stroking his beard in an almost comical fashion. "If she sees, she will know, and if she knows, she will feel."

Ben shook his head imploringly. "Becca—"

"No," the CO interrupted, his voice cold. "She will stay."

Swiftly, his massive body, so much more limber than she would have imagined, leaped from the blankets and seized her arm.

Becca struggled, but the CO only tightened his grip. She called for Ben, but he could barely hold his head upright. When he finally managed to lift it, his eyes were glazed over; he was gone.

No . . . no . . . she cried silently to herself. The CO yanked her arm forcefully, almost throwing her against his blanket throne. "Sit," he ordered and tugged her down. "Bull, son, come over here."

Bull pulled himself away from the bucket and walked shakily toward Becca. "Soldier," said the CO. "I have an important duty for you. She is your prisoner. She is not to move, not to speak. Do you understand?"

As Bull nodded, Becca looked into his eyes, searching for recognition. "We sat on Kath's porch," she pleaded. "We watched a hawk." But it was too late. The chemicals had taken over, and Bull pulled Becca to her knees. Then he knelt behind her and slid one arm around her stomach, holding her still. She felt trapped, like a doll. She wanted to speak his name, to try to break through to him, but she was terrified to be held like this. He could break her neck. Just like that.

"Very good, Bull," said the CO. "Wait for my next command." He picked up a remote control and the hogan walls came to life. Becca saw a dusty, unpaved street lined with cinder-block buildings. The smell of burning trash wafted down from vents somewhere overhead. And the room filled with Arabic singing. The music was beautiful and harsh and so tangible that Becca felt like she could have physically grabbed it—if Bull hadn't been holding her down.

The sound of gunfire burst over the music and Ben dropped to the ground. Then an Arab man appeared from one of the houses. He hurried into the road and laid something there. Then he disappeared back into his house.

Ben was now hiding behind the blankets. He looked up at the CO. "I'll stake out the house," he whispered.

"Good thinking, Sergeant. Report back what you find."

Ben stalked across the room and banged on the door—on the hogan wall—shouting at the man to come out. Nothing happened. Then *boom*. Flames burst across the screen, the explosion so loud that it shook the hogan walls. Becca screamed, unable to stop herself. Bull tightened his hold. He was making it hard for her to breathe. Ben dropped flat and rolled back and forth, crying out as though engulfed by fire.

"You're safe, soldier!" the CO called out. "But the snipers!"

Pops of gunfire echoed through the room, and Ben ducked and dodged like he was trying to avoid actual bullets. He ran toward one wall, and an image of fire burst up in his face. He ran at another wall and met more flames. The CO, meanwhile, was watching intently, pressing button after button on the remote. Becca couldn't stand this. She shut her eyes. She wanted to plug her ears but Bull had her arms trapped against her sides.

"Open your eyes, woman," the CO ordered. "Open them now." Bull shook her hard and finally, she submitted. "Do you understand what you are seeing?" The CO leaned over and whispered hot and close into her ear. "I'm creating the opportunity for his catharsis."

Ben ran back and forth, meeting flames at every turn. Only when the CO beckoned to him did he stop. He hurried to the commander and slid to the ground.

"He is dead in here," the CO said to Becca. He pressed his palm to the Greek helmet branded on his own skin. "I am giving him a chance to live again."

"This is insane," Becca snarled. "Don't you care that you're hurting him?"

Bull seized the back of her neck. Becca whimpered.

"It's okay," the CO said. "Let her go, and start your patrol." Bull did not hesitate. He dropped his arm and started a slow circle around the hogan. Becca crawled to Ben, who was folded into a ball at the CO's feet.

"Those wan, insubstantial relationships of the civilian world," the CO said. "They mean *nothing*. These men died in the jungles! In the deserts! Just look at them!"

He motioned to Ben, and then to Bull, who was still circling the hogan holding an imaginary gun in his arms and mumbling orders to no one. The war scenes flickered nightmarishly. Becca remembered what Reno had said about King fleeing Kleos over and over. It was the one thing that gave her enough courage to speak. "If you keep them here, you're not even giving them a *chance* to live normal lives. You don't have any faith in them."

"If you mean I lack faith in people like *you,* then you're right. There is only one chance for life after death! If a man can embrace his pain and expel it fully, then he may lead others. He may be reborn by leading his brothers and sons. Otherwise, who are we? What life can we possibly . . ."

The CO's voice trailed off and Becca was startled to see tears in the old man's eyes. "It's all right, soldier," he said, and motioned Ben to him. Becca could only gape as Ben knelt before the CO and let the old man pet his head. "It's going to be all right," the CO whispered. "I promise."

"This isn't all right," Becca whimpered, trying to coax Ben from his submissive position at the CO's feet. "None of this." She dared to look the CO in the eye. "Just let Bull win," she pleaded. "Give the heart to him. He's the one who wants this."

For a moment, the CO actually seemed to consider this request. "Bull," he said. But the moment Bull turned, the CO Tased him. Becca was so horrified, she couldn't even cry out. "Bull has been a good soldier," the CO said calmly. "But Durga demands youth. And selflessness. And doggedness. She demands to be exalted by music. Bull cannot give her these things."

Now the cityscape on the walls faded and a sort of metal cage materialized. It was the innards of a vehicle, Becca realized, and it was coated in blood.

A picture of a hand flashed on the wall.

Ben stumbled over and grabbed at the hand. Then there was a foot. Then a leg. Ben jumped and lunged and scratched at the wall as though he could physically pull the images into the room.

"You can't put your friend back together, Sergeant Thompson. You cannot clean up the blood. You cannot disinfect the metal. There is nothing whatsoever that you can do."

"No!" Ben growled.

But the CO only nodded. "This was Coleman's fate. This is what happened."

Ben was crying now, still grabbing at the limbs on the screen. Becca went to him. "It's not real, Ben," she said, desperately trying to steel herself against this psychotic version of her husband. "It's just a picture. Look at me. I'm real." She took his hand and squeezed it. "See, this is me." But Ben kept grabbing at nothing. "This is the leg," Ben cried. "This is the hand. This is the finger." He was out of control, just like the night she'd fled.

"Why don't you tell your wife why you smashed the fiddle," the CO said. "It might clear things up for her."

The images faded and the lights dimmed. "I had a dream," Ben said, turning to face the CO. He seemed to Becca, just then, like an actor on a stage. And the CO was the director, feeding him his cues.

"Go on," the CO encouraged.

"A rope was tied to my waist and at the end of the rope was the sack. Full of parts. Full of Coleman—" Ben waved his hands at the walls. "I had to cut it off me. Cut away the bag of parts! Stop dragging."

"So what did you do?"

"I fought with the knot!" Ben clawed at his waist, pounded his fists against his stomach, pulled at his skin like there was a real rope wrapped around his belly.

"Stop it! Ben, look what you're doing to yourself!" Becca grabbed at his hands, but he shoved her out of the way. She picked herself up from the floor, tears burning.

"Do you see now?" the CO asked. "In the darkness of his mind, you are not his wife. You are not even his friend. You become the knot he cannot untie. You become the enemy." The CO looked disgusted that she'd needed to have any of this explained. "And then what, Sergeant?"

"And then there was music," Ben said. "It was coming from

the sack with Coleman. And I was dragging it, the music and the parts of Coleman."

The CO nodded sympathetically. "And then?"

"I needed to cut the rope. Anything to cut the rope."

"So you broke the fiddle?"

Ben nodded furiously.

"And you used the shards to cut the rope."

Ben nodded.

"Quite ingenious, soldier. But it didn't work."

Ben hung his head, and, all at once, he broke down.

"Do you see now?" the CO asked Becca, his voice blunt.

And of course she did. She saw that Ben had been trapped in a version of this room for a long time and that he wasn't even close to finding his way out. She saw that she was helpless to protect him. She hated the CO for showing her this. And the next thing she knew, she was sprinting at the old man with all her might, as though her anger were strong enough to knock him down. She was going to rip him open. She was going to break him.

But the CO was faster. His arm jutted out and caught her. His fingers dug into her shoulder until the pain made her cry out. And then the hogan was plunged into black. The CO forced Becca to her knees and then released his grip. When the lights rose, a new image played on the wall: a hospital bed and a man, his face washed out in grayish light, his body hooked to machines and tubes. A heart monitor beeped beside the bed.

Music rose out of the silence. It was a fiddle tune that Becca knew well. It was called "Sally in the Garden," and Ben had played it often. The picture it evoked was not a garden, however, but an empty boat knocking against a deserted and rocky shore. Between the notes, Becca heard wind and saw a muddy sky. She'd never really understood why Ben loved this tune so much.

"This is it, Sergeant Thompson," the CO said. "You are the last one." He sounded almost giddy. "Pass this final test and Durga's heart is yours."

"Why is he here?" Ben nodded at the hospital bed.

"He is your last challenge. He is the only thing between you and salvation."

And then Becca realized that the man in the hospital bed was supposed to be Ben's dad.

The fiddle music was growing louder, only instead of notes, "Sally in the Garden" was composed of layers of sadness. You could peel away at those layers forever and still never reach the center. The heart of the song could not be touched, so it would never stop crying.

"It's not really your dad," Becca told him. "He doesn't look anything like your dad." But Ben just stared at the wall.

"What did you tell your dad before he died, Ben?" the CO asked.

Ben shook his head. His lower lip trembled.

The CO climbed off the pile of blankets and walked around Bull, who was now curled in a fetal position on the floor. He went to the bucket of black liquid and drank, long and deep. Then he lumbered to the hospital bed, his massive belly rising and falling to the tempo of the heart monitor. Light from the movie projection streamed out around him.

"I am your dad, Ben. I am dying. So what do you need to tell me?"

"You're . . ." Ben's lip continued trembling.

"Ben, let's go!" Becca pleaded. She pulled at his arm, but he shook her off.

"Come over here, son."

Ben approached. The fiddle music grew louder.

"Son. What are your last words to me?" The CO's lips were inches from Ben's face. Ben was breathing faster now, shaking his head. "What are your last words, Sergeant? How do you honor me, your father, on my deathbed?"

A single note from the fiddle flew long and sharp across room. Ben clutched his chest as though he'd been hit. He mumbled something.

"What?" the CO demanded. He gagged, as though he was about to vomit, but then he swallowed deeply and stood taller. "Speak up, son."

"Traitor!" Ben's voice was louder this time. The CO nodded with a crooked smile. "You're a traitor! To your family. To me! You loved that man. But what about me? I'm your son! But you didn't want me." Ben shook his head furiously. "You only wanted your music. You only wanted him. If he made you sick, then you deserve to die!"

Becca gasped.

The CO shook his head. He suddenly looked very weak.

"I'm your son!" He grabbed the CO by the shoulders. The CO did not resist. He went limp beneath Ben's fury. Ben pushed him with what appeared to be all the strength he had left, and the CO dropped to his knees.

"I tried to honor you," the commander said, his voice barely a scratch of sound. He looked pleadingly up at Ben.

"You. Left. Me."

"I carried the heart for you. I built Kleos for you. All for you." He sank over his knees. "But I left you, Willy. I did."

Willy? Becca thought. The soldier from Reno's story?

"I abandoned you." The CO stared up at Ben, his teeth gritted. "'Just put me in my grave. And give me your hand, Willy, I beg you. Once you've given me the fire I deserve, I'm never coming back.'" From the back of his fatigues, he produced a bowie knife.

Becca felt sick. "Do it, Willy." The CO offered the knife to

Ben. "I was afraid. Of your friendship. Of your love. Afraid of myself. I was ashamed. Oh God. I left you to be slaughtered!"

Slowly, Ben took the knife. Becca said his name and he turned, pointing the weapon at her. In that moment they were back in her childhood room and it wasn't a knife Ben was gripping in his fist but the fiddle. He was going to smash it over her. He was going to break her if he could. "Please don't," she said.

"Come." The CO spread his arms like he wanted a hug. "Purge the past. Save us both from despair. Your catharsis is my salvation." He puffed out his stomach. The jagged scar bisected his hard, white belly like a crack across ice.

The music reached a crescendo, and it seemed as though the hogan was going to come crashing down.

Then a figure bounded between them. Bull pushed Ben over and grabbed the knife. The tackle seemed to have jarred Ben awake. He looked at Becca with a flicker of recognition and scrambled back beside her. The CO lumbered to his feet. He stood to his massive height like a beast rearing up on its hind legs. He spread his arms. "Come and claim my heart, Willy. I give it to you."

Bull stepped in front of the CO and thrust the knife into his belly. The CO grunted, a burst of sound that gave way to a long and throttled groan. He fell to his knees, his arms still stretched wide. Then he fell forward. Bull hunched over the CO's body and pushed him onto his back. Becca gagged, but she managed to help Ben up and to the hogan door. When she glanced back, she had the distinct impression that a lion was ripping into a rhinoceros. Bull's hand was plunged deep into the CO's stomach, and blood poured onto the floor. "The heart," Bull cried out. "Where's the heart?"

Becca shouldered Ben outside to find a line of hoplites facing the hogan, impassive. "Help!" she shouted. "The CO's been stabbed!" But the men did not move, though some of them had tears in their eyes.

Becca turned to Ben, who was naked and shivering violently beneath the cold dawn sky. "It's okay," she said, folding her arms around him. She didn't believe this at all. But she kept saying it, over and over, as though her words might shelter them both.

38

BEN CAME TO in white sheets and a bright pool of sunshine. His mouth was dry and his tongue heavy as a rock. Becca slept in the chair beside the bed, her neck stretched back on the windowsill. For a moment, that was all he could see: the tendons of her throat, fine and taut like fiddle strings. How could she be this perfect? He thought of tiny fossils and petrified vertebrae, too perfectly formed to be accidents of nature —the reasons people believed in a creator. What forces had sculpted this throat. Ben touched her and she woke up. Suddenly, her head was pressed to his neck, her breath hot on his skin. He squeezed her as hard as he possibly could. If it was too hard, she gave no sign.

"Do you feel all right?" she asked, handing him some water. "You've been out for a couple of hours."

He nodded. "Is there more?"

She refilled the cup and he saw that all of the beds in the infirmary were occupied. The men had gauze taped over their chests where they'd been branded. He looked down to see a small square taped over his own. Ben closed his eyes. "Is the CO alive?" he asked.

"He and Bull are still in the hogan. The guards are outside, waiting. Everybody's waiting." She paused to let him drink.

When he'd drained the cup, she said, "Do you know what happened . . . ?" Her voice was tentative, reluctant.

Ben closed his eyes, and in the blackness, he could see it all in detail: the flames, the soldier who was Coleman lying on the ground, the limbs scattered across the street. Ben had counted them, just as he had the day of the explosion and so many days since. Part of him—a significant part of him—was unhinged. And Becca had seen it all. He saw the hospital bed with his father. Finally, he saw the CO hold out the knife. The old man had called him by a dead soldier's name: Willy. It was as though the commander had offered himself up, but not to any goddess. Instead, he'd placed himself at the feet of a long-dead soldier—a mere mortal. How long, Ben wondered, had the CO been contemplating this exit? How long had he yearned for escape? And if Bull had not appeared, would Ben have been the one to set him free? He shuddered, imagining what it must have been like—the cut and the extraction.

He opened his eyes, eager to dislodge this awful picture. Becca was looking at him gravely. "How's King?" he asked.

"He's over his bout of heartburn." This was a familiar and unwelcome voice. Ben propped himself up to see Reno lying a few beds over. He looked disastrous, his thin hair disheveled, his eyes bloodshot. Ben saw the kind—almost intimate—way that Becca observed him. He remembered what Bull had said to him in the desert. Becca and Reno. Something had happened, but whatever it was, Ben made up his mind right then to leave it alone.

"I didn't know you were awake," Becca said.

"I wasn't going to miss the romantic reunion. Also, I was hoping for a thank-you?" He eyed Ben.

"You punched me in the face!" Ben retorted, which made Reno laugh. So Ben laughed too. Which made Becca smile. Seeing her, Ben felt that he would do anything—anything at all—to keep that smile on her face.

The infirmary door creaked open. Arne stood there, stiff and formal. He'd traded his blue jeans for olive-colored BDUs, typical battle dress. His hands were at his sides, his expression grim. Ben recognized this moment for precisely what it was: casualty notification.

"Bull has claimed the heart of Durga," Arne said. "The CO is dead."

39

MUMMIFIED IN WHITE blankets, the CO's body was carried through the desert on a stretcher made from animal hide. Bull walked directly behind, and, as near victor, Ben was awarded the third place in the procession. He refused to go without Becca, however, so she walked beside him. Reno also refused to leave her side, so he followed close. Next came King and Elaine, then the vets who lived at Kleos, and, after them, those who'd ridden in on their bikes. Some of the men had not been able to pull themselves from their infirmary beds and many of those in line looked far too sick to be standing, let alone marching. But they pressed onward without complaint, good soldiers that they were. The Hands of God women took up the rear. Last of all, like the tail of a desert snake, came Lucy and Jacob, holding hands.

The remaining hoplites beat large drums that they wore over their bellies like shields. *Thud . . . thud . . . thud.* The procession walked in step to the monotonous pounding. Heat draped around them like the flaps of a tent. Becca felt her scalp burning, wetness spreading across her back. She prayed for a cloud, for even the fleeting shadow of a bird. After a while, they passed the remains of the fire that she and Reno had driven by the day before. Becca could see it clearly now: blood on the ground, dried to a coppery brown, and animal bones scattered atop the pile of charred wood.

"Ritual sacrifice," Reno whispered. "Four times a month they kill an animal in honor of Achilles and his companion, Patroclus. They say some kind of voodoo prayers over it."

The drums beat heavy and slow. Wind rose up from the vastness and blew the sand around their feet. A black dot appeared on the horizon. At first, it seemed to be a trick of the light, but then it grew, as though pushing straight up from the earth. Finally, they gathered in a semicircle around an intricately stacked pile of logs. The structure stood at least ten feet high and was roughly the length and width of a canoe. "We built this," Ben said, marveling at the odd edifice. "We cut down the trees ourselves."

The hoplites hoisted the CO's shrouded body onto the logs and circled the pyre three times. The other men followed. Then the guards cut off locks of their hair and scattered them over the corpse. The other vets stepped up, one by one, and did the same. Becca wasn't sure what King would do when his turn came. He looked both indignant and despondent. Hurt. She ached for him — for the betrayal he must have felt after all these years of service to the CO. But at the appointed moment, King pulled his ponytail over his shoulder and cut it off. He pressed the gray clump to his heart and then threw it onto the pyre. Reno stepped up and pulled the scissors from the guard's hand. He snipped a few thin strands from his own head and did the same. Becca was surprised. But the CO had once been Reno's commanding officer. Maybe for that reason alone, the old man's death deserved to be honored.

The guards poured red wine from water skins over the pyre and the CO's body. Bull went last, walking fully around the structure, wetting the four corners with the wine. Behind him, the hoplites doused the structure with gasoline until the logs glistened and the blankets covering the CO's body were soaked through. When this action was complete, Bull stood before the pyre, surveying his flock. He had washed the CO's blood from his body, and around his neck he wore a leather pouch. Becca immediately recognized it as one of King's.

The guards beat their drums a final time. And then Bull began to speak. "'I will not forget him, not so long as I am among the living and my knees spring up beneath me. And even if the dead forget the dead in Hades, still even there I will remember my beloved companion.'"

The men repeated these lines. Becca closed her eyes, listening to their voices and breathing in the sweet-sharp smell of gasoline.

"*Currahee!*" Bull pronounced, and the men said, "*Currahee!*"

Bull clutched the pouch and solemnly held it above his head. "The heart of Durga! As the victor of these funeral games, I have won the privilege and burden of its safekeeping. I will suck the poison-grief from your hearts and pour it into the earth. I will heal you as the heart of the goddess has healed me."

Becca recalled those last minutes in the hogan: Bull bent over the CO, his hand deep in the old man's stomach. *Where's the heart?* She hadn't paid attention to his mumblings. She'd been focused on getting Ben out. Now she squinted, trying to gauge the shape and size of the pouch in Bull's hand. It did not appear to be empty, but Bull could have put anything in there. It could be a bunch of rocks for all anyone knew. As she contemplated the possibilities of Bull's deception, her attention was drawn away by an unfamiliar sound: King was crying. Fat tears dripped down his cheeks, dampening his beard. His back and belly shook as if a small earthquake were happening just beneath his feet.

"It should have been mine. I didn't even have a chance to try."

Elaine folded him into a hug and let King shake against her body. She murmured into his ear. Becca had never seen her father accept love or tenderness from another person. She had never seen him cry. She felt embarrassed for him but also angry. *It's not real,* she wanted to tell him. *There's nothing magical inside that sack.*

Her father pulled away. He clasped his dog tags in his fist and yanked them off. Then he threw them on the ground. As a little girl, Becca had climbed into King's lap and slid her fingers across the punched-out letters and numbers, reading them like they were reverse Braille: *Keller, King F., US53864910, O positive, Protestant*. She'd asked her father why he wore a necklace. "It's identification from the army," he told her. "In case something happened to me."

"Did anything happen to you?" she'd asked, not understanding the euphemism. At this question, King had pulled the tags away from her. "No," he said, his voice heavy. "Nothing happened to me."

It wasn't true, of course. And it was because of what *had* happened that King believed in the impossible story of Durga's heart and put so much faith in her specious salvation. King's country had asked him to experience unthinkable things. Nightmarish things. So it made sense that he would have little faith in ordinary medicine. In civilian medicine. He needed a remedy that was as powerful and terrible — perhaps as unthinkable — as his trauma. But now that remedy had been denied him too. Just like everything else that had been denied him, throughout his life.

Reno clearly shared Becca's anger, because he now said, "Why don't you show us the heart, Bull? Before you cut your own belly open and tuck your little prize into it."

Jeanine pulled her cigarette from her mouth and snorted. "Yeah, Bull, why don't you show us."

"Shush!" Becca hissed at them.

Reno and her mother were asking to see a god they knew full well did not exist. But they had not considered the consequences of proving this god to be a no-show. Her mother should have known better. She, at least, knew the result of testing believers. Reno wanted only to reveal the truth to King—to help his friend. He didn't see King's need to believe the way that Becca had seen it.

"Come on, Bull." Reno grinned. "Let's see the source of your newfound power." He took a step forward.

"Reno," warned Ben and tried to grab his arm. But Reno shook Ben off. It was then that Becca noticed movement from the four corners of the pyre. The guards were closing in.

"Look at us. Look what we've done to ourselves!" Reno looked wildly at the other vets. "We've allowed ourselves to be mutilated. We allowed a man to die. We're not this sick. We don't have to be this sick."

"CO Proudfoot sacrificed himself," Bull said, clutching the pouch.

"It's not right, Bull. It's insanity."

The guards reached for their guns.

"Reno, if you don't back off, these men are going to shoot you," Ben said.

"Let them." He kept moving toward Bull. "Show us the heart. If this is real, then fucking prove it!" Reno grabbed for the pouch.

"Hoplites!" Bull shouted.

And then the pyre exploded. The bubble of orange and yellow flame was like the sun crashing to Earth. King grabbed his daughter and pushed her down so hard that she was momentarily stunned.

How long did they lie there cowering? When her head

cleared, she pushed herself up and looked around. Smoke billowed from the pyre, and flames crackled between its wooden bones. Bull lay nearby on the ground, groaning. She did not see Reno or Ben or Elaine or her mother. But King was right beside her, coughing and gripping her arm for support. Becca brushed the sand from his face and beard. "Dad, are you okay? Can you breathe?"

"I'm fine." King waved her away. She ignored this signal and threw her arms around him. "Becca." He coughed. "Becca, please."

But Becca didn't care what her father wanted or didn't want. She squeezed him tighter and tighter until he stopped protesting. And then, miraculously, he hugged her back. He rocked her, cupping her head with his large, wrinkled hand. Everything she had witnessed and felt and feared over the last twenty-four hours burst up from inside of her and poured out of her eyes in a rush. King held on tight, his beard scratching her face, his breathing lumbering and wet. He needed a shower. He smelled. They were both covered in sand and dirt. But they didn't care. Becca closed her eyes against her father's shirt and tried to let herself simply exist in this space, this small compartment constructed not so much from her father's body but from his comfort. It was like a shelter that they had built, painstakingly, together.

The smoke had begun to clear and Becca saw that Ben was helping Elaine to her feet. He brought her to King. Then he reached for Becca. His embrace was strong, but it did not compare to the fleshy fullness of her father's arms.

The guards flocked to Bull and lifted him onto the same stretcher that only moments before had held the CO. Hurriedly, they started back toward Kleos. Some of the vets followed, but most remained and stood watching the pyre. The Indian women prayed over the CO's body, now encased in a sarcophagus of flame.

As all this was happening, Becca finally spotted Reno, sitting dazed on the ground. He too was covered in dirt and ash. His face was purple; he'd swallowed a mouthful of smoke and was coughing uncontrollably. His clothes were scorched. Becca searched among the vets for a canteen and quickly brought it to him. Ben came over and offered his hand. Reno looked at it for a moment as though assessing whether this was some kind of trap or trick. But then he clasped Ben's hand and let the younger man pull him up.

"You almost got yourself shot," King said, walking over.

Reno raised his eyebrows. "Yeah, but I was saved." He nodded at Jeanine, who stood by herself, a wavering specter beneath the sun's glare. "Saved by the Hands of God."

Jeanine watched the flames with a look of stoic resignation. Her arms hung listless at her sides. Her cigarette was gone.

The group kept vigil over the CO's body for some time, the wind blowing the smoke overhead in thick white plumes. The desert air was dry and sharp in their throats. When their water was nearly gone, most of them started the long walk to camp. Jeanine and the Native American women had already left, Lucy and Jacob with them. Twenty men remained at the pyre. They would watch over the body, King told Becca, until the flames finally died. Then they would collect the ashes and bury them in the graveyard. Whenever a man died at Kleos, he received a pyre cremation and burial among the letters. The CO had run Kleos for over thirty years, and in that time, several men had passed away, either from sickness or old age. But never suicide, he assured Becca. Never once.

"Did either of you see this coming?" Becca asked as they

walked to the camp. "Couldn't this have been stopped?"

King and Reno looked at each other, then at their feet. Whatever they were thinking would remain locked inside of their heads, probably forever. And that was okay, Becca knew. Not all stories, not all feelings, were meant to see the light.

40

EARLY THE NEXT morning, King crept out of his hogan and into the adjoining hut where Becca was sleeping. He shuffled as silently as his heavy feet would allow, past Lucy, who was zipped up to the top of her head in a sleeping bag, and Elaine, whose hair was fanned out on the pillow like a beauty queen's. Jeanine, who refused to share a room with Elaine, had chosen to sleep elsewhere with her fellow faithful.

Becca was curled up in a tight ball, her hands folded up beneath her chin. She looked delicate and childlike. Peaceful, King thought. And this made him happy. She deserved more peace than she'd had in her young life. He tapped her gently, and her eyes snapped open, almost as though she hadn't been asleep at all. "What's wrong?" she asked in an urgent whisper.

King put his finger to his lips and motioned for her to follow him. They walked through the slumbering camp until they reached the spot where Reno had parked his bike. "Hop on," King said and inserted Reno's keys into the ignition.

"Reno gave you his keys?" Becca hesitated.

"I'm riding his bike. I'm not sleeping with his woman," King said.

"Exactly!" Becca said, which made King laugh.

"Unless you want me to swim back across that river, climb on," he said.

They sped east. White light pooled along the horizon like the froth that collects on waves. Here were spindly bushes tipped with small yellow buds, flowers that resembled sea anemones. King had always loved riding out here. He loved the combination of space and isolation. Nothing to hem you in or slow you down. He loved feeling like he was close to the earth's center. He tilted his face to the wind, letting his beard whip against his throat. The cold air chafed his lips, but he didn't care. He'd felt so heavy ever since the CO had betrayed him and passed him over in favor of Becca's husband or Bull or however it had happened. But it *had* happened, and time was moving on, and what could King do about it? He was resigned. Resigned to that betrayal, just like he'd resigned himself to the war and its aftermath and everything he'd lost. He was thankful to be healthy enough to ride. And he was conscious, in a way that he'd never been before now, that the girl sitting behind him was a product of himself: the ruined parts, the good parts, and even the parts that were ruined for good. She was a young woman who, for reasons he felt intuitively but could not explain, had chosen her husband because of him.

It remained to be seen whether that decision was the best thing she could have done or the worst. Probably it was somewhere in between, like most things. But he was partly responsible for the outcome, which meant that he had to step up. He had to stick with her and see it through. And the reason he had to do this was so simple, it was a wonder he'd failed to see it before: Leave no man behind.

They were a good ten minutes outside of Kleos and coming up fast on the mining tunnel.

Tracks lined the floor, and King went slow, his headlights barely piercing the dark. They rode downward, then upward again. The darkness echoed with water crashing from a great height. Finally, they rumbled out into the open. King turned right and proceeded down the center of a wash. He wove around scrub bushes and cacti in the riverbed and then gunned up the bank. Within five minutes, they hit highway and the silky pavement, which provided a clear view of the river and the buildings of the two ghost towns, old and older. Somewhere beyond was the graveyard of crosses, and Kleos. Out past that, the CO's body still smoldered.

King pulled in beside the Death Star. It was covered with dust, as if it hadn't been washed in years. "Not in the worst shape," he said.

"Dad, it's filthy!"

King laughed. "I did right handing this car over to you, huh?"

Did her father really not know what the car meant to her? What the *gifting* of the car meant? She rubbed away some dust with her forearm. The surface was newly scarred, covered with nicks and cuts.

"Broken beer bottles," King said with the certainty of a forensic detective.

Becca's excitement sank back to her stomach. But then King did something unexpected: he picked up his daughter's hand. She turned to him, surprised to feel the roughness of his fingers. Two physical displays of affection in just twenty-four hours. Who was this man? He even looked different now, without the ponytail.

"Listen to me, Becca," he said. She listened, watching his marcasite eyes sparkle. He pressed his thumb against her palm. "I'm a disappointment. I know."

She shook her head.

"No, I am. Because I don't have any good advice. I'm sure Ben got blind drunk and did that to your car."

"Yeah."

King looked at her sternly. "I'm also sure that he followed you here when you ran. Kind of like your mother ran after me."

"You're telling me that I'm like you, and Ben's like Mom?"

"All I'm saying is that Jeanine wouldn't let me go." King looked down, bashful. Discussing important, painful topics, he always felt as though he were walking along a ledge; one wrong step and he'd tumble. "I'm just laying things out for you, Becca. In case you have so much muck in here" — he tapped his chest — "that it's clouded up your head."

"It's *your* heart I'm worried about, Dad."

King smiled. "I got your keys back from the hoplites last night."

Becca took them gratefully and climbed into the battle-scarred car. Something was different. There was a strange object attached to the wheel. "Dad, what's this?"

King peered inside the car, saw the hose that his daughter was holding with bewilderment, and started laughing to himself. It wasn't funny. But Reno's ingenuity — oh, how he loved his friend. "Reno said your car needed fixing. And this was the fix. To make sure Ben drove sober."

King could not read the expression on his daughter's face. Was it relief? Hurt? Plain surprise? Shouldn't he be able to tell? Becca lay back against the seat and closed her eyes. For a full minute, he let her sit and feel however she needed to feel. But the road pulled at him. The past few days were rushing up behind him, nipping his tires. "Becca?" he asked and she opened her eyes. "Do you think you can find your way back to the compound through that pass under the river?"

"You're going somewhere?" she asked, quick and helpless. "Does Elaine know you're leaving? Does Mom?"

"Elaine, I'll see before long. Your mother . . . I'm not sure we'll ever really make our peace."

"But where are you *going?*"

"I've always wanted to see Canada. British Columbia, maybe. There's good riding up there, I hear." There was a look in her eyes. It said, *Deserter.* But she had it all wrong. "I'm worried about my heart too, Becca. I've got a lot to think through. After all this . . ."

In fact, King did not want to think about it. He needed to ride, to let the wind sweep his many questions out of reach. The trouble wasn't simply that the heart had gone to another man. More difficult to understand was the CO's deception; he'd promised King a fair chance and then, without warning or explanation, he'd taken that chance away. *Leave no man behind.* It was the one promise you didn't break. And the CO had. He'd left King out, then he'd left them all – all the men who relied on him for guidance and strength. What would happen to them now? Could Bull really carry them?

Because maybe the competition wasn't about selecting a capable leader. Maybe Durga's heart wasn't as strong as the CO said, and the pain that he felt was about more than toxins flowing through his bloodstream. Maybe he was so desperate to ease this pain that he'd gone looking for one of his disciples to take it away. And if this was true, then King was forced to ask himself whether he could have been that man. He didn't know.

And, of course, there was one final question, the one that King needed to escape most of all. Now that the CO had broken his most fundamental vow, King had no choice but to wonder whether any part of Durga's story was true.

"I need the road, Becca." King paused to see how this was going over. Becca's eyes blinked quick and anxious. "And maybe you need some time too. After what's happened."

"You mean time away from Ben?"

"Or with him? I want to help you, Becca, but I don't know what's right for you."

When he said this, she almost burst out laughing. What had she expected him to give her? Hadn't she known from the start that her father was a dead end? "But I need you to listen carefully," he continued. "I'm done with this place. And before long, I will come home. I'll be there for you. Like I'm supposed to be."

"Why should I believe you?"

"Because I'm your father and you are my daughter. Because that, right there, is the oath I'm making."

In any other situation, between any other people, these words would not have sufficed. But King had never made a promise to her. And so his words weren't simply good enough. They were everything.

"Can I just see that tattoo once more before I go?" he asked.

Becca held up her wrist. There it was: KING.

He nodded, still looking perplexed by the finality of the thing. "I love you, Becca," he said and touched her shoulder. "You are my child."

They hugged once more. A real belly-to-belly hug, with her father giving her a heavy slap on the back. Then King climbed onto his own motorcycle, parked nearby, fitted the helmet over his head, and turned the key. A lion's roar cracked the quiet. King raised his hand in farewell. He pulled out onto the road and sped away.

41

All morning, Ben and Becca ferried the vets and the Hands of God women out of Kleos by way of the mining tunnel. Bull and the hoplites paid them little attention. They were involved in an elaborate series of mourning rituals, and the vets who called Kleos home were too exhausted and grief-stricken to do anything but follow along. Ben wondered what would happen once the processions and ceremonies were over and the CO's remains had been buried. Given the commander's charisma and his unchallenged control over the community, it was difficult to imagine that Kleos's inhabitants would simply accept their new leader. Could they really believe in Durga so much? Could their allegiance truly be to the goddess instead of the man? But Ben had also seen the power of belief in action. When you truly believed in something—when you needed it desperately—you could go to extraordinary lengths. Ben did not share the same beliefs as the vets of Kleos, but he knew something of their sacrifices. He could still feel his own, throbbing beneath the bandage on his chest.

By noon everyone had assembled on the road, though they all seemed oddly reluctant to get going. Ben stood in front of the smashed-in post office watching Jacob pick his way carefully through the rubble.

"I know you saved him."

Ben started. He hadn't noticed Becca standing there.

"You saved my dad too. You saved . . ."

Us, he thought. Please say *us.*

". . . Elaine and Reno a lot of heartache. And me too," she finished.

Ben frowned. She seemed to be talking about a group of people — an entire family, in fact — that excluded him. He wondered if the savior was always destined to remain separate from the saved.

"We going soon?" Lucy said, coming over. She yelled for Jacob and he scampered over to them, calling shotgun. "You don't get to do that," she said sternly. "This is Becca's car and she decides who rides where."

"As long as I get to drive, he can sit on the roof for all I care," Becca said.

"Lucy and I will sit in the back," Ben said and swiped his hand through the boy's hair.

They headed east, caravan-style: the vets, Elaine and Reno on his bike, the Death Star, and the Hands of God van. A couple of the vets who'd come in with King elected to stay at Kleos, but most were leaving. Whether it was because they'd lost the competition or because they didn't want to live under Bull's new leadership, Ben didn't know. Maybe, like him, they just wanted to be home.

As Becca drove, Ben drifted off. He dreamed that the four of them were on a family road trip. He saw himself teaching them how to fly-fish. He imagined them sitting on the bank of a glittering lake beneath tall western pines. He dreamed that he was stretched out on a sleeping bag across from Jacob, teaching the child how to scratch out "Twinkle, Twinkle, Little Star" on the fiddle. He did not dream about Coleman or Majid or Ali's Alley. He would later on, but in those brief hours, snug in the Death Star's back seat, he was peaceful.

For the next two nights, the vets camped out at KOAs while the rest of the caravan slept nearby at motels. Both nights, Elaine pushed her way up to the desk and announced that Becca would be sleeping in her room. "We girls need each other," she'd told Ben, kindly but without apology. Ben longed to have Becca close to him, to bring her into his bed. He did not want to let her out of his sight. But the two of them had fought a kind of war, and you couldn't just return from battle pretending that nothing had changed.

On the second night of their trip home, he sat with Reno and Becca at a decrepit picnic table outside the Waffle House beside their motel. Darkness was elbowing its way in, but nobody suggested moving. They were deep in conversation about the CO's war stories, lingering over the fate of Willy Owen.

"KIA," Reno said. "But I don't know how." He'd been surprised that the CO failed to carry Willy's body out of the jungle. "It was totally uncharacteristic. The CO always put his men first. And those two were especially thick."

Ben knew why the CO had not done his damnedest to save Willy, but he didn't think it was his place to share. As deranged as the commander had been, the man's secrets deserved to be protected.

"The inevitable product of love, battle, and abandonment is guilt," the CO had said during their drug-infused conversation. "And guilt is heavy. You drag it behind you, just like Achilles dragged Hector's corpse through the dirt. It's not body parts you're dragging around with you in those dreams, Ben. It's your guilt. I don't need some army shrink to tell me that. I've lived it."

Now Ben looked over at Becca. He had to squint to make out her face clearly, even though she was right beside him. He'd felt so guilty for leaving her that he had dragged his shame all the way to Iraq, through his missions, and back home again. With the first tour, it had been different. He hadn't left anything behind. His mother was sorrowful, sure, but she was happy with a new husband. His father was dead. He had no other attachments. But then, suddenly, he had a person to love, not just an inanimate object that produced a bunch of beautiful sounds, but a living person who filled him with joy as not even the most beautiful music could. And he'd left her behind.

The CO was a warning for Ben. The man had done so much to unlatch himself from his guilt. He'd turned to drugs and goddesses and ancient warriors. He'd held confessionals for his men, urging them—forcing them—to confront their shameful stories. He knew that to release the pain, you had to face up to it. No matter how ugly and shameful it was, you had to turn around and look that story in the eye. The CO had tried to do this himself, but he had not succeeded. So he'd dragged that story behind him until he couldn't drag it any longer.

No, Ben would not end up like the CO. But he now understood that you could not sever the rope. You had to use the rope to raise that sack up from the dust. And sitting beside him right now was the one person he wanted to lift.

Just as he realized this, like it had been preordained by some higher power, the entire table was bathed in glorious yellow light from the Waffle House sign.

"Ugh, it's hideous!" Becca made a show of shielding her eyes, but Ben jumped up, ecstatic from his revelation. If he could just explain to her what had only now happened, he was sure all transgressions could be forgiven.

"Whoa, boy, you got ants in your pants?" Reno said.

Becca jumped up after him. "What's going on?"

Ben grabbed her hand and pulled her across the grass, across the asphalt, and down to the road. He felt her stumbling to keep up, but he needed them to be alone. Finally, he stopped at the roadside, in a pocket of darkness. He opened his mouth, but she preempted him.

"Why didn't you tell me about your dad?" she demanded.

Ben cleared his throat. A couple of cars sped by and disappeared. "I don't—"

"You're not allowed to say 'I don't know.'"

Ben swallowed and looked down into her face. "I didn't tell you about my dad because I didn't want to expose you to that part of me."

"But you did, Ben. You exposed me."

"I know, Chicken."

"You hurt me," she said. "Over and over. Long before that night. Everything you didn't say while you were gone—all that silence hurt me. But when you came back, the things you said to me—called me—that hurt more. Nobody who really loves a person should—" Her voice quavered. "Should ever . . ."

"I know." He cupped her shoulders gently with his hands. She was so small compared to him.

And now there was something she needed to ask him, but every time the words climbed up her throat, they slid back down. She took a deep breath. "How could you not have known"—she paused—"what you did to me?"

"I don't—" he started, but he managed to stop himself. "All I've ever wanted to do is protect you. I've been so deluded, Becca. So fucked up. I feel like I don't exist anywhere. And then I see you and I think, *Becca knows where I am. She can get to me and bring me back*. But that's not fair. It's not your responsibility to fix me."

"No," she said. "It's not." Her voice was barely a whisper and it was almost drowned out by the passing cars. "And the thing is . . . I've got a scholarship." She did not meet his eyes as she said this. Instead, she stared at the road. "To the University of Oregon. To be on their team. It's the best—"

"It's a shot at sponsors, the Olympics. God, I know." He took her hands. "Chicken, that's incredible. Hey, would you look at me?" He squeezed her hands, ran his thumbs over her knuckles. "You," he said, holding her eyes, "are going to be a star."

She wiped forcefully at her face. Why was she crying? he wondered. A fear began to well up inside him. Was this her goodbye? They were so much closer to Oregon than Tennessee. Tomorrow morning he could wake up to find her gone.

"At first, I told them I needed to defer," she said. "Until after my husband got out of the army."

Ben's relief was almost too much. *Defer. Husband.* These words meant their future remained intact.

"But that was a few months ago. I've changed my mind now. I'm going to start in September."

He felt a wave rush up inside of him. He felt like he was going to be swept away. He couldn't breathe. *Husband,* he thought. *Husband.* The word floated before him like a life preserver that was just out of reach. "As soon as we're back, I'm going to see the doctor at the base," he said.

She did not respond to this remark. She wasn't buying it, or it wasn't enough of a promise, or it simply wasn't the right thing to say. And yet, he had to stay afloat. He had to do something. "Becca Thompson," he said quickly, "I want to buy you a waffle."

"What?" She sounded pissed off. "What the hell are you talking about?"

"No, you don't understand." He stepped as close to her as he could without actually touching her and looked down on her beautiful head. “Becca Thompson, will you have waffles with me so that I can tell you a story about my dad?”

She didn’t speak. He saw that she couldn’t.

“For every bite I take, I will tell you one hundred stories. I will answer every question that you can think of to ask. I swear to God, you won’t be able to make me stop talking.”

42

SLOWLY BUT SURELY, the group dwindled. Every fifty miles or so, a couple of men peeled away onto some northern- or southern-bound road. They headed back to their towns and their women or their empty beds. They returned to their day jobs and disability payments and hours spent on hold with the VA. They checked in with their AA sponsors, with Jesus, with their grown children. They went back to feeling steady and stolid or disconnected and discounted. And on parade days —Memorial, Veterans, the Fourth of July—they gave motorcycle rides to the white-haired Gold Star mothers; mothers like their own, except without sons.

And King? Becca envisioned him riding north into Canada, the air growing colder by the mile. She knew it was summer in Canada too, but she imagined her father's nose and cheeks turning red and the tips of his fingers burning as they clutched the Gold Wing's handlebars. She imagined him growing increasingly uncomfortable until the cold forced him to reverse course. To head south again, to his house with its fifteen door locks. Becca did not doubt that he would return as promised; she only hoped that it would be soon.

Elaine seemed unfazed by King's sudden departure. When Reno dropped her back home, she gave Becca her phone number and e-mail. "I expect you and Ben to visit," she said as they stood outside of her apartment building in town. "If your daddy's still gone, maybe I can drag him back for one of the holidays? We'll be a big, cozy family."

At this, Becca glanced back at the Hands of God van. Her mother stared out the window, her mouth set in a tight, flat line. Elaine was going to be just fine, Becca could see. Whatever contentment she'd found with King wouldn't suit most people, but it was good enough for her. For Jeanine, things were less certain.

By the time they reached Hands of God, the hearty pack had shrunk and scattered; just the Death Star, the van, and Reno remained. From the highway, they turned onto a series of smaller paved roads, which soon gave way to dirt. Up and up they climbed, their narrow route hemmed in by pine trees. Soon, Becca began to anticipate the summit around every bend. But these priestesses had sequestered themselves high atop their Parnassus, as though striving to be that much closer to heaven.

Finally, a boxy one-room building appeared among the pine needles. The Hands of God van was parked, and the women, Jeanine among them, filed immediately inside, like they were worker ants returning to the nest. Only the crucifix nailed above the doorway signaled the structure's intention. Becca had not stepped foot in a church since her childhood. Sometimes, when King raged, her mother took her to the First Methodist, just to get her out of the house. For a while, she sent Becca to Sunday school, hoping some lessons about humility and piety would sink in. Then Becca asked why the church spire was giving God the finger, and the pastor had kicked her out.

Now the remaining five travelers—Becca, Ben, Lucy, Jacob, and Reno—hung back. Becca could see that Ben was bursting to talk. He was like an overstuffed duffle bag, packed full of apologies. Two nights before, Becca had accepted her husband's waffle bribe, and for over an hour, she'd listened to him toggle between his father and the war. She began to see that another life—with its own set of fears and regrets—was hiding inside of him. She felt guilty for not pressing him harder, earlier on, about his father. He'd cut her a trail straight to his heart's core, but she had not followed it, preferring not to push him or cause tension. And, then, when it came to the war, of course Ben wasn't going to talk to her. He wasn't going to share these new heartaches, because he had no reason to trust that she could handle them. He'd had no clue how she would respond. She'd been so selfish, letting him prop her up but never considering that she bore him an equal responsibility. She was his load-bearing beam too, but since she'd never asked him how much weight he needed her to carry, she hadn't been able to perform her role very well.

With the war, things were more complicated. Reno had shown her the gravity of those tales, the weight of those heartaches. Only now did she understand why Ben had withheld his war stories. He didn't know whether she'd be able to accept what he'd done and failed to do over there. And if she couldn't or didn't—that would break him.

Still, despite her newfound knowledge, Becca worried that they were both too damaged to move forward. She worried that Ben would hurt her again and keep on hurting her. She worried that despite his best intentions, the man she'd fallen in love with was gone for good. How could she possibly help him get better? And what if better didn't exist?

These questions weighed heavily on her as she wandered around her mother's home. In a clearing behind the church sat several small shacks with concrete porches and metal doors. Pine trees towered above, dwarfing everything. Becca followed a short path through the woods and was suddenly standing at the edge of the gardens, a buzzing world of lush fertility. Here was God's benevolence, exploding in leaves and flowers and rich, dark earth.

She roamed among the snap-pea vines and into a thicket of sunflowers. She took one of the sunflower heads in her hand, closed her eyes, and pressed its soft brown center and bursting yellow petals to her chest. For a moment, she imagined that this flower really could pour light and warmth into her body, heal her bruises from the inside out. But when she opened her eyes, she suddenly saw this place as it surely looked in winter, after the flowers and squash and snap peas had withered. Without these gardens, her mother's whole world looked bleak. Hands of God was not for the faint of faith. Which was probably the point. A person would come here only if she was fully committed to this life or if she needed total escape — a means of forgetting the world beyond these pine trees. Hands of God, Becca thought, wasn't so different from Kleos.

And what if her mother hadn't come here for escape but to somehow emulate King's experience? Just like Ben had done to reach his own father, picking up the fiddle and joining the army. "Please don't let that be true," Becca whispered to the sunflowers. "Please let her life be something more than a shadow of King's."

"Home, sweet home," Jeanine said, appearing through the thicket as though she'd been summoned. She seemed thin as the sunflower necks but just as tough. Not nearly as happy as the flowers.

"The service over already?" Becca asked, afraid that her mother had heard her plea.

"I was worried you all were going to take off. I wanted to say goodbye to my daughter."

Jeanine was jittery. She probably wasn't allowed to smoke here. Becca suddenly felt a strange need to comfort her. "I wasn't going to leave without saying goodbye," she said, trying to coat the words in kindness. Her mother nodded. "Mom, are you sure you want to stay here? You can have the house back. I'm transferring schools in the fall. To Oregon. To run."

Jeanine raised her eyebrows. "It's my house, Becca. It's not yours to give back to me."

"You know what I mean."

"I don't aim to see Dry Hills anytime soon."

"Do you want me to rent it out, then?"

Jeanine shrugged as though she didn't much care. "I know you don't want to hear it, Becca, but you're a lot like me."

Hadn't King just said something similar? After all this time, suddenly each of her parents was trying to claim her.

"You want a regular kind of love, Becca. A love you can count on. A love that doesn't have to hurt so much."

Becca didn't respond. If her mother really wanted a stable, reliable love, then why had she hung on to the other kind for so long?

"You're making the right choice, going to Oregon," Jeanine said. "I hope my saying so won't cause you to change your mind."

"I have a lot of pride, Mom, but not that much."

But Jeanine, being who she was, couldn't leave well enough alone. "You can still break it off, Becca. You're still free. Don't lose your momentum."

Becca couldn't keep her mouth shut either. "I didn't say that I was making a break, Mom. There's a difference between —"

But Jeanine only shook her head as if she couldn't stand to hear another word. "Hug your mother," she said. So Becca did.

When they broke apart, Jeanine held her daughter at arm's length. The light showed the older woman's deep laughlines, but Becca saw that her mother was still beautiful. She could have remarried. She could have been happy. Or maybe not. Her love for King had taken a long journey, from Dry Hills to Hands of God to Kleos. It had been exposed to the worst of the elements. It had been beaten and battered. But it did not break. It was stubborn. As stubborn as the woman who felt it.

Jeanine smiled her brittle smile. "I'm going back to the service now. Let me know when you get to Oregon." She turned and walked off through the garden.

Back at the church, Ben and Lucy were saying their goodbyes while Reno stood slightly apart, puffing on a cigar. "I don't think you're allowed to smoke up here," Becca said, walking over to him.

"Does the Bible have a rule against cigars?"

"I think that's beside the point."

Reno continued to puff as Becca listened to the subtle pop of his lips opening and closing.

"So would you reckon we're friends now?" he asked. He didn't look at her. He kept his eyes on the others. The adults were laughing, fawning over the boy.

Becca was suddenly flooded with feeling and could not speak. That night at Motorcycle Mountain, she had felt something for Reno—a feeling so particular that she would never have it again, not even with him. Somehow, it would remain tucked inside of her, unshared. She would try to preserve it, to keep it strong and clear, all the while knowing that it would eventually weaken, its power draining by degrees. She knew that one day she would call upon the memory of them dancing that night and find it merely a pleasant moment, a powerless if happy reminiscence. It seemed unfair. The best memories faded so soon, while the worst of them kept on battering the psyche like gale-force winds.

"Yup," Reno said, yanking Becca back to the present. "I reckon we're friends now. We've been through the shit together and neither of us can go back."

"You're saying I'm like one of your war buddies?" Becca replied, sarcasm being the only way she could recover her voice.

"More outrageous claims have been made, Becca." He put the cigar between his teeth.

She left him to finish his smoke and walked to the others. Ben gave Jacob a hearty handshake and Jacob grinned back, his smile as electric as his silver jacket. Becca's heart swelled. In these simple gestures, could she dare to see a vision of their future? She didn't know. She and Ben would have to match each other's rhythm. When the war pulled at him, they would both lose momentum. They would give up ground together, even fall behind.

"You can still break it off," her mother had said. "You're still free."

But her mother was wrong. Because here was Ben, reaching for her, pulling her into his arms. He held her tight and close. She let him.

Acknowledgments

I AM ENORMOUSLY GRATEFUL to the men and women of Carry the Flame and Rolling Thunder for their service, and especially to the amazing individuals who carried me three thousand miles across this great continent. That journey remains the pinnacle of my career as a journalist and one of the defining experiences of my life. Special thanks to John Dooley for offering me a spot on the trip (and suggesting that I write a book about it), to Frank Bair, Steve Britton, and Leon Curley for sharing their stories and keeping me safe on the road, and to German Hernandez, Deno "Paco" Paolini, and Vinny Scotti for always speaking the truth to power. Last but not least, thank you to King Cavalier II for his leadership on the road and for serving as this project's motorcycle guru.

Dan McArdle, I wouldn't have had the balls to take this journey without you. Thank you for being such a wonderful photographer, roommate, and friend — and for coding up that alarm clock in a pinch, so we didn't get left behind in New Mexico.

I am honored to have had translation assistance from Marian Makins, whose ancient Greek is clearly good enough for government work. Dr. Nicole Herschenhous was a fastidious early reader and expert counsel on all matters PTSD. Karl Marlantes and Chuck Pfeiffer kept my military facts straight. Books by

Jonathan Shay, David Finkel, David Maraniss, Robert D. Schulzinger, and Brian Castner proved to be invaluable research sources.

Mollie Glick, you were once again my dedicated early editor and advocate; I am so lucky to have you on my team. To everyone at HMH, I am thrilled to have worked with you again. Jenna Johnson, you always support my vision while pushing me to mature as a writer. I will cut thousands of words for you any time.

Thank you to my parents for taking me to the National Mall each Memorial Day and for introducing me to America's most badass subculture. You have long supported my far-reaching, sometimes risky explorations. And to my husband, Jason: You had enough confidence in me and in this book to drive the highways and back roads of Tennessee, Missouri, Arkansas, Kansas, Colorado, New Mexico, Arizona, and Utah in search of nothing specific, which turned out to be absolutely everything. Without you there would have been no Motorcycle Mountain and certainly no heart of Durga.

And, finally, thank you to George from Denny's, wherever you may be.